Also by James A. Lyons

"A" Different Kind of Superpower

Out in Greenwood

The Paper Boy

Half the World Away

James A. Lyons

SRL PUBLISHING

SRL Publishing Ltd
London

www.srlpublishing.co.uk

First published worldwide by SRL Publishing in 2025

SRL PUBLISHING
THINKING DIFFERENTLY, DELIVERING CHANGE

ISBN: 978-1915073-51-8

1 3 5 7 9 10 8 6 4 2

A CIP catalogue record for this book is available from the British Library

SRL Publishing is a climate positive publisher offsetting more carbon emissions than it emits.

Hello,

Thank you for picking up this book, whether you purchased from a bookstore, borrowed from a library, or found a discarded copy by the bins behind your local Tesco Express. All are welcome.

Before diving in, please be aware of the following content warnings: This book contains on-page mentions of cancer, terminal illness, and parental bereavement. There are also homophobic terms used as insults in dialogue spoken by school-aged characters, and discussions around the historic treatment of the LGBTQ+ community.

Although a work of fiction, I hope this story helps establish how it could feel as a gay child being educated under Section 28, the 1998 UK Government legislation that not only prohibited local authorities from 'promoting homosexuality', but also from schools teaching/discussing homosexuality in a positive manner.

Scotland overturned the legislation in 2000, however it took a further three years in England and Wales. In 2003, my local MP and future Prime Minister, David Cameron, voted to keep the legislation in place. He, alongside seventy-seven other MPs, did not succeed.

Progress has been made since the nineties, however I ask you to find an overview of Section 28 as you will see the language of the time being mirrored in today's society, notably language targeting the trans community.

If you enjoy this book, please let me know, and recommend it anywhere you have an audience. LGBTQ+ authors like myself rely heavily on word of mouth to raise our voices and share our stories.

I can be found on all social media under @JALwrites.

Many thanks,

James

One

September 1995

According to Nan, I'm four times more likely to be eaten by a shark than I am to win the National Lottery. Well, the joke is on her. I have never paddled deeper than my shins in the sea, and in front of me sits a winning lottery ticket.

It may only be three matching numbers and worth a tenner, but I will take any positivity I can get. Life has been one kickback after another recently. Ten pounds won't change that, and I often wonder if I'll ever get a real lucky day.

Today is my second ever first day of school. With the way Mum has been making a fuss, I should have an adventurous excitement flowing through my veins with each ripple from my heartbeat. The truth is my stomach is knotted as I stare down at three soggy Weetabix. They swim around my bowl, turning to mush, whilst *Take That* remind me from the radio to never forget where I came here from.

"Theo, are you looking forward to big school?"

I've been asked this question far too many times over the holidays, ever since it was announced Mum's illness was terminal. My answer has always been the same. No. (Also, calling it "Big School" when I'm heading into Year

Nine hasn't exactly helped me prepare for the more adult educational experience).

The thought of going back brings me out in a cold sweat. It's played on my mind so much I've had many an anxiety dream where I arrive at the school gates in nothing but my M&S undies, being introduced to the other pupils halfway through an assembly like Macho Man Randy Savage arriving mid-match at *WrestleMania*.

I never even wanted to leave primary school, instead wanting I could stay in the safety of my small classroom with its bright red walls and having weekly games of Wink Murder.

As I slowly tie my shoes, Ian McKellan is being interviewed on GMTV. His face vanishes as Mum flicks the set off quickly, shaking her head as she tosses the remote on the sofa next to me.

"You best get a wriggle on," she says, kissing me on the top of my head.

I grab my schoolbag and head to the front door. Stokewood Secondary is a tsunami of new experiences ready to flood over me. Sadly, nothing I can do will stop it. As I sling the bag over my shoulder, I find myself pinned against the door, Mum opposite with disposable camera in hand.

"Mum, this is embarrassing," I complain, my vomit-green jumper suffocating my body and my arms rigid by my sides.

She winds the camera on before squinting through the viewfinder. "Look at my big boy off to big school." It looks like she's about to cry, which will play havoc with her thick Avon eyeliner. I help by hugging her quickly before hot footing it down the cracked garden path. Things are changing, so what's the point of delaying any longer?

As I cross the dew-carpeted playing fields, I realise the 'big' that mum has been referring to also relates to the buildings, not just the concept of secondary education itself. I draw in a long breath of the cold air as I prepare for whatever lays ahead to engulf me faster than a bag of nerves caught in an avalanche.

Crowds of students trudge towards the imposing concrete, brutalist-style structures, like a sea of uniformed ants returning to their government-funded nest. I pull a badly photocopied map out my pocket to get a sense of direction. Nan had offered to bring me in, but I can't afford to lose any cool points this early (especially with her hair in neon pink rollers).

At the main reception, my wet socks squelch inside my new Kicker shoes as a petite lady with a sensible haircut grins at me. She's standing with a large sign, my name scrawled across it in marker, along with the names of three others.

"Hi, I'm Theo," I say, shaking her hand when she offers hers.

"Good morning, Theo. My name is Miss Houghton, and I teach music. You're the new Year Nine, aren't you?"

I nod and give her my bravest smile.

She pushes her glasses up with a scrunch of her nose. "Marvellous. Go and take a seat with Vicky and I will take you to your form room shortly."

I look across and see a small girl devouring the contents of her lunchbox, gnawing at sandwiches like a hungry, blonde-pigtailed gerbil. She's eating them in a bizarre spiralling motion from the crusts inwards, and as I sink into a chair opposite, I watch in disgust as she squashes the remaining sandwich into a ball, before trying to fit it into her mouth. I involuntarily let out a sick burp, which burns when I swallow.

There's a strange atmosphere in this waiting area, like a sense of apprehension hanging around me in a cloud. I expected it to be modern and chic, yet the multiple class photos hanging on the wall have been left to fade, a skin of dust nestled on their brown frames. The yellow foam from my chair puffs out the side as I get comfortable, pulled from the lining by those who've been in this position before. The double doors nearby are tempting to run through.

During Year Six, when Mum first received her cancer diagnosis, Nan thought it'd be in my best interest to stay at home to learn. I'd been in and out of class during my final year at primary, Mum's health a constant worry. She'd been a sprightly fitness class leader before the illness took hold, and as the early signs of extended fatigue kicked in, it was hard for her to educate me. With fewer funds for a home tutor, and Nan being freshly retired with a dodgy hip, I have to accept that today is my new normal. This is where I belong for the next three years, my educational routine altered for structured lessons and actual homework.

As Vicky gnashes the top level off a Mars Bar, Miss Houghton is back, with two identical twin girls in knee-high white socks flanking her either side. She eyes Vicky and gives me a pitying smile. "Follow me."

My breath forms a mist cloud as I sit in my form room, my hands tucked into the sleeves of my jumper, my ankles chilled where the trousers don't meet my shoes.

I've been placed in 9 Elm, and my tutor, Mr Richardson, is stood at his desk in a beige, pinstripe suit, ensuring all his pens are present in the terracotta cup on his desk. I'm so close I can smell the stale coffee on his breath, which keeps being refreshed every time he takes a sip from his *World's Best Teacher* mug.

"Do you think he bought that mug himself?" asks Bethany who has set all her new stationery neatly on the other half of our table, making me look unorganised with my non-matching, discount store bought, equipment.

I nod. "Bet there are some students who love to suck up to teachers, even at secondary."

"There are a few in this class, believe me," she says, gesturing her head towards a table of girls sat near the windows as she ties her long dreadlocks into an aquamarine scrunchie.

I'm so glad to have Bethany with me. We started in nursery on the same day and were in every class together until Year Six. When she left me to come here, we promised we'd never lose touch, but in the last twenty-four months, our interactions have been limited to birthdays and Bonfire Night. I glance around at the others, all packed into their own friendship groups. I've never felt like such an outcast.

"Attention please, class," says Mr Richardson as he strides in front of the board, running a thumb and index finger across his dark blonde moustache to straighten it, revealing flecks of grey pebble-dashed throughout. "Welcome to Year Nine, and welcome Theo, to Stokewood Secondary. As you know, I'm Mr Richardson, and I'll be your form tutor for the final three academic years." He grabs a pile of paper and puts it in front of Bethany. "This is your timetable for the year. Please take one and pass it on, et cetera."

I grab one off the top and pass the pile to a pair of boys sat behind. They look so similar they must be twins. Blonde curtains frame their pale faces, blue eyes staring in my direction. I quickly lick my palm and attempt to put some style into my unruly mop of brown hair.

"Practical Studies is first," says Bethany. "That's in this room so makes things easier."

"What's Practical Studies?" I ask, already lost. The only practical thing I did during home schooling was to make cups of tea for everyone when I was allowed a short break.

"Stuff which helps in life, like making anti-bullying posters and getting to watch all those ancient videos about smoking. There's a stranger danger one too with this girl called Tabitha. It'll haunt you. If we're particularly unlucky we might have to sit through another God-awful theatre production in the main hall by this student group who call themselves The Squirrel Brigade. The last one was on road safety and it was S-H-I-T."

"Sounds dull. Least we get a good view to daydream to from here," I reply as my eyes drift to the outside world. From the second floor of Middle School, a small car park gives way to the main football pitches, with a new housing site under construction on the far side where the old park 'n' pick used to sit. I spent time every summer gathering fruit there with Mum before the illness took away her ability to do so. I hope she's doing okay without me. I bet she hasn't had a cuppa since I left.

After an introduction about what to expect from the next ten months, we are made to write our names on sticky labels and place them over the gold oak tree emblem on our jumpers. I am sure this is for my benefit only. I turn to the twins and say hello, noticing they've only written their first names. In fact, everyone has only written their first names. I tried so hard to fit my entire name on mine and it looks squished as a result. Barker-Hall isn't exactly the shortest surname.

"Hi, Theo Barker-Hall," says blonde boy one. "I'm Matt Houston, this is Sam Baxter," he adds, tilting his head towards to the other.

"Heya. Are you related?"

Sam frowns. "No, just friends."

"You look similar, sorry."

"Everyone says that," laughs Matt.

"Bethany, this is Sam and Matt," I say as she finishes turning her name badge the correct way.

"Oh, hey guys, nice to meet you," she replies, before laughing hysterically.

"We've known each other for two years," says Sam.

"Sorry, yeah of course." I keep forgetting I'm the new fish in this pond. "Do you like it here?"

They both shrug in unison.

"You'll be fine, Theo. Trust me," Bethany says as she turns to the front, digging an elbow into my ribs to bring my attention back to Mr Richardson.

He takes yet another swig of coffee. "Now, I'm obliged to remind you registration is at 8.50am, and again for afternoon lessons at 1.50pm. You must be on time, no exceptions, as I will get in sh…trouble. As some of you may have heard, this school has seen a few upgrades over the summer. You'll be pleased to know we now have a fully functioning set of computers available in the IT block."

Mr Richardson leaves a pause and stands with eyebrows raised, half-hoping for more excitement, but instead everyone remains silent. He takes another drink and continues. "Anyway, these computers are state of the art. Top of the range! You must only use them for academic work, and your printing will be monitored. If you wish to use photographs in your work, Mr Teale in the computer lab has a new scanner he will help you with."

Matt leans forward and taps me on the shoulder. "Teale is gay."

"Matthew, none of that," responds Mr Richardson.

"Mum goes to aquarobics with his boyfriend," Matt continues.

Mr Richardson strides to the side of Matt's desk and slaps down a ruler. "I have said we will not have any of that discussed. Final warning or you'll be spending your first lunchtime back with me, okay?"

A chorus of *oooh*'s ring out from across the room at the threat.

"I mean it," Mr Richardson says, his voice a few decibels louder. "You're in Year Nine, now, so you best all act like it, do you understand?" He stares at everyone until there is a deathly silence blanketing the room. "I said, do you understand?"

"Yes, sir," we all mumble in response.

"Good. As you can see from your timetables, you have Practical Studies first with Mrs Bosnich. She is also new, so you won't be on your own, Theo," he says, looking directly at me. Sorry, but 'make friends with a teacher' was NOT on my imaginary to-do list.

"It would be easier if you all remained in the same seats. Mrs Bosnich can then use my seating plan. After the lesson, Theo, you will join myself on a school tour with the other newbies. The room numbering system is pretty straightforward, however, I appreciate it is a larger space than your previous school."

Mr Richardson shuffles from the room after giving a final reminder about our behaviour, and a fearsome-looking lady appears in the doorway, blocking out the artificial light spilling in from the corridor. She's about six feet tall and her eyes are hidden by smoky-lensed glasses jutting out from under a large mop of curly black hair. I note she's carrying a *World's Best Teacher* mug. One of them is clearly lying about their title.

"Good morning, Elm," she says. Her face softens as she smiles, and my nerves about entering the world of proper education ease a little. "My name is Mrs Bosnich and I will be taking you for Practical Studies and English for the whole of this year, unless anything happens. Touch wood it won't!" she says, tapping at her forehead with a closed fist. "So, before we begin, can I get a quick show of hands; who is feeling a little apprehensive about being back here today?"

I raise my hand but notice Bethany doesn't. I spin my head and look across to the other twenty-eight people in the class. They all stare back. The only other person with their hand raised is a girl sat at the back chewing on a spare cartridge from her fountain pen, her lips now looking like she has applied striking blue lipstick.

"What are you worried for?" whispers Bethany.

I lower my arm slowly. "Just am."

Mrs Bosnich sits with one buttock on my desk. "Being nervous is normal when it comes to a new school. I was a little nervous myself when driving in this morning. I admire the honesty of…" she squints at the seating plan, "Theodore and Molly."

"You can call me Theo," I say, quietly.

"Sure thing, Theo," she replies, her voice bouncing along with each word. Her accent is summery, and definitely doesn't belong to a Stokewood native. The farmer twang we all have is not present at all. We wait as she opens a window and a gust of wind rattles through the room immediately, blowing a selection of papers to the floor.

A girl on the front row with a well-styled dirty blonde bob jumps from her seat and picks them from the floor.

"That's Katie Barlow. She's such a suck-ass," spits Sam from behind me, and I chuckle at the hate in his voice. I'd love to know the history between the two.

The chattering that started from a number of people in the room, me included, stops as soon as Mrs Bosnich slaps her hand down on the desk. I jump and crack my knee on the underside of the table.

"Fly on my desk, sorry," she says. "Sorry."

She takes a new piece of chalk and scribbles WRITING LETTERS across the board. "Over the past year I have spoken to many parents regarding key English skills your age group should know. One skill which was raised as potentially lacking was the ability to write letters. Writing a letter is an important skill to have these days, whether when applying for a job, or even staying connected with a relative. So, today, letters are what we will be focussing on."

"Will there be homework?" asks Katie from the corner. Bethany turns to me and mimics shoving her fingers down her throat.

"No, there will never be any homework from this period," says Mrs Bosnich. "Now, I think I have planned something fun for you all. Who here watches *Blue Peter*?"

My hand goes up again, but this time it is joined by the majority of the class. *Blue Peter* is one show I look forward to, mainly as the pirate-style theme music used to signal the end of my homeschool day. I even had a go at making my own Tracey Island a couple of years ago, although it didn't quite look the same as the one Anthea Turner made. The fact I'd no green paint to hand was a disadvantage. Using red instead made it resemble a group of people escaping an erupting volcanic island rather than the renowned base of International Rescue.

Mrs Bosnich takes a stack of blank, lined paper from the shelves by the door and hands the sheets out. "On last Friday's *Blue Peter*, you will have seen they launched *The Great British Pen Pal Project* for Year Nine pupils. After a brief discussion with the headmaster, we thought it might be a wonderful idea to get you all involved." Everyone lets out a long groan. "What is the problem, Theo?" asks Mrs Bosnich. Sitting at the front seems to be the prime position for my every move to be noticed.

"I don't want a pen pal, Miss. I need to make friends with the actual people here first."

"Nonsense," she replies as she paces around the tables, becoming more animated with each step. "It will be good practice for the future, and if you make a new friend from it, well, then that is an added bonus, isn't it?"

"Who should we address it to?" asks a girl at the back.

"No one in particular. Ideally, in a real-world situation, you would start with *To whom it may concern*, so maybe use that. Once complete, your letters will all be bundled and sent to the BBC, and they will then pass onto another school who have registered for the programme. From then on, every month, you will take it in turns to write to one another."

"Every month?" Sam asks.

"Mrs Bosnich lowers her glasses and whispers. "Only until next July."

Bethany crouches over her desk, her tongue poking out the side of her mouth as she furiously scribbles away. She stops and screws the paper into a ball before throwing it at the waste bin. Despite two years on the school netball team, the paper bounces off the side and rolls across the carpet tiles.

"Bethany," starts Mrs Bosnich as she bends over to pick it up, "please ensure paper is taken to the bin rather than thrown. Elm, you have twenty minutes to write your letter. After which, we can take a few examples to read aloud."

"I dunno what to write," I say to Bethany.

"Just tell them about yourself."

"I'm boring, though," I protest.

She smiles. "If you were boring, I wouldn't still be hanging out with you. Tell them your favourite things."

I take a ballpoint from my Pepsi Can-shaped pencil

case, ready to do my first piece of work in this new life. After writing the school address, my mind goes blank. There is absolutely nothing about me which might interest a mystery person. Living at home with your Mum and two budgies, with a few visits from your nan thrown in, would hardly set the world alight.

I think about telling the (un)lucky recipient about the fact I know the dance to *Saturday Night* by Whigfield, but decide I should keep it more formal. I write a load of nonsense, talking too much about my budgies (Kylie and Jason) and their love of cuttlefish.

Having exhausted anything even remotely interesting, I put my pen lid on and sit back proudly in my chair, staring at my completed page of A4 paper. That's until I notice Bethany has already written almost three times as much. "What have you even got to talk about?"

"Telling them about my summer, my singing at Gospel church, that kinda thing."

I look at my poor effort and feel inadequate. I glance behind to the boys, and they're also on a third sheet of paper. "Let me see yours," I tell Sam.

He pulls the paper closer and wraps an arm around it. I should have stayed at home. Academically, these people are much more advanced than me. I'm gonna be chewed up and spat out in no time at all. No one will reply to my letter.

Two

October 1995

The first month and a half at Big School™ flew past. I still haven't adapted, and the homework is stressing me out more than it's meant to. My chance of getting a coveted one hundred percent attendance certificate vanished by the end of my second week. I don't understand how everyone else is managing so well, yet here I am, stood with Sam at lunch on Friday after returning from my sixth sick day in the last three weeks.

Mum is trying her best to encourage me to attend, but I hate leaving her at home, especially when Nan isn't about. Mum had a particularly bad weekend, and I spent most of Sunday in the hospital with her, watching her get more tests and poked about by a variety of medical staff. In between, we were served anaemic looking meals and played Connect 4. She won our best of seven tournament five games to two. I would've won if I weren't so tired. After victory, she gloated she was the Connect 4 reigning champion again, as always.

"Are you feeling better?" Sam asks as we lean against the tennis court fence, our assigned break location.

I don't want to let on it wasn't an actual illness. "All good, thank you."

Sam looks me up and down. "I'm rubbish with

words, but, you know, it must be hard. Me and Matt will keep you occupied if everything at home is too much."

"Thank you, I appreciate it."

He looks off across the courts, fixing his eyes on a fight breaking out in the distance. "My dad was ill last year. The school were good with me, and during the worst times I actually preferred being here than at home. He might not seem it on the outside, but Richardson is helpful if you've any problems."

"Even if I'm off at least once a week?"

"Yeah, make sure you let him know what's on your mind, I guess."

Some parts of school have been enjoyable, and I've found myself to be much more adept at Geography than I expected. I even received my first Merit in German last week for my snooker-themed colours homework. In another moment of success, I also got to pick a chocolate from a plastic jar of Roses after being deemed sensible in the way I descended the Maths stairs. It may appear patronising, but I count getting a free Golden Barrel a win.

One substantial change, which has caused multiple levels of corridor whispers, is that Bethany and Matt are officially 'seeing each other'. Basically, from what I can tell, this means they sit next to each other on the small wall outside the lower school building every breaktime. Someone said something about Matt visiting first and second bases, but he claims he hasn't been there. They aren't on my map, so they can't be important.

"They'll break up before Christmas, I bet you," Sam says as he looks across to Matt while throwing a tennis ball against the wall. "Just like last year. Until then, it's me and you." Sam pulls out his lunchbox and punches me on the arm. "By the way, are you gonna join the football team with me and him?"

I let out a small laugh as I take the Babybel he's offering. "You've seen me in PE. I've never been picked first."

"You're quite good, though."

It takes me a moment to realise he is being genuine. I've never been known for my footballing ability, unlike Sam and Matt, who already have the interest of most girls in our year due to their good looks and sporting prowess. "Actually, why not? Playing football might help distract me from you know what. How do I join?"

Sam, as always, gets excited when he can talk about sport. "Training is on Mondays for an hour after school. We have some fixtures soon so it's a good time to get involved."

"Who are we playing?"

"All the other local schools. The fixtures were all in Daley's letter a couple of weeks back. Did you not read it?"

"Nope. I didn't even get sent one. Maybe he only wants people like you."

"Rubbish. We're proper shite so any new people might help. Come along and give it a go."

"Fair enough. I'll chat to him in the lesson this afternoon if I get a chance."

I'm glad training won't clash with the rehearsals for the school play, at least. Bethany and I both auditioned for a role in *Oliver!* and found out yesterday morning we will be forming part of the chorus. The audition results were pinned to the noticeboard in the drama corridor, and as I scrolled from the top, the feeling my name wouldn't be on Ms Fenton's cast list grew stronger the further down the page I got. I kept my fingers crossed she hadn't forgotten me. The main roles all went to the confident kids, unsurprisingly. That could never be me, especially here.

Oliver is being played by Abdul from 9 Pine, as Ms Fenton has been constantly gushing about him being an 'actual actor'. This results from him having played a small role in *Mother Goose* at the Corn Exchange last Christmas, and his uncle being a deceased extra in one episode of *Casualty*.

When I spotted my name near the bottom, a weird sense of pride hit, even if Ms Fenton had spelled my name as Theodora, much to everyone else's amusement. But there I was, picked from the abyss to be on stage! I've never acted before.

Saying I auditioned may also be stretching the truth a little, too. I only went to give Bethany some moral support as she tried, and failed, to steal the role of Nancy from Katie. The rest just happened. I was holding a prop food bowl stage left when Miss Houghton spotted me from her piano.

"Adorable. You look the part with your makeup!" she shouted across the hall. Ms Fenton clapped her hands together in agreement.

I went red instantly, too embarrassed to tell them the 'soot-stain makeup' on my face was actually a result of me scratching at my blossoming acne shortly after slipping in a puddle in the staff car park on the way to the drama rooms. Rehearsals are on Tuesdays for seven months and I'm already furiously trying to learn the words to the songs. Some are actually quite good! Luckily, I have until May to nail them.

When Mum last had a prolonged stay in hospital, we took her a box set of Rodgers & Hammerstein adaptations on VHS, so she's naturally thrilled I now have a shared interest in musicals, even if it was not my intention. She still puts her tapes on from time to time, but the music of her favourites in particular make me realise the songs will, one day, only act as a soundtrack to my memories of her sitting in her armchair, boxes of pills nearby to ease the pain.

Nan is even more excited about coming to our opening night, and she even got me the cassette of a West End recording from her bingo friend, Diana, after I had told her the news.

"Are you any good at ice skating?" Sam asks as he wipes his mouth with his sleeve after finishing a Nutella sandwich.

I shrug. "Never tried. Why?"

"It's my birthday in January, so I'm having a party at the rink. You can come if you like?"

"That's ages away."

"You have to book in advance there, especially if you want the food or cake package. It's well busy now the swimming pool is being refurbished."

I sit and think for a moment. "Maybe. If you need me to make up the numbers then I guess there's no harm."

Sam smiles at me, before nudging my shoulder with his. "I want you to come, you muppet. And not just to make up the numbers."

Even though everyone is being kind, it feels strange to be included, as if I am waiting to discover a catch that I'm too stupid to figure out. His grin as he told me he wants me there brought a warmth to my body. "I'd love to, thanks."

"Awesome. It will be my first time skating, too, by the way, so don't be nervous. My pen pal said it's great fun, and it will make a change from having to host a party at home."

I turn and face him. "Your pen pal actually replied?"

"Yeah. Some annoying posh kid. Did yours not?"

My heart sinks a little. "Nah. Bosnich didn't say anything on Monday, anyway."

"Maybe she assumed everyone had collected their

letters. When did you last check your pigeonhole?"

I furrow my brow. "My pigeon what?"

"Your pigeonhole! On the first floor of Art block?"

My blank look must've made him realise I wasn't following. Sam laughs as he pulls his sleeves over his goosebumped arms. Even though it isn't funny, and the fact I'm still confused as to what is going on, I laugh too. I feel comfortable around him, more so than any other pupil.

"Go and check it now, Theo. If you don't, then you might not have time after PE and then you'll have to wait until Monday. I'll meet you in the changing rooms in ten."

He messes with my hair. "I'll take your sports bag. I'm off to speak to the lovers. See you in a minute."

I watch him leave, almost forgetting I should be rushing to find these pigeonholes.

The art department is up two flights of stairs near the main school entrance and with each step, the smell of paint and glue grows stronger. The walls are covered with colourful pictures, including a selection of self-portraits showing that getting the right skin tone is not a skill many in Year Ten have mastered. Most look like the person depicted has been lying in the sun for a few days, the brightness of their faces making my pupils shrink.

As I reach the top floor, a laminated sign is pinned to the landing wall. I follow the arrow pointing me to the post room, which now does sound familiar from something Mr Richardson mentioned on the tour. My thoughts must've drifted after the tour had passed the thirty-minute mark.

The heavy door creaks as I enter, and the dim light coming through the narrow dirty windows illuminates a million dust particles, making me feel like I'm travelling through space. All walls are filled with wooden framed slots, class names written in marker pen at the top of each. There is a box of supplies in the centre of the room and I make sure I'm alone before helping myself to a new Pritt Stick and a bottle of Tippex.

I scan around the room until I spot Elm, running my eyes along the pigeonholes. It isn't difficult to find mine. It's the only one about to burst with post. I pull all the envelopes out, dropping most onto the floor, before sitting on the hard tiles to rifle through them. The majority are invites to clubs and events, including Mr Daley's football practice announcement. There is also a note regarding the Year Nine residential to Aachen at the start of July. Hopefully we can afford the £75 fee by the Spring deadline. I put the letter into the front pocket of my bag so I don't forget to show Mum at tea.

At the bottom of the pile, there it is. An actual letter addressed to me, and the only one not sent by the school. The handwriting is neat, big, and loopy. It looks identical to Bethany's. Maybe it's a prank from her and the boys. No girl would want to write to me. Why would they? To discuss my fascination with Monster Munch? Hardly seems likely.

I want to read it immediately but the clanging of the school bell thrashes through my head. I put the letters in my backpack and pace as fast as I can to get changed for cross-country.

It rained for the entirety of P.E.. Mr Daley remained sheltered in the cricket pavilion and offered, no, *shouted* support at us through a megaphone in the distance, his words lost at times in the swirling winds. The cold had continued to penetrate through to my bones on the journey home.

"I'm back!" I call as I enter through our back door,

before turning on the oven so I can cook some potato waffles and sausages for me and Mum. I quickly shower, and take a seat at the table, powering through three bourbons from the broken biscuits box Mum got from the market last week.

"How was your day, darling?" Mum asks, her cane clicking on the torn linoleum flooring as she comes over to kiss me.

"All good, thanks. I'm gonna try out for the football team."

"That's wonderful, I am proud of you." She takes the biscuit box away, revealing my pen pal's letter that I'd hidden underneath. "What have you got there?"

I take it before she can get her hands on it and hold it close. It's too personal to open in front of a crowd. I can't remember ever getting a letter from someone who wasn't in my family. I pray the girl who sent it has some similar interests and doesn't think I'm a weirdo. "This is an English project. I'll show you after dinner. I've got one for you about the residential, though," I add, as I pass it to her. "Why don't you have a sit and I'll bring dinner through shortly."

"Thank you, darling. Nan will be here soon so put some extra sausages in for her. Don't forget to feed the budgies, too. There's a new box of cuttlefish under the sink." She kisses me on the top of my head and clacks off to the front room. Her pace is slowing by the day and I try to forget the times when she could chase me around the garden trying to soak me with the hose.

I walk silently into the hall and press my ear close to the door. She's humming along to the Record Breakers theme tune. I pull the letter from my pocket and carefully slice it open with a butter knife.

I was right. No girl has written to me.

Three

Alexander Beauchamp
9 Tolkien
Saint Martin's
Rutherford-On-Thames
Oxfordshire

09/10/95

Dear Theo,

Thank you for your letter! We had to pick one each from a box and yours was the one I chose at random. My name is Alexander, but like you and Theodore, I hate my full name, so please call me Alex.

School has started very well, thank you. It hasn't been too much of a change for me. I have been in the same location since nursery, moving through Lower School, and now into Middle School. The main difference is I am now officially a boarder! This is what happens at Saint Martin's from Year Nine. It feels strange, still. The way it works is I arrive here on a Monday morning, stay all week, before getting picked up on a Friday by Felicity, who helps my parents in the house when they are busy with their jobs.

My dad has worked in the financial sector for twenty

years, and he often gets to travel to his company's sister offices in Chicago, New York, and Adelaide to work. I think he is currently in Australia, although it is hard to keep track. I will finally get to see him this weekend for the first time in four months. It is my Mum's fortieth birthday this week, so on Saturday we are travelling to a rented farmhouse to help her celebrate. I have been told I must take some schoolwork so don't get jealous that I will be having fun!

I am so sorry to hear about your Mum. I will keep her in my thoughts. I appreciate it may be difficult for you having to help provide care for her. I am sure she is ever so thankful for everything you do for her. It is lovely your nan is with you also!

I apologise if my writing looks a little shaky. I am sat writing this on the minibus as we head home from rowing practice. In three weeks' time, there is a regatta on the Thames near Oxford, and our school is one of nine competing. My training partner is Brian Jacks, and we have been a pair for around a year. My arms ache so much from pulling on the oars for an hour so hopefully you are able to read what I am writing!

I must admit, I can't say I have heard the new *Take That* song, but my sister mentioned she likes their music. She is called Isabelle and is three years older. She is in the sixth form of St Agatha's Girls School, which is virtually next door to Saint Martin's (we even share the same sports field). She plays hockey and was selected to represent Great Britain in the Under-17 nationals, held in India recently. Everyone expects me to follow her so I am working hard in the boat where I can!

Most music I listen to is classical, unfortunately. I am part of the school orchestra, playing piano, although occasionally violin. I am only Grade 4 in both. Aside from classical, there are times when someone will bring in a new CD we can play during our free time. There is a music system in our dormitory so I do hear some bands from the charts. The latest is the new one by *Oasis*, which is not too bad. I prefer the guitar bands to the pop bands, sorry.

Kylie and Jason sound great! It must be so nice to have such colourful birds in the house with you. When I am older, I would love to own a pet. I used to like cats, however, now I am leaning towards wanting a dog. My Grandma used to own a German Shepherd named Plato, and during previous summers we used to walk him together along the meadows closer to the family home.

I wasn't sure about the pen pal project initially, however your letter brightened a dull Monday, so thank you! I am extremely interested to hear more about you, and your time at your new school.

Sorry for all the exclamation marks. Too much adrenaline from rowing!

!!!!!!! haha.

Yours sincerely,
Alex

Four

November 1995

Despite a week-long frost, we are still forced to head out onto the icy pitches on the Wednesday morning for a shambolic hour of football. The girls are in the distance in their hockey gear, and I am pretty sure they're shivering as much as we are.

Nan was forceful in convincing me to leave the house this morning, not allowing me to throw another sickie. I reckon she wanted me gone so she could watch the Princess Diana documentary she taped off ITV last night. She didn't let me have my Frosties so must have bought my compassionate plea a little.

I rub at my leg, a perfectly circular burn stinging my scrawny thigh after it was slapped with the over-inflated football from short distance as Mr Daley was picking teams. He ensures those on the school team are split for a level of fairness. It doesn't matter after our disastrous inter-school football campaign (played three. Won zero. Lost three. Goals scored - two. Goals conceded - thirty-six – I think. The scorers lost count at one point).

A whistle blows and Matt bumbles across to join me, his maroon cheeks puffed as he gasps for air. Fog is encroaching the pitches, and steam rises from my limbs after I unsuccessfully chased the ball around for the entirety of my matches. Hopefully, my commitment might see Mr Daley promote me from unused substitute at the next school match.

"Are you still coming to Sam's party in the new year?" asks Matt as he takes a swig from a bottle of fizzy Lucozade.

I wait for him to finish an extremely audible belch before answering. "I'll be there. Mainly for the pizza."

He nods and pulls mud out the hairs on his legs. I don't have that problem yet, being a few months behind him puberty wise.

"How are things with you and Bethany?" I ask.

"Why? Has she said anything?" The panic in his voice is kind of cute.

"Nope. I was just asking."

He looks at me suspiciously. "You'll tell me if she does, won't you? I don't want her to dump me."

"I promise," I reply, wishing I hadn't asked. This is why I don't want a girlfriend. It's so much trouble.

"We have to choose dorms for the German trip later this week," he says. "You can bunk with me and Sam, if you like. We'll need a fourth but we can see who is spare during Geography."

I shift uncomfortably and wrap my arms around my knees. "Um, yeah thanks. I am not sure if I can go yet, though."

"Why not?"

"Mum," I say quietly. Things have remained tough at home, and the hospital visits seem to be becoming more frequent, like relentless reverse ripples washing towards our family. "Money is tight, too. Don't tell anyone, though. I don't want people to be horrible about it." He shuffles closer and puts his arm around my shoulders. I shrug him off immediately. "I'll be okay, honest," I whisper.

Fifteen minutes later I am walking with Bethany towards double science, my damp PE kit dripping onto the corridor's wooden floor through my *Happy Shopper* carrier bag. I have already eaten the two bags of prawn cocktail crisps from my lunchbox so I don't pass out and wither away from starvation.

"These decorations are tacky," Bethany says as she tugs at a hanging homemade star, one of many those in Year Seven have made in order to make the school feel Christmassy, even if it's far too early for them to be up.

"I'd rather make them than have double science," I reply. The decorations aren't too dissimilar to the ones at home, made during my time at primary school. Every year they shed a new layer of glitter across the front room carpet.

As we walk into the science block, Bethany becomes quiet, and she nervously plays with one of her dark locks as she stares at the boys. "Is everything alright between you and Matt?" I ask.

"Why, what has he said?" she says quickly.

Again, I wish I hadn't asked. "Just being kind."

"Sorry. Yeah, things are great."

I give her a smile. "Good. I was worried because you're being a bit quiet."

"Girl problems," she says, waving a hand around the outside of her skirt. I definitely shouldn't have asked. She jabs my bicep with her finger. "Anyway, how about you? Is there anyone you have your eye on?"

I push out my bottom lip. "No one."

"Genuinely?"

"Genuinely."

The truth is there isn't anyone I fancy. Even the popular girls don't appeal to me. I'm much happier hanging around with Bethany, Matt, and Sam instead.

Even though I do not have a crush as such, I have become fascinated by one person.

Alex.

It isn't like I'm in love with him or anything like that, but something about his letter struck a chord as soon as I read it for the first time thirty-one days ago (not that I'm keeping count).

We are completely different to each other; Him with his family, his money, his orchestra, and his foreign holidays. Me with Mum, our off-brand food, my *Take That* CD and our occasional caravan holiday in Weymouth, if I'm lucky.

It's the differences that draw me to him. I'm looking into the life I could have been living if the circumstances had been different, being shown behind the curtain to what I could've won.

I sometimes wish he could be in my position instead, worried about a mum constantly having medical treatment, being left to watch *Antiques Roadshow* with their Nan. I wonder if he feels the same. I doubt it. Why would he?

In my first reply I told him about my role in *Oliver!*, the school football team, Bethany and Matt, and other general ramblings of someone writing to a pen pal to dump all their problems on. Every day before registration I dash to the post room, hoping for a letter with his neat curly handwriting to be sticking out my pigeonhole. So far one hasn't come. Maybe I was too forward. After Christmas I'll send him another, in case it got lost.

Ms Fenton is stood at the front of the dark-walled drama room, her glasses balancing on the end of her nose. She stares at us over the top of their half-moon lenses. "Shakespeare is not confusing, it just requires concentration."

The start of November brought a change in topics in drama, and I find myself one week in a two-month plan of studying *A Midsummer Night's Dream*. The biggest response Ms Fenton has received to date is when half the class laughed a bit too long at a character being called Bottom. She's already aware we'll never make the RSC. Still, she perseveres. She continuously looks at the clock, likely glad it's Friday and a glass of wine can be in her hand in under six hours. (She keeps a bottle in her filing cabinet's top drawer and thinks we don't know.)

"We have thirty minutes left, and then you can all go and get something from the tuck shop so you have more energy than this in Double Maths." I'm amazed she knows my timetable better than me. "Please get into groups of four."

Everyone shuffles around the room, aside from our gang of four, who are already beside each other. Bethany is leant back onto Matt's legs. Their display of affection is quite something considering they've split twice in the last four weeks. I stay sat cross legged, hoping the holes in my socks don't show.

We're assigned a task to sketch out a two-minute play that sets Shakespeare in the modern world. I hate the idea, but it gives us time to chat rather than do the actual work. Whilst we are not the most productive quartet, Ms Fenton will be too preoccupied with Adam Boxhall and Stacey Cockburn, who haven't done any work in any lesson since I joined. Their disruptiveness taking the focus away from us means they do have their uses, though.

"I've got a detention at lunch," says Sam as he takes some chewing gum from his pocket.

"What for?" asks Bethany.

"For laughing at Stacey's surname."

"You got detention for that?" I asked.

"Barrett heard me. Didn't realise he was stood so close. Have to go and spend lunch in his geography room."

"Gay," says Matt. "Gimme your football before you go, though. We need it for the kickabout."

Sam takes the ball out his backpack and chucks it to Matt. "At least in detention I can sweet talk Barrett giving us a dorm together for Achen."

"Apart from me," says Bethany.

"Well, obviously, not you," Matt replies. "But me, Sam, and Theo."

I wish people would stop mentioning the residential. I mentally draw a list of ways to earn some money to help Mum pay for the trip. When I was at Cubs we did a sponsored carwash one Saturday, so that's an option. There are loads of cars on my estate, and if I charge a fiver I'd only need to find fifteen people. Easy. As Christmas approaches, they might be more willing to help a poor kid out. Christ, if I get any more desperate I'll be worthy of that lead role in *Oliver!*

If the plan proves successful, I could continue doing it and get spending money for summer. Most people will be getting paper rounds in a couple of years, so I can get a head start. I'd never have my own paper round, though. Nan is convinced someone will kidnap me and always shuts the idea down. Her neighbour's son has one and she complained to me about the risks all the way through *Live and Kicking.*

"Did you guys all get the Aachen itinerary letter Barrett sent out?" asks Matt.

"I didn't," I reply.

Bethany runs to her bag by the far wall.

"Not in your pigeonhole?" asks Sam.

"Definitely not this time."

"I've got a copy in my bag you can have. It sounds

like it'll be fun. Teale is coming, though," says Matt.

"And?" I reply.

Sam punches Matt on the arm. "Give it a rest. You're like a broken record and it ain't funny, okay? Teale is alright."

The boys stare at each other for a good few seconds.

"When does the bus leave?" I say, breaking the tension.

"Like, 6am?" says Sam.

"Yeah, it takes twelve hours to get there," Matt confirms.

"And back," Sam replies. "It's gonna be so boring. We only stop in Brussels on the way."

"I've never been abroad," I admit. "Unless Wales counts."

"I've only been once," says Sam. "We went to Calais, which was basically like being in Cogges, but more French. The only part I saw was the inside of a warehouse when Dad was buying crates of lager."

Bethany comes back over carrying a selection of envelopes. "I was meant to give these to you yesterday, Theo. Sorry. I bumped into Matt on the way and then forgot all about them."

She hands me my post as she falls back into Matt's arms, and I immediately feel my heart jump a little when I spot Alex's handwriting on a firm square envelope. Uh-oh. Maybe I do have a crush. Help. I try my best to hide any excitement. Letting on will only lead to questions that I can't answer.

"Did any of you hear about that exhibition in the summer?" asks Bethany as she puts some new gum into her mouth. We all shake our heads. "They're doing something at Earls Court as part of Fashion Week. Gonna have a load of old Hollywood dresses."

"You want me to go, don't you?" says Matt from

above her head.

"Not if you don't want to go. It'd be cool, though. They have Audrey Hepburn's dress from *Breakfast at Tiffany's* there."

I sit up a little. "I'll go with you."

Matt squints at me oddly. "Why'd you want to go and see that for, weirdo?"

"It's interesting, ain't it. Seeing costumes from films."

What I don't want to tell them is I was obsessed with *Breakfast at Tiffany's* I am. When I was off school at five with measles, Nan put it on whilst she made tomato soup (from a can, of course). I've seen it over fifty times since. Every other boy my age would never admit to liking it. They're far too worried about their masculine image, which unfortunately, I must pretend to have, too. "If Bethany wants someone to go with her, then I'm happy to do it," I confirm.

"See Matt, that's how you should answer," Bethany mocks. "I've asked Dad if he can take me. He'll give you a lift, too, I am sure."

"Awesome, thank you."

A boring week has turned back positive in the nick of time. A chance to see Hepburn's dress AND a new letter from Alex, all in the space of sixty seconds. As soon as I can escape Fenton's classroom, I'll be dashing home as fast as my sore thigh will allow.

Five

Alexander Beauchamp
9 Tolkien
Saint Martin's
Rutherford-On-Thames
Oxfordshire

27/11/95

To Theo,

Thank you for replying. I was so extremely excited when it was delivered by the school Postmaster that I had to reply straight away! There is a bonus item in here, too, but open that on Christmas Day so everything in this envelope counts as a December letter. I am not making any sense am I haha! Or am I? I may have eaten too many Quality Street.

Firstly, never apologise to me for sharing your troubles. I can't begin to understand how hard things can be for you. Being at a new school is tough enough as it is, and considering your Mum's illness, it must be so difficult. I wish I was able to help you in some way. I am glad you have made some new friends around you. Sam and Matt sound wonderful. Hopefully, Matt doesn't become weird now he is dating Bethany!

If you are unable to speak to them about things on your mind, from this moment on you have my permission to tell me anything you wish to in your letters. Anything. There will be no judgement from my side.

Personally, I feel a bit freer when writing to you. I know we barely know each other, but it feels like we do. I don't know, I feel like I can be myself with you. In terms of schoolfriends, I am closest here with Brian (my rowing partner from my first letter), Barnaby, and Felix. Felix's dad works alongside mine in the City so we have known each other all our lives, however, never became good friends until a couple of years ago. Me, Felix, Barnaby, and Brian all share a dorm together here at the school along with five others.

Congratulations on getting your role in *Oliver!* I am sure you will be amazing. Have the rehearsals gone well so far? There hasn't been a production announced for next Summer here yet. Our annual Advent recital in The Chapel is next weekend, which I am looking forward to a great deal. The Chapel is always decorated with candles and real holly. It is so magical!

Now, this will sound horrendously upper class, so brace yourself: The summer productions are held in a purpose-built amphitheatre towards the lower end of the school grounds. I am even cringing a little telling you that! I promise I am not your stereotypical posh boy. The rowing and orchestra probably do little to shatter the illusion, I know.

We had to attend a university event this morning. They like to prepare us super early. The thought of going to Oxford or Cambridge (as my parents are expecting), fills me with a sense of dread. I would rather be able to travel and find a different path in life. If I end up working in the same way as my dad, then I believe I will have wasted my life. I need something different.

All my friends' parents are the same. They assume we are all academically gifted and love studying. Everyone's favourite time here is when we are in the dorm together playing on the PS1. My friend Barnaby managed to get the console confiscated a couple of days ago, so I am currently staring at the blank space underneath the television. He was throwing a potato about (for reasons unknown), and due to some incredible inaccuracies, it took out a pane of glass. He is an idiot.

If you ever need any tips for being on stage then please do ask. Last year we performed *The King and I*, but I didn't have a major role. It was a blessing as it allowed me to mime my way through most of it. My voice is breaking so it never can quite hit the notes I want it to. I am much more comfortable when I can hide behind my piano.

How did your recent football matches go? I hope you didn't lose. Our regatta was fun, thank you. In the coxless pairs, Brian and I came fourth. We were so close to third but my oar slipped and we lost valuable seconds. It was disappointing, however, the school did win overall Team Silver, which is fantastic. It is the first medal I have ever won. It was cold on the river so I am glad I don't have to go back out for a month at least. We have three months before the next competition, so I will be spending the majority of winter inside the training facilities.

The March regatta counts as the County Trials so it is an important day. Succeeding there is the main focus. The Dean even allow us time away from our real studies in the week leading to the event to ensure we do the best of our abilities and achieve a good result for the school.

Are you looking forward to your trip to Aachen? I have never been to Germany and don't know much about it. I study French, however, I am not sure how good I am at it. It is fine in the classroom, but listening to a tape is a lot different to actually being in France and having a conversation with a native speaker! I will have to try it out at Easter when I go to see my aunt in Cambes.

I asked Isabelle about *Take That* and she says to tell you she is definitely still a fan too, so you are in good company. Her favourite was Robbie. I remember her crying for an entire weekend when he left them in the summer. She is such a child haha.

In our free time recently we have been listening to a band called *Pulp*, who are my new favourite by far. Someone borrowed a *Now* compilation from his older brother so we have had that playing a lot too, but *Pulp* have mainly taken residence in the stereo. *Disco 2000* is everyone's favourite. I will have to do you a mixtape one day of all the music I listen to (but not the classical, I promise).

Speaking of that song, do you ever wonder what we will all be up to in the year 2000? It seems so far away but I bet it comes around quickly. Maybe if we are still writing at the end of the year we could make a pact to meet somewhere when we are eighteen. Won't it be strange when we are fully grown?

I am just eating some cake which was leftover in the canteen from the Open Day our school recently held. It's a little stale now it is two weeks old but is still better than the desserts we have had recently during lunches. One chef always gives us the leftovers. She is definitely not meant to, but we keep quiet.

Before I go, I want to wish you the most amazing Christmas. I am already looking forward to your next letter. Please find enclosed a small card with an added extra. I hope you do not find it strange!

Yours,
Alex

Six

January 1996

It has been three weeks since I received Alex's last letter, and I have a face to the name. He surprise was a sweet Christmas card, with a half-decent drawing of a holly bush on the front. Inside, he had paper-clipped a polaroid. It's stuck to the side of my wardrobe on my left, next to a 3D picture of a T-Rex I got in a box of Cornflakes last week.

I got the camera for my birthday in the September! Alex had written on the back. He's stood in his school uniform by a massive (I mean GIGANTIC) real Christmas tree outside the main school reception. It made the fake, sparsely branched trees at Stokewood Secondary look a total embarrassment.

It was weird seeing him in reality. I'd had version of him in my head and was only fifty percent correct. He's skinny, but not as skinny as me. You can tell he does a lot of sport by the tightness of his blazer around his biceps. Under a bush of light ginger hair, he has the most piercing set of green eyes. It feels like he's looking into my own. The number of times I've stared at the photo is getting, quite frankly, ridiculous now.

I don't own a polaroid camera, and nor does anyone else in my year, however, I needed to send him something in return. My car cleaning scheme raised a total of £15 over the Christmas holidays, so I used part of the funds on a disposable camera, using every frame to take a photo of myself. Nan helped on most (under the premise it was a for a history project), and I waited patiently for a whole day for the *Kodak* shop to develop them.

Out of the twenty-four images, half had Nan's thumb over the lens. Of the remaining twelve, there was only one I deemed suitable. I attached it to the letter and hope he'll be happy to see who I really am. I also told him about Aachen not happening. Him asking me in his last letter has made me realise how much anguish it's causing, knowing I'm not likely to be on the bus in late June.

As I fight to get my feet into my jogging bottoms, I'm interrupted by the doorbell. I quickly finish dressing and bound down to open it. Bethany stands on the welcome mat with a pair of ice skates hanging around her neck.

"You ready?" she asks, glancing at her watch.

I nod. "Do I need a jumper?" I reply, eyeing her gloves.

"It's an ice rink. Of course you do."

Five minutes later I pull on my shoes, a dark blue jumper Mum knitted me covering my torso. The rink is only fifteen minutes, and we meet Matt at his house at the halfway point. It's the first time I've been there, and it's at least twice the size of my own. Even though it's winter, the garden looks immaculate and there are even stripes on the lawn.

I turn my back as he kisses Bethany and follow close behind as a third wheel whilst they walk hand-in-hand for the remainder of the journey. They best not be like this when we are all watching *Toy Story* at the Odeon later.

"Hey guys!" calls Sam as soon as we enter the rink

reception. He is wearing dark loose trousers and a tight, white long-sleeved top which shows off his pecs.

"Happy birthday," I reply, handing him a homemade card. He smiles, before placing it onto a growing pile of cards in the hands of a blonde woman in the corner.

"This is my mum," he says. "Mum, this is Theo."

"Nice to meet you, I've heard so much about you," she says.

"Likewise," I reply, even though I know nothing.

"The others are getting their skates on, come through," says Sam, as he leads me away.

"One second," calls Sam's mum as she pulls out a camera. "Say cheese!"

Sam puts his arm around me and we stand there with exaggerated grins. "Sorry about her, she will be like that all day," he tells me, before gesturing me into the shoe changing area.

I join the long queue, standing on the damp floor in my socks as I get closer to the front. On the counter, a girl who I recognise as a sixth former asks what size I need, her voice hanging with boredom.

"Seven, please." I hand my dirty trainers across. She holds them at arm's length and sprays them with an unknown liquid from an aerosol can. The audacity. They do not smell *that* bad.

I sit next to Sam as he tightens up the straps on his skates. They are bright red with a union jack emblazoned across the heel and much better than the dirty recycled ones I've been given.

"I got these from my uncle for my birthday," he says, catching me staring.

"They're awesome! You're totally gonna show me up."

He laughs, his braces catching the spotlights above. "They aren't magic boots. I'll be rubbish. We can both fall over together."

"I'd love to!" He gives me a glance through narrow eyes. "I mean, I'm happy I am not the only one who's gonna to be useless."

"You'll be fine. The trick is to go slow, apparently. I'll be holding onto the edge for most of the hour." He stands and holds his hand out, and I take it and rise to my feet. I feel like a new-born giraffe and fully expect to hobble away from here with a sprained ankle.

Bethany is on the far side of the ice with Matt, and they're gliding effortlessly. They complete two laps before I have managed to get both feet on the rink.

"The secret is to put your weight on each leg in turn," says a voice from behind. I turn and spot Molly from our form heading towards me.

"Oh, hi!" I say. "I didn't know you were coming."

"I love skating. Want to follow my lead?"

"I needed to ask her so we had the ten people needed to qualify for the food part," whispers Sam, before he slaps me on the shoulder. "Go on, Theo, I wanna see you go first."

I hold onto the side and immediately lose my footing, my legs flying in the air as I crash onto the cool surface. All the oxygen escapes my lungs in one hit. Am I dying? Sam offers out an arm and I struggle back upright, the venue spinning around, and then follow Molly's instructions gripping on to her hand for dear life. It isn't exactly Olympic pace, but I am moving! I hold the side each time I feel my balance slip, but this becomes less frequent quickly. I'm a natural.

After a few minutes, we have completed an entire circuit with no mishaps. I'm about to set off again when the lights dim and flashing lights fill the venue. The DJ, who I didn't know existed, turns on the speakers and *Relight My Fire* by *Take That* blares out, bringing a vision of Alex. I can't wait to tell him how well I am doing. I wish I had another camera with me so I could send him pictures, but hopefully Sam's mum is taking a few rolls worth from the sidelines.

"Left, right, left, right, that's it, just gliiiide," says Molly as we to turn to the left. Sam is still holding on to the barrier and we pass him again.

"You go ahead," I call to Molly over the music, and I allow myself to slide in a straight line until I come to a stop a metre or two from the birthday boy. "Are you okay?"

He nods. "I told you I'd be bad."

"It's okay, you're doing well."

"Don't patronise me."

"I wasn't, honestly. Do you want to skate with me?" I hold out my hand, retracting it quickly. He releases his grip on the side and pulls mu sleeve as he skates. Every time he stumbles, I grab his arm tightly to make sure he stays upright.

"You don't have to hold me, I'll be fine," he says as he pushes me forward at twice the pace I've previously reached. There is a problem, though. A massive, huge, enormous problem. I don't want to let go of him. I can see Bethany ahead, laughing and joking with her boyfriend and I turn my head and see Sam heading towards me. His blonde curtains waving at the side of his head and I am transfixed on him and his toned upper body. Urgh, why him? This is literally the worst thing that could happen.

"Theo!" he calls. "Look forward!"

I turn my head back to see the barrier approaching at an alarming rate. It's too late. I am going too fast and the barrier is too close, approaching me at breakneck speed. I cover my face with both arms and hold my breath. My body crunches against the wooden hoardings, the music stopping and the lights disappearing immediately.

Voices seem distant as I lay with my eyes closed. My back is freezing, so I'm still on the ice, but the coldness is hardly noticeable compared to the pain shooting through my left arm.

"His leg just moved, he's coming round," says an unknown voice nearby.

I let out a groan and open my eyes, squinting into the bright artificial lights beaming on me from above. I sit myself up, but the pain increases ten-fold.

"Stay laying, Theo," says Bethany, who is on her knees, leaning over me looking concerned.

"I'm alright," I say, even though I am wincing constantly.

"Mum is gonna run you to the hospital," says Sam who is stood by my feet.

"I'll be okay, give me a couple of minutes."

"You ain't seen your arm," he replies.

I raise my head a little. My arm is bending at an angle that arms definitely weren't designed to. The pain becomes even worse now I can see it. Even if my jumper hadn't been cut back with a pair of scissors it'd be obvious I've done some serious damage.

"What's your phone number again?" asks Bethany. "I'll call your mum and let her know what's happened."

"01850 20 16 00." I put my head back onto Sam's hoodie, which has been thrown across to form a makeshift cushion.

A rink worker with first aid written across their chest skates to me and flicks ice onto my face as they grind to a halt. "You've had a bit of a crash and bumped your head a little," he says as he crouches and takes something cold out of a green box and puts it to my temple. "Hold that on there with your good arm."

I manage to sit up and sweat pours from my armpits

as he unties my skates before tossing them aside.

"We're gonna take you slowly to the car and then get you checked out properly."

It takes four people to get me upright, and the room becomes a whirlpool as blood races back down my body.

"You were so funny when you were coming round," says Bethany as she drapes Sam's hoodie over my shoulders. "You kept saying you wanted Sam." I hate my subconscious brain right now. Hopefully, I've got away with it. As I'm lifted on to the carpeted flooring, Bethany lets go. "I'm gonna stay if that's alright? Sam's mum will take you to the hospital."

"What about the party?" I ask.

"You can't stay in your condition," she replies.

"No, I mean, is it still happening?"

"Yeah, don't worry. Matt's dad is here so he'll look after everything."

I am taken to the back seats of a chocolate brown Volvo estate, my dignity left in the building. I can't believe I have managed to mess this up so badly. I lay myself across the back seats and put a hand over my eyes in an attempt to shut out the shame of being so useless. "Tell Sam I'm sorry," I call to Matt as he picks Sam's hoodie up from the tarmac and throws it at me, before closing the car door.

I was only allowed the Monday off school despite doing my best 'sick boy' routine. Apparently a broken radius and cracked ulna is not a good enough reason to be allowed to sit at home and eat ice cream in front of *This Morning* more than once.

The first lesson on my return is Geography and Mr Barrett has set up an information hour about the upcoming Aachen trip. The most worrying part is the confirmation that payment is due by the start of March.

I've convinced him I'll pay, and my name is on the list, but in reality, I know I am just chasing dreams. Mum has another round of treatment coming up next month, and I may have to live with Nan for the fortnight she's in hospital for.

"Can I sign your cast?" asks Sam as he sits on my table with a board marker in his hand. I pull my sling back far enough for him to scribble on. All this wouldn't have happened if I didn't realise I was crushing on this boy whilst on a slippery surface.

"Sorry for ruining your party."

His tongue pokes out the side of his mouth as he concentrates on his signature. "You didn't ruin it. I'm sorry you weren't there. It's kinda my fault for pushing you too hard. We all missed you."

"Back to your seats please," Mr Barrett calls, and Sam hurries off to his desk.

Once he has gone, Bethany leans over to me. "Did you hear Sam and Molly kissed?"

This does nothing to boost my mood. "When?" I ask, annoyed but still curious.

"At the end of the skating. She held her hand out to guide him around. That could have been you if you didn't fall on your arse."

I snap my head in her direction as my heart beats fast. "Me with Sam?"

"Ha, obviously not. I mean with Molly. You were holding hands, if you remember?"

I slump back in the seat. "Oh. Yeah, Molly. Yeah, we were."

"Nothing will come of it, though. Rumours are they haven't spoken since."

My Sam-crush needs to stop, and thankfully this revelation does the job a little, even though the jealousy is causing a vein in my temple to throb. If I maintained my

Sam crush, I'd follow him around like a lost puppy and then the rumours would start. And then the bullying. Crushing on your straight, male, best mate is the biggest NO there can be. Especially at this school. I'd be a target for all the abuse. I'm the new kid and not enough people care about the real me here. Last in, first out. I'm getting carried away. Sam wouldn't feel the same about me anyway, so I'd only be on a long painful road to rejection.

By the time the *Oliver!* rehearsals start, I've firmly put thoughts of wanting to hold Sam into a box labelled "pubescent hormonal abnormality". He's still pretty cool, though. And yeah, he's attractive. Actually, maybe the feelings haven't gone.

All my mishaps meant sending quite a lengthy and detailed to Alex. He probably thinks I'm nuts. I like his idea of meeting up in five years' time and agreed we should definitely go ahead with it if we haven't fallen out by July. The chances of it happening are pretty slim, but it's a nice thought to be able to hold on to.

"Line up, everyone, line up," shouts Miss Houghton from the front, her piano music in hand. Rehearsals have moved into the main hall now there are only five weeks until opening night. Next week we are staying late on Thursday for costume fitting and a full-dress rehearsal, which we have been told will be a disaster.

"Nothing like being told that to boost your confidence," says Bethany a little too loudly.

"Bad rehearsals give you motivation to improve," Miss Houghton says in reply. "Now, where is my Nancy?"

Katie Barlow strides out to the front and does a spin. "Here," she calls out in case we missed her entrance, which, despite our best efforts, we didn't.

"Dick," says Bethany, and I give her a nudge to remind her she isn't the quietest person in the room.

"She is, though."

I'm inclined to agree. Katie is an absolute dick, with a capital D. She always needs to be the centre of attention, and her two closest friends, Jenny and Laura, stick to her side like they've had an accident with the glue guns in the Materials block.

During rehearsals, we run through half the songs and they go okay, much to Miss Houghton's surprise. Michael from the year below has been cast as the Artful Dodger, and he keeps putting on an exaggerated mock cockney accent, but I've heard worse.

My broken arm restricts my movement during the more upbeat numbers, and a plaster cast isn't the most Victorian of accessories. Today is the first time we get through *Food, Glorious Food* without getting the order of ingredients mixed up. It's a rare win in a long week of losses and by the time I'm home, I make excuses to Mum so I can lay on my bed in the dark.

The heating in my room has not kicked in, so I put on Sam's hoodie to keep warm. (Yes, I stole it.) I can smell his Lynx on the fabric. I catch myself breathing it in, certain something is definitely wrong with me. Like Alex's letters, Sam makes me feel a bit fuzzy. Saying his name whilst dazed and confused at the rink might be evidence I'm not like the other boys in my year.

Crushing on boys would explain why I don't feel any affection to any girl either, even the ones I'm told are pretty. There was even a magazine passed around in tutor time the other day. It had a double page picture of Pamela Anderson in her red swimsuit. The other boys were fascinated by her breasts (or jugs, as they call them). Not me, though. I preferred the picture of Lee Sharpe on the following page, dancing by the corner flag in his Manchester United shirt.

It's clear I'm different and I need to find a way to

change that. Urgh, why can't I be normal?

I'm much happier spending time with Sam and Matt than trying to win popularity contests with the girls. And as for the jealously of Bethany and Matt's relationship, who is it I am jealous of?

I sit quickly, disgusted at myself. I've heard the 'gay boy' taunts enough during lessons to know everyone would destroy me if it were true for me. And do the teachers step in to tell them to be quiet? No. The *technical* term is they do absolutely bugger all. I've even seen Mum turn the TV over quickly when two men have been shown kissing, and I know she's doing it to protect me, but maybe life has other ideas. I wish I could speak to someone, *anyone*.

I'm broken and I need to be fixed.

Against my better judgement, I grab my English workbook from my bag. Tearing out two pages from the middle, I start to write.

To Alex.

Seven

Alexander Beauchamp
9 Tolkien
Saint Martin's
Rutherford-On-Thames
Oxfordshire
27/02/96

To Theo,

You broke the rules this time and sent me two letters in a month! I'm only joking, I appreciate you writing to me as always.

I am so sorry to hear about your arm. How much longer do you need to keep the cast on for? I've never broken a bone so not sure how long the pain lasts, but hopefully you are able to sleep without too much discomfort. Please sign your cast on my behalf.

When you spoke about Sam's birthday party, it made me realise I never told you exactly when mine is. Well, it is on the 18th of September, so I am the oldest in my academic year. We held a small party in the dormitory, like we do for everyone who is trapped in this academic prison. Even at the weekend of my birthday week I didn't do anything. My parents were too busy and Isabelle was away on a trip, so instead I spent it alone with my Grandpops in Buckinghamshire. He owns a very big house in the country, complete with swimming pool and a white Rolls Royce.

A birthday near a May bank holiday would be much better I reckon. The weather will always be nicer than September where I am pretty sure it always rains. Hey, maybe your 18th could be the day we can meet! 22nd May 2000. Put it in your diary. I'll meet you by the fountain in Trafalgar Square at 2pm sharp haha!

I liked the picture you sent through, thank you. You look exactly as I imagined you to be. Your smile is so nice so I am not sure why you dislike it. The picture fits with your personality as well.

Despite what you say, we are both quite similar. We like music, like sports, and have a good group of friends around us. I can understand how my life may seem half the world away from yours, and you telling me how you wish you had my life sometimes broke my heart.

I realise I am lucky, but I would love to have a life like yours. Imagine how bad it can be *living* in your school. Everything is so strict and there are not many opportunities for me to be myself. The rowing and the orchestra are things I was forced to do because that is what is expected. Even though they are enjoyable, often I wish I was able to do other things which interest me. If (and a big if) I wanted to walk to town and buy a *Take That* single, I would have to get a permission slip signed by our Dorm Master.

I am sorry to hear your Mum is still unwell, and the trip to Aachen is causing you stress. I believe everyone should be free to take part in events without anything holding them back. I am worried how you will take this, but there is another separate envelope again. Please understand it comes from a place of care and not that I see you as a charitable cause.

Thank you also for telling me about how you are

feeling. You aren't alone, and being confused about who you are is common with people our age. I know there have been some crushes between the boys in our school, and it is all normal. There is no rush to figure yourself out, and if I am being totally honest, I did have these feelings too over the summer.

There was a moment where I was swimming with the others in a nearby lake, and at one moment I caught myself staring at Felix, wondering if I saw him as more than a friend. I didn't have anyone to speak to at the time. In fact, this is the first time I have ever put it into words. We can both get through this together. Life has a way of figuring itself out, so stick in there and let me know if anything changes.

How are your rehearsals going for *Oliver!*? Not long until you tread the boards. I am excited to hear how it goes in a few weeks. As for my top tips:

1. Sing as if you are trying to get your voice to hit the back wall

2. Do not picture everyone naked. You will gross yourself out.

I am busy training and have been moved into a new team. I will be in the foursomes for the next regatta. We were all out of sync in the first practice we had, and we caught the wake from the lead boat which caused a large amount of water to enter our boat. I genuinely thought we were going to sink! I believe being in this new team will give me a better opportunity in qualifying to row for the county, so I am going to work harder than I ever have to earn my place on that team.

I am meant to be studying for a history test so I will leave this letter there but will look forward to your next, as always.

Stay safe,

Alex.

Eight

March 1996

Mum stares at the four twenty-pound notes on the table. It took a few minutes to build the courage to show them her. She has launched into fifty questions about Alex and how he could afford to send the money.

Having survived the interrogation, Nan helps Mum back to the front room before returning to make an omelette.

"How important is your school trip to you?" she asks as she sips a glass of water.

"Very," I reply. "It will help with my German and Geography classes, and if I don't go I'll have to sit in the hall with all the other losers for three days."

She reaches across and puts out a wrinkled hand, which is cold to the touch. "I will speak to your mum, okay."

"Thank you," I say, excitement bubbling up inside of me, before it bursts and drifts away. "It might not make any difference though. The deadline to pay was Friday."

She takes the money and folds it into a small brown envelope. "I know life is difficult, but we must keep going. Also, just because we don't have a lot of money, that doesn't make us losers."

I nod my head as I put the envelope into my

rucksack. "Sorry."

"It's fine. Make sure you hand that money over to your teacher and explain things have been a little hectic. Make sure you send Arthur a thank you note."

"His name is Alex."

"Of course. I have some cards in my drawer you can use if you like."

She shuffles off towards the make-shift spare room where she sleeps when helping us during the harder weeks. I busy myself making cheese and ketchup sandwiches, and double check I have the preparation notes for my science test this afternoon. We have been let loose with Bunsen burners and are running an experiment in pairs which has something to do with salt dissolving. Bethany ditched me in Science to work with Matt, so I'm spending the afternoon with Sam (trying not to watch him as he constantly chews his pencil).

He's on a final warning after setting fire to his homework diary last week, with the flames spreading onto the chipped edge of the big desks. Miss Staunton had to come to the rescue with the red fire bucket, dumping sand across both the tables and us. I'm sure some of it is still in my shoes.

"Here you go," Nan says as she drops four cards on the table.

I flick through them, deciding the one depicting a bunch of red carnations is the most appropriate. The others are so dull and morbid they could be condolence cards, and that is not the vibe I wish to portray.

Nan takes her purse and pulls out a stamp. In the card I tell Alex this doesn't count as sending a letter. As a little gift, I include a programme for *Oliver!* I spotted in the drama rooms yesterday, which thankfully had my name spelled correctly.

Three hours later, I'm stood outside the staff room waiting for Mr Richardson to arrive. Located next to the school hall, you're normally only ever summoned here when in trouble. Matt calls my name and approaches, his face covered in cream from a bun he's quickly ramming into his mouth.

"Yo," he says as he punches me on the shoulder, leaving a small dairy deposit on my jumper. "We're gonna play some basketball if you wanna join?"

Before I can answer, Mr Richardson appears, grinning widely. After a quick glance over his shoulder, he invites me in.

"I'll meet you out there shortly," I tell Matt, who looks at me suspiciously before wandering off.

I don't know anyone who has seen inside the staff room before. I'm a soldier behind enemy lines. My presence causes all teachers to spin around and hurriedly look like they're busy, and I'm pretty sure Mrs Cox threw a lit cigarette out the window into the small herb garden.

"Come and take a seat," Mr Richardson says as he bites into a slice of Battenburg. The staff room is covered in posters giving guidance on how to influence and improve behaviours, but the untidiness makes me realise all their talk about us being organised is something they might need to practice as well as preach.

"How is your arm today?" he asks.

"Same. Off to get it checked next Wednesday."

"Make sure you let me know the time so I can notify your teachers." Mr Richardson takes a custard cream from a packet on the table. "So, Theo, how can I help you today?"

I pull the envelope from my pocket and pass it across. "I've got the money for the school trip. I know it's late, but if there is any way I can still go, I'd love to."

"I see." He takes the money and counts it, before

putting it into his top pocket. "I will make sure this is all sorted and that Mr Barrett adds it to the accounts."

"Thanks, sir," I say, and sit smiling as I wait for him to continue.

"It will do you good to come on the trip. How are things at home?" I know he feels as awkward about asking as I am answering.

"Nothing much has changed, I guess."

"And your mother? Is she well?"

"Still the same." I know she is getting weaker from the questions she's asking. *"Theo, can you open this for me?" "Theo, can you take the sewing box from the top of my wardrobe?" "Theo, will you run to the shop, we are out of custard."* These small moments make me realise her getting back to full health is never going to happen.

"Well, send her my regards as always. If there is anything I can do to help, either with school or pastoral support, you know where I am. I am glad you have the school trip to look forward to, and the play, of course."

My shoulders relax and a sense of calm falls over me. "I'm oddly excited about performing."

"You will be fantastic. I already have my ticket." (I know he gets a free ticket, but it's nice of him to say.("I was thinking, actually, how would you feel about performing in assembly next Wednesday morning?"

"I'm only playing a street urchin, Sir."

"I meant the whole cast." He looks at my arm. "No pun intended."

Katie will relish showing off in front of middle school. "I'm sure we'd all love to," I confirm. We need all the practice we can get.

"Wednesday morning it is then. Look, you best go and have your lunch so you don't flake out this afternoon. Is there anything else?"

I might be gay, sir. I obviously don't say this out loud,

but the words sit in my throat. "Nah, all good, sir, see ya later."

The science room is on fire again.

This time it isn't Sam's fault. The girls were being boisterous on the table in front, and as one swung their schoolbag around, it collided with our desk, and now the Bunsen Burner has toppled on its side and is firing golden flames horizontally towards Sam.

I jump from my stool and turn the gas off at the tap, but I'm not fast enough to stop the flame connecting with our safety precautions sheet.

Sam grabs a folder and wafts the small fire, causing it to spread along the desk at an alarming rate, and two months' worth of science notes turn to smoke.

Miss Staunton hits the red alarm button and bellows at us to follow procedure. As we file out, she's perched on a chair with a fire extinguisher in her hand, covering the room in a layer of water.

During the commotion, Mr Atkinson enters from the classroom next door.

"Call the fire brigade," Miss Staunton shouts as she continues attacking the problem area.

Our class, and also the Year 11's of Mr Atkinson's descend the metal staircase and out onto the gym playground. As we form an alphabetical line, the alarm continues to screech like a goat caught in a tornado. One by one, everyone else takes their positions in a neat, regimented order.

"It's well cold out here," says Bethany from two places in front. She is shivering, even with her arms wrapped around her body. Snow has been forecast to fall this afternoon, and I'm hoping to retrieve my jumper before I freeze to death on the spot.

I bring Bethany into a hug with my one good arm,

with Matt and Sam standing close by, too. We resemble penguins fighting for survival in a cold Antarctic breeze (or is it the Arctic where they live? I can never remember).

There's some chatter from the front, and it pulses towards us. Everyone looks to the left as light smoke swirls gently from the upper floor windows. A few squeaky gasps puncture the atmosphere.

Mr Richardson strides down the line to calm matters. "Nothing to worry about, everyone, all is under control," he reassures us. After taking a register, he tells us to remain outside until the fire brigade allow us access. My feet are now blocks of ice.

"What was you doing in the staff room earlier?" asks Matt, his voice muffled from being squished onto Bethany's shoulder in a way that puts his face quite close to my own. The beginnings of a wispy moustache are visible on his upper lip.

"Was just paying off the school trip," I say.

Bethany screams and hugs me tighter, pressing into my bad arm. Pain fires up it like an electric shock. "So glad you're coming!" she shouts in my ear.

"Seriously chuffed," says Sam. "That's so cool. It means we can defo dorm together."

"We still need a fourth," adds Matt. "The only other person I know who's free is Pyjamas." (Pyjamas, or Graham to give him his birth name, is so called because he once wore lime green jogging bottoms on non-uniform day.)

"I don't wanna spend three nights in a dorm room with someone who has to sleep with the light on," says Sam. "I bet we get thrown with him anyway."

I look around and make sure everyone else is busy in conversation, and I gather the three of them close. "Can I tell you a secret?" They all look at me expectedly. "Alex paid for my place."

"Who the hell is Alex?" asks Matt.

I slap at his arm to keep him quiet. "As in my pen pal Alex," I whisper.

Matt becomes animated quickly. "I knew these kids were rich, but not *that* rich. Fair play, I guess. Wish mine paid for me."

"Mine hasn't replied for three months," says Bethany.

"That beats me," Sam adds. "Mine never even replied to my first letter."

"Who hasn't replied?" asks Katie as she strides into the group, obviously in need of a shot of attention. Her fake eyelashes flutter as she poses in front of us.

"Just talking about pen pals," I say, feeling embarrassed.

"I gave up on it a while ago. Mine was so boring. What a bunch of rich, entitled tossers."

"Well, mine isn't," I snap, surprised at how quickly and vehemently I defend Alex in public.

"Maybe yours found you boring, Katie," says Bethany.

Katie screws her mouth in disgust, before leaving, staring over her shoulder with narrow eyes.

"Be careful with Alex, Theo," says Bethany once Katie is out of earshot.

"There is nothing to be careful of."

"I mean, well, don't you find it strange a randomer gives you like a hundred quid for no reason?"

"It was eighty quid," I retort.

"Even so," says Matt. "They might see us as a social experiment. Them being rich and us being at this hellhole, I bet they're loving looking down on us."

"Mine is different. I mean, Alex is different. He confirmed it wasn't charity, and he wanted to give me the opportunity to be able to experience new things." I want to tell them even rich kids seem to struggle sometimes too, like we all do. "He's just being kind."

"Well, I think it's great Theo has managed to bag the one pen pal who actually wants to make an effort," says Sam.

Matt laughs. "All I get from mine is gossip. This month it was all about him saying one of his friends could be a bummer."

"A bummer?" Sam asks.

"As in a bum bandit. I haven't bothered replying to him yet as I don't know what he wants me to say. They're from a totally different world."

"Why is him being gay a bad thing?" asks Sam. There it is again. The crush. It has crept up on me and I'm reading into every syllable he says. Him saying the word makes me wonder if he's trying to tell us something.

"Maybe it's his way of trying to have a conversation and get to know you, Matt," I say, trying to remain diplomatic.

He shakes his head. "Like Katie said, it's boring. If gossip is all he thinks I care about, then frankly, Felix can kiss my arse."

I tuck my good hand into my sleeve nervously. Felix isn't that common a name. It has to be Alex's dormmate and ex-crush. Does that mean the suspected gay friend is Alex? I try not to let the thought stick in my mind, but it's hard to think otherwise. Maybe he fancies me. Maybe that's why he said he liked my smile. Oh God. Maybe that's why he paid for Germany.

If the others put two and two together, then suspicions will fall onto me, too. I need to somehow raise it to Bethany. There are only four more months of letters to go, so if any of my friends become weird about Alex, I only need to get through to July.

After another twenty minutes in the cold, our

headteacher enters and stands on an upturned milk crate, megaphone in hand. "Can I have your attention, please?" he calls out, finger in air waiting for the chatter to dissipate. "Due to the small incident earlier, we will be sending you home rather than stay for fifteen minutes. Those who have items in the science room, these are being taken to the staff car park. Everyone else, back to your classrooms to gather your belongings."

He stands down and disappears quickly back into the building.

Bethany puts an arm around me to keep us both warm as we head to collect our belongings. "Oh, forgot to say," she says. "I phoned Dad at lunch today to remind him about something and he said he has bought three tickets for the Hollywood exhibition in the summer."

I bounce on the spot a little. "That's amazing, thank you. How much do I owe you?"

"It will be my birthday present to you."

"Are you sure?"

"Definitely. I've heard they're gonna have over a hundred dresses. I'm so glad you're coming with me."

"I'll be your date in place of Matt."

She laughs. "You'll be more fun to be with. It isn't his area of interest so would be quiet all afternoon. He's going to some football thing with Sam anyway, so at least he will be enjoying himself elsewhere."

"Oh yeah, Sam did mention about getting tickets for them both to the Euro's this summer at Villa Park."

"Yeah. I'm glad you chose the dresses over football for me."

We walk on in silence for a minute before I come to a stop on the edge of the car park. I take deep breaths as I chew on my next questions, hoping it is a good idea.

"What is it?" she asks. "Is it your arm? Did you want

me to get the nurse?"

"No, just listen." I swallow. "Bethany, if someone was gay, would that matter to you?"

"Are you trying to tell me something?" she responds, tongue between her teeth.

I want to scream yes, but the fear hits me. "No. I just wondered." Bethany narrows her eyes, and I'm not sure if she has bought the lie. "A few minutes ago, I think the person Matt said Felix was gossiping about being a bummer, as he eloquently put it, is Alex."

"And you wanna know if that's why he paid for Aachen?"

I can be read like a book. "I guess. Not that it matters. He's nice, but if he is gay, I want him to know I have his back."

"We have his back," she confirms, and I relax a little. "He probably paid because he was able to. Has he said anything about being gay?"

"No, not at all. He did say all crushes at our age were us being hormonal."

Bethany smiles. "He's at a proper school so knows more about science than we do. I mean, we can't even sit in class without setting fire to the place."

"Very true," I say with a laugh.

"Anyway, if he liked you more than a pen pal, there would be a bigger sign. Like a grand gesture of sorts."

"Isn't paying for a school trip a grand gesture?"

"Well, yeah, but you did say it was because he wanted you to experience it. Some people are decent. And to answer your question more directly, no, being gay doesn't matter to me. Just don't go shouting about it. You know what they're like at my church. From what you've told me, which is minimal by the way, he seems kind. He's helped you settle in."

Bethany is right. Alex gives me the chance to reflect

on things, a safe place for me to be more open than I can with most at school.

"I sent him a thank you card this morning."

"You should probably buy him a German fridge magnet from the trip."

"Yes, amazing! And I do have a fiver left over."

Blood rushes to my cheeks as I think about him again. Bethany gives me a side-eye before nudging me with her shoulder. Have I revealed my secret without having to say it?

Nine

Alexander Beauchamp
9 Tolkien
Saint Martin's
Rutherford-On-Thames
Oxfordshire

23/04/96

Hey Theo,

I hope you are well. I am furious. Three days ago, we took part in the Spring Regatta, and indeed the county trials. On the face of it, the result was fantastic. Ours coxless fours won both our semi-final and then the final, so I have my first ever gold medal. I have not allowed myself to display it in our dorm room, and the whole event has been tainted by the absolute farce which followed when I arrived back to school on Monday.

The County Selection Committee had confirmed the teams for the South of England championships, which will be held this July in Eton Dorney. Progressing from here would lead to the nationals, where scouts from the governing bodies of Great Britain and Northern Ireland would be present to look at potential rowers for representing the country at under-15 level.

I did enough for selection. That is not me being boastful, it is the truth, yet when I viewed the selection for the county, my name was not present. The three others in my team had been selected, yet my position on the bow side has been given to Maxwell Fanshaw from St Joseph's Boys. His team were seventh (out of eight!!!) in our semi-final and were at least thirty seconds behind us in that race.

The championships are sponsored by KDM Solicitors, and their CEO is Jacob Fanshaw. Now I am not saying Maxwell got chosen because his father has paid for part of the championships, but it is extremely suspect, don't you think? The narcissism is outrageous, and I have already told Mr Pallister there is no way I will continue with the school team this year after this debacle.

I am sorry to dump all of this on you, but I need a space to vent my disgust at being overlooked this way. Absolute joke, that's what it is.

Are you all set for the opening of *Oliver!*? I read the programme you kindly sent, and even spotted you in a rehearsal photograph inside. I hope someone has a camera on the night so I can see you in action. Have you learnt all your lines? I have asked Felicity to keep an eye out for a CD soundtrack so I can listen to it here whilst studying for my summer exams. I will be thinking of you when the curtain raises for the first time!

Our summer production has been announced for the amphitheatre. We will be doing *A Midsummers Night's Dream*. I knew it would be yet another Shakespeare production. I wish we could do something a little more contemporary. Some of our year group asked if they could write an original play of our own, however this idea was closed down, borderline laughed at, by the performing arts teachers. Mrs Sealey joined the school in September and is obsessed with Shakespeare, so she won't allow to do anything else aside from worship 'The Bard'. I reckon she has a crush on him with the amount of time she pushes the creases out the poster of him on the wall.

I appreciated your thank you card you sent recently. It is pinned to the corkboard above my study desk. I am happy you did not take my gesture the wrong way. I was so worried after I had sent it that it might have come across badly but knowing you will be on the bus and looking forward to the trip makes it all worth it.

How is your arm feeling now it is back to health? Next time you go skating you will need to wrap yourself in cotton wool!

On Friday, Felix invited me to his family's summer holiday in Valencia. His parents own a villa around half an hour drive away, so I am looking forward to it. We will be there for the last two weeks of July, and the first week of August. It will be nice to spend some time with people as Dad will be in New York this summer, and Mum is super busy with work. Have I ever told you what she does?

For the last ten years she has been part of the royal household, helping to arrange royal visits for family members. As you will have seen in the news over the past few months, there have been talk of troubles in the marriages of both Charles and Diana *and* Prince Andrew and Sarah Ferguson. It has meant extra work has come her way to ensure all engagements are updated. She is feeling the pressure a little now, and there are signs she may be ready to move to a different career. Before I was born she was working in the same company as Dad, but she would not go back to that. If she did, Isabelle and I would hardly see anything of either of our parents.

She is a talented interior designer, and I have tried telling her she should run her own business. Our family home is wonderful to look at thanks to her hard work so I am sure she would be a success. Do you think I should keep pushing her to do it? It would keep her occupied whilst dad is on his long trips. Dad is far too focused with work to notice us sometimes. His business partner, Joanna, rarely has to go to such lengths. Joanna is pregnant now, so all her work is being put on dad and I don't know when I will get to see him again. I wish I had family around me more, like you do.

Do you have many plans for your birthday? I hope you are able to do something fun with your friends (but maybe not ice skating…). I understand you may not feel like having a party, but you are only fourteen once, so why not have a movie night with Sam, Matt, and Bethany or something? If you are yet to see Jurassic Park, I would recommend that. It's out on VHS so go and get a copy! It is still the best thing I have seen at the cinema. I want to read the book yet we only have two copies in the school library and I am really quite high on the waiting list!

Writing has helped calm my mood a little, however now I am off to throw darts at the county team announcement in the common room. Only joking. (Or am I?!)

As ever, I am keeping your Mum in my thoughts. Please pass on my regards.

Yours,
Alex

Ten

May 1996

I stare at the clock on the kitchen wall. Three hours until the curtain lifts on what is looking likely to be the most shambolic performance of *Oliver!* ever to grace the world of theatre. Over the last month we have upped rehearsals to twice weekly, and even had to attend on Saturday to make sure as little as possible can go wrong. Forgotten lines, incorrect costume changes, and an orchestra member dropping their tuba and denting the end. We have had it all.

I sit at the table, squeezing a stress ball over and over in my left hand. Since my cast was removed, I've to keep it active to build strength. My forearm looks like it's attached to the wrong body, as pale as milk with rose red marks where plaster pressed against skin for ten weeks. My potato waffles remain on the plate smothered in beans, my stomach in knots ahead of this evening.

The door bangs, and Mum enters. At the weekend she reluctantly agreed having a wheelchair would be beneficial for mobility. With the illness robbing her of her strength, she rolls beside me, breathing heavily. She has one of her old posh dresses on, which now sadly hangs loosely to her frame. Her April hospital stay lasted for nine days. Due to our home being closer to the school than Nan's bungalow, Nan moved in to look after me. She did her best to keep me upbeat, yet every night we would make the ten-mile round trip to visit Mum, a different set of tubes and medicine around her each time.

"You look lovely, Mum," I tell her, before helping her move across to the table. I haven't seen her this elegant for a long while.

She smiles at me, and for the briefest of moments the old glint is back. "Thank you, darling. How are you feeling about tonight?"

"Honestly? Shitting it!"

"Language, Theo," she says with a small laugh, which turns into a guttural cough. "It is expected, though. I remember being the same when performing in Mary Poppins. Did you need Nan to drive you tonight?"

I move some waffles and beans about with my knife. "I'll walk up shortly. I said I'd meet Bethany at six. Doors are an hour later. I'll ask them to reserve a place for you, if you like?"

"Yes, please. One with a good viewpoint so I can get some photos."

I stand and give her a hug. Even her scent has changed. It's clinical, medical.

"I hope we don't put you off," she says.

"Having you there is the only thing that won't be rubbish."

"I'm proud of you," she says as she kisses me on the cheek. "Anyway, have a waffle, get your stuff ready, and stop panicking!"

I arrive at school, navigating my way through the assembly chairs which are now acting as the stalls for the makeshift theatre. The atmosphere is different out of school hours. Ms Houghton and Ms Fenton are in casual clothes, and don't look like teachers at all.

On stage, the scenery produced by the sixth form art students has transformed the usual black back wall into the cobbled streets of Victorian London. Cotton wool smoke clouds rise towards the spotlights from the cardboard chimneys high above my head.

It isn't long before the double doors at the far end crash open, and Bethany enters carrying four bulging carrier bags. Her hair is shorter than during classes, and it glows with moisture compared to the dull lifeless cut that sits on me. I could do with seeing her semi-professional stylist aunt. She looks incredible. Bethany is the one stand-out performer from rehearsals, and her Gospel church educated voice carries everyone else in the chorus. She should have got the role of Nancy. Part of me hopes Katie Barlow is awful.

"Hey, Theo," she says as she drops her bags to the floor. "Just taking this backstage. Take the Sainsbury's one for me. There are some cakes in there for energy from Mum. I'll be back in a second. I need to talk to you urgently."

"How can I be of service?" I ask as Bethany returns after I've shoved a whole lemon cupcake into my mouth.

She lets out a sigh. "It's about the exhibition in London."

"Oh my God, I cannot wait," I say, spitting crumbs in her direction. "Have you seen the previews of the Hollywood Stars exhibit? It looks incredible. The dress from *Breakfast at Tiffany's* is definitely there, and so are some of Monroe's shoes!"

"I have yes, but Theo, look, I'm not sure if I can do it anymore. I'm sorry." She doesn't make eye contact, instead focusing too heavily on stirring a coffee she has stolen from the machine near the drama rooms.

My heart drops and I throw my second cake onto the table. Bethany had been keener than I had, and that's saying something. "What? Why not? It's gonna be amazing!"

She takes hold of my hand. "I know, it looks great, it's just my parents have decided to take me away on the Saturday after the last week of term."

"Well, that's OK, the exhibition is on until the middle of August, so we will delay it until you're back."

"But Theo, I'm gonna be away for at least a month."

"A bloody month? Where the hell are you going for a month?" I lean forward, resting my chin on folded arms.

She smiles widely. "The Caribbean!"

Of all the places in the world, it had to be there. Her grandparents still live there, and I know I should be happy for her, but I can only think of how lonely that will leave me. It already feels like her being with Matt has left me behind. I haven't hung out with her on a weekend for a month. She's always too busy. No Bethany, no Hepburn dress. She was going to be my security blanket this summer, and for the first time in years I was hoping I wouldn't have to spend the majority of it with Mum and Nan.

There's no way I'll be allowed to go on my own. "What are you gonna do out there for a month?" I ask, exhausted, as I clean the table with the sleeve of my jumper. She holds out her arm, and I take a serviette and wipe my crumbs from her sleeve.

"It's my Granny Best's eighty-fifth birthday and they wanna get the whole family together. We only had to pay for the flights as we will be hopping around the various Caribbean islands staying with my many uncles and aunts. Jamaica, Trinidad and Tobago, St Lucia. Everywhere! It's gonna be such an experience."

I ease a little. "It does sound good," I tell her honestly. "I'll allow you to go, but what about me?"

She takes my hand. "I know, I'm sorry, but Sam and

Matt will be here so I'm sure there are things you can do whilst I'm away."

"I get bored at weekends already, Bethany. I'll be a recluse after a month without you."

"You can see if Matt and Sam have a spare ticket for the football, maybe?"

I raise my eyebrows. "Tickets are like gold dust, especially for the England games."

"Okay, how about doing something special for your birthday?"

I take another bite of cupcake. "Alex suggested a film night. Have you seen *Jurassic Park*?"

"I haven't. Which reminds me, Matt has promised to take me on a date to see a film, but he still hasn't sorted it. Have a word with him, will you?" I nod in agreement. "We have the summerhouse at mine remember, so how about you come over on Saturday for a film, and then we can sit out in the garden with pizza or burgers or something. Hey, why don't you invite Alex?"

My hands become clammy, and I get hot as my stomach gurgles. "Um, yeah. Maybe. He wouldn't want to make a forty-mile round trip. Anyway, he's already seen *Jurassic Park*. If he did come, then what would I wear? I don't want him to think I'm a scuffer. Maybe I can borrow one of Sam's nice shirts? And my hair! Is it alright like this or should I cut it short like Matt's?"

Bethany stares at me with wide eyes. "I was only joking."

"Oh."

"Your hair is fine by the way. You'll be a catch for someone one day. Actually, ask Alex if you want, he seems cool."

"He's amazing, honestly. We've got into a rhythm now where we can spill all our problems. Fair play to Mrs Bosnich for pushing this pen pal thing." I look at

Bethany and bit the inside of my cheek, looking around to make sure no one is in earshot. "If I can be totally honest, I've started to care about him. He doesn't have family near him, and I worry he's forced into doing things he doesn't enjoy when he does get to spend time with them."

"I get what you mean. I bet it must get boring not being able to chill with friends."

"One hundred percent. That's why the movie night will be good."

I have another bite of cake and then I get hit by a bolt of confidence. "Bethany, can I tell you something important?" The words leave my mouth before I think.

She puts a hand on my knee and smiles. "Of course."

As I stumble over finding the right words, a commotion comes from the foyer and four other chorus members tumble into the hall. Bethany flies out her seat. "We defo need to get a move on. I've some new Rimmel glittery eyeshadow from Superdrug I'm dying to upstage Katie."

I want to protest and tell her glitter isn't in keeping with the production's Victorian theme, but when she feels determined, there is no point in trying to distract her. I sit, slightly slumped, and watch as she leaves. I'm left on my own finishing the most depressing cupcake I've ever had, wondering if the universe is convincing me my secret is too shameful to share.

Eating three cakes before going on stage was always a bad idea, my stomach is doing somersaults, but they helped get me out the slump.

"In positions, everyone," says Ms Fenton as she claps at us as we stand in line behind the curtain.

I tune in to the murmurs of the audience on the other side of the fabric, knowing in a few seconds the overture will drown out their mutterings. I check my shirt is tucked in three times, before Bethany hurries to my side. Her eyes are glowing with the brightest green glitter, and her cheeks reflect the lights into my face.

"There are some flowers backstage. I've put them in a vase," she says.

Katie Barlow strides in front of us. "Ha, they will be for me no doubt. My boyfriend is that kind of person."

"She's still a dick," I whisper to Bethany, her laugh catching the attention of Ms Fenton.

Bethany pulls my arm until my ear is pressed to her cupped hand. "Theo, the flowers aren't for Katie."

"Good. I'm glad you got them and not her. Bonus points for Matt. Who knew he had it in him?"

The school band in orchestra pit (i.e. The small roped off section by the piano) blast out the first notes and it's almost in key. I jump, my brain doing acrobatics inside of my skull. I've forgotten all the words. I've forgotten where I'm meant to be standing. Bethany can't stop grinning at me, which doesn't help.

Ms Fenton sprints across the stage one last time, clipboard in hand, with a second to spare before the curtain is pulled across, exposing us to two hundred pairs of eyes. Front and centre, Mum is sat beaming, tears falling onto her cheeks. It sets me off straight away, and I struggle to hold myself together.

The first half flies by in a blur, and fair play to the teachers, we're managing to pull this performance off. Admittedly, there has been the odd lyric missed, and at one point Bethany left the stage in the wrong direction and had to spend ten minutes hiding underneath a table in Fagin's house, but everyone, including Houghton at her piano, was expecting worse.

As act one closes, we slink out to the largest drama room which, for two nights only, is acting as the costume and snacks room. I fall onto a solid metal chair and take a drink of Lucozade. I'm so nervous I need to spend five minutes on the throne in the PE bathrooms, but not so much I'd want to be anywhere on my own. Out the large windows, a group of Year Elevens are slyly sharing a cigarette, with each in the group taking it in turns to be a look out. They've failed to realise everyone in the dark drama room, including the teaching staff, can see them.

"Not too bad so far, is it?" says Bethany as she crouches in front of me.

"I'm actually enjoying it."

She smiles and looks over both shoulders, the light catching the glitter, which is slowly transferring itself from her eyes to the side of her face. She looks less like a Victorian and more like a face drawn onto a disco ball.

"You need to come with me," she says, holding out a hand. She virtually drags me over to the opposite corner and I stumble behind her. "These are the flowers I was on about."

"Yes, lovely." Me faking interest in the fauna here is Oscar-worthy, even if nothing else tonight will be.

She punches my (newly recovered) arm and I wince. "Theo, listen. They aren't for me."

"I thought Matt got them you?"

"Nope. Look."

She puts a hand on the back of my head and pushes me towards the vase. Inches away from my nose stands a bunch of red carnations tied together with a royal purple bow. In the centre is a small brown envelope poking out from the stems, my name written along the centre in a familiar, loopy handwriting. I pick it up, turning it slowly around in my hands.

"For God's sake open it," shouts Bethany.

"Alright, alright, keep your smock on."

I lift the flap and pull out a white card.

> *Theo,*
> *Break a leg, but not an arm!*
> *Alex*

I show Bethany and puff my cheeks out.

"Now that," she says, "is a grand gesture."

I take a moment to run my fingers over the petals whilst I regain my composure, trying to slow the heartbeat that is pounding blood round my body so hard that it throbs in my ears.

"Are you okay?" Bethany asks. "You've not said anything for nearly a minute."

I don't know how to respond. No one has ever done anything like this for me. For it to be another boy is something I'd never expect. I appreciate him sending them, but I'm awash with a sense of embarrassment, knowing everyone else in the production will catch on to what is happening if I don't act fast. I can sense the faces of others in the room staring as I hide in the corner with my back turned. The noise dies out and tunnel vision sets in.

Before I know it, my feet are carrying me into the corridor and I throw myself into the nearest boy's loos, quickly locking myself into a cubicle. I sit on the closed toilet seat and regulate my breathing, staying completely still when I hear someone enter.

"Theo?" Bethany's voice is soft and kind, but I'm too shellshocked to reply. "Theo, can you come out?"

"No."

"I shouldn't have sprung them on you. I'm sorry. It might be us reading too much into it. We shouldn't jump to conclusions." I sit still, remaining in silence. "Look, come out. We have to be back on stage in five, and you won't be much use sat in here."

"What if he does like me?" I say, my voice barely audible. "As in, *like me* like me?"

"It's better than not being liked, isn't it?"

"I guess." I stand and pull the chain out of habit, before unlocking the door and heading to the sinks. Bethany stands behind, watching me splash cold water on my skin. As I dry myself on my costume, she ties her arms around my waist from behind.

"It's okay. In fact, it's cool. You've bagged the only decent pen pal."

I spin around and pull her into a hug. "What if I like him back?" I say, as much to myself as to her.

She pulls her head back slightly so she can look into my eyes. "*Do* you like him back?"

I shrug. "I dunno."

Bethany looks concerned. "You know the answer as much as I do."

I lean back on the sink. "Argh, Bethany, I dunno. I've never felt anything like this. I've been thinking about it for ages. Maybe I should tell him how I feel, just in case?"

She holds me firmer, almost squeezing all the oxygen from my lungs. "Theo?"

"What?"

"That's a terrible idea."

"Is it?"

She lets go. "Yes. We don't even know for certain if that was his intention. Like when he paid for the trip, he might just be a decent person. And if he does fancy you, then I'm cool with that. And if you like him back too, then that's cool too."

"Would you disown me if I was gay?"

"Of course not. If it's just friendship, then make sure you keep that friendship."

"But what if it's more?"

"We can come to that another time. Gay or not, I still love you. Let's not tell anyone though, yeah?"

Despite my brain fog, inside my feelings are clear. I do like Alex in that way, and I'm secretly praying he does fancy me too. I don't have the funds for a grand gesture, but I need to give a hint. In theory, after this month, there will only be one more letter between us. I need to save my confession for the final letter. At least that way, the project will be over, and I'll be under no pressure to open any reply.

"Your eyes are a bit puffy," says Bethany. She draws a thumb gently across my cheek to remove an escaped tear, leaving a snail trail of glitter. "Just play it cool, yeah, and don't think about it."

Is she serious? It's impossible to not think about. It's less of an elephant in the room and more the entire cast of Noah's Ark sneaking past the window. Bethany keeps hold of me and I kiss the top of her head.

"You two. Stage. Now!" Ms Fenton stands staring. I'm always amazed by the stealth-like movements of the staff. They're like ninjas in knitted tops. She drags a finger up and down in our direction. "You know the rules about heavy petting in the schoolgrounds. We will discuss *this* tomorrow."

Eleven

Alexander Beauchamp
9 Tolkien
Saint Martin's
Rutherford-On-Thames
Oxfordshire

30/06/96

Hey Theo,

I LOVED the article you sent through from the *Stokewood Gazette* of *Oliver!* How does it feel seeing your face in the local paper? You all looked like you were having fun, and the scenery looked good. It's better than what we have so far for our Shakespeare performance. Rehearsals have been going well, and I am lead piano for the performances now for the first time!

I am so pleased you liked the flowers I sent. Felicity helped arrange their delivery for me. The idea came after your March letter. I was on a date with Melody, and I was telling her all about you, so she recommended giving you a little gift to wish you good luck. Melody likes *Take That* too, but she says she prefers *Eternal*. (I don't know who they are, but I haven't told her that!)

There are only two weeks left at school to go before

we get to have some time off over the summer. I am looking forward to Valencia with Felix and his family. It will be lovely to spend time in the sun with people around me. Dad's recent trip has been extended by a further month, much to Mum's anger. I heard them shouting at each other down the phone last weekend. I will be glad not to be stuck at home with them, especially if they continue to bicker with each other.

Isabelle is heading to another tournament soon. She is playing for England in the Home Nationals. They are being held in Belfast, so I have asked her to buy me a Titanic souvenir. I can't wait to see the film they are making with Leo in it, so it will definitely be worth watching. I'm not sure when it is out, but Melody loves him so hasn't shut up about it!

We received our exam results last week, and I did well, so I'm quite happy I can relax a little now. I got a Grade C in Woodwork, and as the expectations on us are ridiculously high, a letter was sent home explaining ways on how I must focus to not fall behind. It's literally mad. This is why I hate being here. You always have to be better than you are, be the best at sport or music or performing. There is no time to just exist. To breathe. Why do they pressure fourteen-year-olds so much?

Sometimes, I look out over to the woodland from our dorm window and wonder what would happen if I packed a bag and snuck out one night. If I timed it right, I could be a few miles away before sunrise. Knowing my luck, the rumours about teachers roaming the grounds boundaries during the night would be true, and I'd be rounded up with any other escapees and dragged back and punished with chores.

Two more years, that's all there is. I cannot wait for the day when I am free. Felix and I have a world map on the wall, and we have stuck coloured pins in all the places we wish to visit. Me with blue pins, Felix with red. He is most keen on Southern Asia (he has a weird fascination with Vietnam War trivia), whereas I want to go East. I'd love to visit Japan, especially Tokyo. There was a picture in my Children's Encyclopaedia I used to read obsessively as a child. It showed a street scene with neon lighting illuminating all the people below as they headed into the night for food or drink.

Then there is Mount Fuji, of course. I don't want to climb it, but to sit far away and take in its beauty. The other place I have pinned is Yoshinoyama. This is reportedly the best place to see the cherry blossom on the trees. We would have to time our trip correctly otherwise they'd look like any other tree, I guess. If it happens in a few years, maybe you could come too!

At the Spring Regatta, our county crew got knocked out before the final, missing out by 3/10ths to Durham in the repechage. We would have qualified for the final had I been in the boat instead of Maxwell Fanshaw. I spoke at length to Mr Pallister on the bus home from London, and he understood my frustrations, especially as the selection process was out of his hands.

The decision has been made to move me back into a doubles team with Brian. This time next year, I WILL be rowing for the county.

Are you all set for Aachen? I should have sent this letter earlier, but I will ask Mrs Sealey to make sure it goes first class as I want you to receive it before your long journey. I am writing it before I head to the hall to watch Germany and the Czech Republic in the Euro final. We all want the Czechs to win after what the Germans did to us AGAIN, so I am doing my best to write fast whilst not leaving important news out. Make sure you have plenty of snacks for the trip, and if you do stop in Brussels, see if you can get some of their delicious chocolate. It is even nicer than *Cadbury's*.

I learnt a phrase from my friend Kristian you can use. He is originally from Bonn so is fully fluent with it being his first language. He said if someone is a bit odd, then you can say *Sie hat nicht alle Tassen im Schrank*. It is a bit like us when we say someone is a few sandwiches short of a picnic. See if you can use it on the trip!

I'm feeling a little weird because that is all my news for now. Knowing this is the last letter I have to send as part of the *Great British Pen Pal Project*, something about it feels off and I don't know exactly what it is. What I am trying to say is this: Thank you.

Getting to know you during this past academic year has been amazing, and it has helped me appreciate the small things more. Every so often, I will catch myself thinking, "I must tell Theo about this."

Receiving your letters has been a highlight. I have loved hearing about *Oliver!* and the fun you have with your friends. I got extremely lucky in finding you. There are only a few left who kept in contact for the ten months. That reminds me, Sam is still in touch with Barnaby (the one who smashed our dorm window with the potato). I saw a letter from him on a desk. I didn't read it because I am better than that, but there was a picture underneath of you with a blonde guy taken at what looks like the ice rink, and it had both of your names on the back. He is shorter than I imagined.

Wishing you, Bethany, Matt, and Sam the best summer ever. Make sure you spend as much time as possible enjoying any sunshine, and don't lock yourself away whilst Bethany is in the Caribbean.

Finally: May 22nd, 2000. 2pm. Trafalgar Square. I will meet you by the fountains.

I will miss this.

Alex x

Twelve

July 1996

I was on a date with Melody.

Seven words proving I got everything wrong. Again. I finally read the letter on the coach, having been allowed access to the post room after the art block was out of bounds for a refurb. I'll miss those paintings on the staircase. As we are waved away by our families, I already want to smash the emergency window and get off.

"You'll see them again in few days," says Bethany as I slouch back in the bus seat, waving at Mum and Nan out the window as the sun rises above the school. Mum's wheelchair use is increasing, and Nan being around the house is much more frequent. Another round of treatment is three weeks away.

I wish there was a magical fix, but the treatments don't seem to be making her stronger. Even with the power leaving her body, I still imagine getting home in four days' time to see her striding along the hallway, picking me up and spinning me in a tight hug. I know it won't happen, but it's the one thought stopping me from breaking completely.

Nan called me to help fix something on Mum's chair at 3am this morning, and I failed to get back to sleep, instead staring at the glow in the dark stars on my ceiling, wishing I didn't have a long journey ahead.

"I said, you will see them again in a few days," Bethany repeats, tapping me on the head with a closed fist.

"What? Yeah, sorry." I close the thin curtain and rest my head back, eyes closed. As I drift, a bag of sweets is opened next to me, the rustling bag resembling the crackling of a campfire. I open one eye and see the confectionary thrust towards me.

"Liquorice Allsort?" Bethany asks.

I let out a sigh. "Only if I can have a coconut one."

"I've obviously already kept those ones aside for you." I put out my hand and Bethany piles around a dozen into my palm. "Don't eat them all in one go. We have ages on this bus, and I don't want to sit next to you if you're complaining about a stomach ache before we get to Dover."

I open the sickbag from the seat pocket in front and put them inside for safe keeping and put my head back again.

"What's up with you?" she asks.

"I'm alright," I lie.

"Tell me."

I sigh again and have a quick check over both shoulders. "Alex has a girlfriend."

"Shite."

"Utter shite. It's in his latest letter."

Bethany strokes my knee. "I'm sorry."

"It's alright. I guess it helps clarify things in my mind."

"Was Alex just a crush, like a one off?"

"If you're asking if I'm gay, the answer is still maybe. Don't tell anyone." The coach becomes claustrophobic, as if the sides of pushing towards me, crushing me under the pressure.

Bethany gives me a hug, and I can smell the fruity scent from her hair. "Are you sure he meant girlfriend?" she whispers. "Let me have a look at the letter in case you've got the wrong end of the stick."

I'd pass it across if it didn't reveal Sam had secretly been writing to Barnaby all this time. "I put it in the bin before we got on. He's dating someone called Melody so it's hardly ambiguous." I push my legs against my bag in the footwell on the off chance the letter will magically spring from the inside pocket into Bethany's hands.

As we head along the new bypass that circles Stokewood, the inevitable chant of *It's Coming Home* starts from the backseats and slowly makes its way towards the front like a tsunami of heterosexuality and Lynx Africa. Not only did football not come home, ten days ago it technically went to Germany.

Sam and Matt are doing their patriotic best by wearing England shirts, complete with their names written in big blue lettering across the back. The shirt is the outfit of choice for the majority of boys, actually. I sink into my seat and pick at my Allsorts. Eleven and a half hours to go.

As I wake from a slumber, I open the curtain to an unfamiliar landscape, my brain taking a moment to understand why we're driving on the wrong side of the road.

"Morning," says Sam as the fizz from his bottle of coke splashes my face.

"Where did you come from?"

"Bethany asked to swap so she could tongue Matt. Want a chocolate?"

I sit and readjust my seatbelt, taking a box of Belgian truffles from his hand. "Where did you get them from?"

"From the services in Brussels."

I twist my head to the window. "We're in Belgium?

Why didn't you wake me?"

Sam shrugs and speaks with his mouth full of food. "I wanted to, but Bethany said you were knackered, so we left you on here with the driver. You missed Katie Barlow singing along to the radio. She was awful as per."

"Where are we?"

"No idea. There's only like twenty minutes left, though. You've been asleep since the ferry."

"I'm never gonna sleep tonight."

"Probably not. Trust you to get jetlagged on a bus."

The coach chugs and lurches forward as the driver manoeuvres it into the car park of the Sonne Jugenherberge, our home for the next three nights. After a quick headcount, we collect our suitcases from the hold and gather in the reception as Mr Richardson speaks in German to the staff, returning soon after with a stack of envelopes containing room keys.

Me, Sam, and Matt have been allocated room 54, and we squeeze into the lift together with our inevitable dorm-mate Pyjamas, who has his night light tucked under one arm. We all stand back as he lets out a phlegmy cough.

"Bagsy not sleeping above his bunk," says Matt as he darts out the lift as soon as the doors open. I follow him to our room, which takes a minute or two to unlock due to a dodgy handle, and immediately head to the tiny en suite.

As I come back into the main dorm, an argument has already broken out between Matt and Sam.

"Theo, help us out," Sam demands as I climb the ladder to the bunk above Pyjamas, the plastic mattress cover sliding beneath my knees. Sam hangs onto the railings as he stares at me. "Who's fitter? Geri Halliwell or Emma Bunton?"

I try to remember which is which. "Um, the one in the Adidas," I reply.

"Mel C?" Sam says as he jumps with thud onto the floor. "All she does is backflips and stuff."

"Mel C is better than Emma," says Matt. Pyjamas stays quiet in the corner, nervously eating a pack of crisps, his eyes watching us as we advocate for our favourite Spice Girl.

The back and forth between Sam and Matt continues for another ten minutes, and I wonder if Alex has to listen to this in his dorm every night. He has an extra four people, too. It must be a nightmare. I try and push thoughts of Alex out of my mind, the magic having gone now he is, and will always be nothing more than 'just a friend'.

I'll find time to write, making sure to leave the parts about him maybe fancying me, and vice versa. I still have the spare five pound for a keyring, and I'm a boy of my word, so I have to send him a letter regardless. Without him, I wouldn't be laying on this creaky bed in central Europe.

I barely slept last night and Mr Richardson is being weird. I filled a bowl with Cornflakes and then made a cup of tea, and he somehow managed to ask me twice if I was feeling alright. My immediate and obvious thought is that he's worked out my secret. Aside from the tiredness, everything is fine, and I'm looking forward to exploring the town with the class soon. Richardson looks odd in normal clothes, opting for a Welsh rugby jersey, chinos, and open-toed sandals. He seems to have a lower sense of authority when not in his suit.

"I am *still* fine," I say, as he checks on me for a third time. I smile and sit next to Bethany who has reserved a space at the end of her dining bench.

"Thank God you're here," she says, looking pristine as always in yet another set of new clothes. "These two are being disgusting," she adds, waving a milky spoon in Sam and Matt's direction.

"I was only saying it was something I read. It said in *Nuts Magazine* they're bringing in a new range of flavours," Matt says, his eyes wide and elbows on the table.

"Like tropical fruits and black forest gateaux," adds Sam.

I take a spoonful of cereal. "I love black forest gateaux, so whatever it is, count me in."

Bethany punches my arm. "Don't encourage them!" she says pointedly.

Sam holds his hands up in defence "We're not talking about lollipops, Theo."

"In a way, we could be?" says Matt before they both roar with laughter.

Bethany leans forward on her elbows. "If you don't shut up, I'll dump you," she says to Matt, who only chuckles in response. "I mean it."

Half an hour later, and still none the wiser as to what confectionary they were on about, we have changed into waterproof trousers and have been driven across the town for a morning of water-based geography research in Westpark.

The water is cold, and if I move forward any further, it will spill over the top of my trousers and freeze my legs. Sam is stood to my left, waving a net around haphazardly trying to collect algae from the surface.

"Why did they nominate us to get in this cesspit?" asks Sam.

I look towards him. "Probably because you wouldn't shut up on the coach ride over here, despite us being told a million times." He remains silent, continuing to collect samples. "Sorry, but it's definitely your fault."

On the banks I can see our class sitting in the sunshine, filling in some forms attached to clipboards and passing around a giant bag of marshmallows.

"Can I ask you something?" I say, needing to break the awkward silence. Sam grunts, which I assume to be confirmation I can continue. "Why didn't you say you were talking to your pen pal?"

"I'm not," he says, unconvincingly.

I wade across towards him, which is difficult to do in water when you're trying to move fast to make a point. Even though we're marooned in the middle of a pond, I whisper when I reach him. "He's called Barnaby, and he's in a dorm with Alex, my one." A look of panic crosses his face, and he licks his lips nervously. "It's okay," I say. "Alex said he saw a photo of us you'd sent. I shouldn't have mentioned it, sorry."

Sam tips a splodge of green algae into the bucket hanging around his waist. "I dunno why I didn't tell you."

"Hey, it's alright. I won't tell anyone."

"I guess I was a little jealous, that's all."

"Of Barnaby?"

He shakes his head. "Of you."

I'm taken aback for a moment. "Really?"

"You're so open about Alex, and I know you like him, and I was worried for you. I didn't want people bullying you. I wish I was like that."

I can feel my cheeks turn red. "We're just pen pals. Well, *were* pen pals anyway."

Sam drops the net and lets it float near us on the surface. "Theo, I know you like him, and not just in a pen pal way."

"Has Bethany spoken to you?"

"No. But it's obvious. I know you're as close to him as you are to me or her."

"I'm not."

"Theo, it's fine, honestly. I saw the flowers and you said you're planning on meeting."

"That's not for a few years."

"Even so." He draws his hand through the water, creating small whirlpools on the surface. "Also, how many times have you said, 'I'm gonna tell Alex about this' whenever we're doing anything fun?"

"I've never said that. Well, not knowingly anyway."

"Trust me, you do. And do you know why I notice? It's because, every time we do something fun, I always stop and wish I could tell Barnaby, too."

The chatter from the banks recedes, my whole attention tuned into Sam. I allow him some space, but he doesn't say anything more, instead moving away to escape the pond. I chase after him in slow motion through the hip-high water but fail to get close enough to grab his arm. "If you feel the same way about Barnaby as I do about Alex, tell me." He shakes his head and wades away.

Sam didn't make eye contact for the rest of the pool study, and swapped places on the bus so he could hide behind Matt across the aisle. For the whole journey, he is sat with his head against the window, staring into space. As we approach the hostel, the bus clips the kerb making a left turn into the car park. Bethany screeches and spills orange juice from a paper cup all down my favourite t-shirt.

I grab a napkin, but it's soaking through to my skin. "Good job I was gonna wash this anyway."

"You can borrow this," says Matt, throwing his England top at me as we jump onto the gravel.

"Cheers. Is Sam alright?"

"Yeah, he'll be fine. Just homesick."

"Already?" I reply. We've only been gone thirty

hours.

Matt shrugs, and walks off with Bethany, taking her hand as they go. Sam is the last off the bus, and he gives me a nod as he trudges down the three stairs onto the driveway.

"Wait here, you two," Mr Richardson says as he moves around to the hold. He pulls out two large sacks containing the waterproofs. "Before you get showered, take these to the washroom."

"But Sir, we were the ones who had to get in the water," Sam complains.

"It's your fault for being last off the coach," I moan.

Mr Richardson lifts the sacks, one in each hand, and tosses them across. I sling mine over my shoulder, and it nearly takes me over backwards. "The washroom is that door over there," he says, pointing to a haunted looking entrance, half covered with sinister dark ivy.

As the class bundle into the hostel, me and Sam cautiously enter the dingy washroom. The walls are plain brick, and a city of cobwebs glow from the low unvarnished beams when the naked lightbulb finally buzzes to life.

"Are you alright?" I say as I take off my orange-soaked t-shirt, throwing Matt's England shirt on in its place.

"Everything is fine," he says, but I know he's lying. I can tell by the way he's drawing circles in the dirt on the floor with his left shoe. "I'm sorry," he says eventually as he leans back on a washer.

"I don't mind. We're cool."

He puts his hands on his head. "Theo, when did you realise you fancied Alex?"

It's not something I've thought of before. It's hard to pinpoint the exact moment everything changed. "Maybe when he sent a photo through, so like, his second letter."

"How did you feel?"

"Excited. Confused. Awful. Actually, yeah. Awful is probably the best description."

"Why?"

"Sam, being gay is disgusting. Everyone knows that. I dunno how to change it, though."

"You don't have to change it."

I let out a fake laugh. "I'm sure school would be an absolute party for me if everyone knew." He goes back to being quiet, so I move towards him a little. "Do you feel the same about Barnaby?" It's a probing question, and Sam buries his hands in his pockets, fighting through all the ways he can respond.

Eventually, he looks in my eyes. "No, not exactly. Well, I did, but, I dunno." I don't think even he believes what he's saying. "I mean, at Christmas. I told him about my birthday, and he sent that pair of ice skates."

"The ones with the Union Jack on them?"

He nods. "Yup. I was too embarrassed, so I told you they were from my uncle. It made me think Barnaby is gay, but he isn't."

"Nor is Alex."

Sam lets out a sigh. "It's difficult, ain't it?"

"It's hard." I leave a short gap, wondering if my next question would change everything. "What about you? Are you definitely… y'know?" I allow myself to trail off a little.

He makes a weird shape with his mouth. "I mean, a part of me must be, mustn't it?"

"Not necessarily." My heart pounds as I walk across to him. I've built up moments like this in my head so many times before, but now it's a reality, I've never felt so sure about who I really am. As I reach him, I put my arms around him and hug him tightly, realising I've wanted to feel a connection like this for months. "It'll be alright. There's no rush."

"Maybe everyone our age is confused," he says, whilst his right arm strokes my back.

"You don't have to say you're gay because I've told you I probably am."

Despite us having been in the pond, the scent on his t-shirt matching that on the hoodie I stole on his birthday. I lean my head back and put my forehead on his. I don't know why, but in my head, this is meant to be happening. "Thanks for being cool," I say. He smiles, and I decide to go for it. I kiss him, and he doesn't pull away.

We stay embraced, and in the distance, I can hear the crunching of gravel. I wait for it to stop, before kissing him again. A few moments in, he throws me off and I stumble onto my knees in a dark corner.

"What's going on?" I hear Katie Barlow ask from the doorway. Her eyes are squinting, adjusting to the light.

"We're on our way back," Sam says, stumbling over each word as he strides towards the door. I remain hidden, waiting for his footsteps to disappear. "We weren't doing anything, I promise," I hear him say as he makes his way up the stairs and out of sight.

I rush to the door, and poke my head outside, hidden by the foliage. "Katie, wait," Sam calls, but he's a few yards behind her. "We were just sorting the washing."

I walk back into the washroom and slump onto one a sack of waterproofs. I pray she didn't see what was really happening.

We left Aachen at 8am this morning. Half the class are asleep as we travel along the M25 towards Stokewood. The descending sun's glow illuminates the horizon like a golden orb, providing enough natural light for me to write my final letter to Alex.

For the rest of our time in the hostel, I made sure Sam and I were mostly apart. If we are going to keep the kiss a secret, it'd be easier if we kept a bit of a distance between us. We're still speaking, but all conversations are in groups and usually involve pretending which pop star we find 'the most fit'. We decided on sticking with Emma Bunton so we can cover each other's tracks if one of us slips.

I hate writing this letter. I *do* hope Alex is happy, and I tell him to say hello to Melody, congratulating her on her great choice in music. It's a shame it's all over. I'll miss hearing about the rowing and his dorm mates.

He was right all along. It will be strange when we're all fully grown. We had a fun year, regardless of outcomes. Ships in the night, as Nan would say. On that day in May in four years' time, perhaps I'll have someone new in my life and Alex will be a passing silhouette from the past, no longer required to meet me at the Trafalgar Square fountains.

"Are we home yet?" asks Bethany as she finally rises from being doubled over in her seat.

I rub the back of her neck, which, if anything like mine, must be ceased up. "Still got a few hours."

"Have you slept?"

"Nah, I had way too much sugar on the ferry." My mind was stuck on thoughts of the youth hostel washroom all the way through Kent, but now the day is closing, I'm battling against drifting off. "Do you have that fridge magnet handy?"

Bethany pulls it from her bag, polishing crumbs from its face until Aachen Cathedral is visible again. "Is it for Alex?"

"Uh-huh," I say, trying not to give my tongue a papercut as I lick the envelope closed. I put it into the seat pocket in front and watch planes take off from

Gatwick in the near distance. "Fancy running away?"

Bethany smiles and places her head on my shoulder. "Maybe one day."

The crackle of the coach's intercom wakes me from my slumber. I glance out the window, wiping dribble from my chin as the school comes into view.

"Please remain in your seats," says Mr Richardson, much to everyone's annoyance. We're all tired and irritable. He darts off the coach and becomes deep in conversation with Mrs Bosnich. They are huddled just below my window, and he nods along and strokes his moustache as he listens to what she has to say. He lets out a long exhale and comes back onboard with a blank expression.

He takes the microphone and coughs to clear his throat. "I need everyone to remain seated for a couple of minutes. I know you all want to see your families, but we won't be too long. Where is Theo, please?"

I cower in my seat, panic setting in, wondering why I'm being singled out. "Here, Sir," I say, hand raised in the air. Bethany looks across and puts her hand on my knee as we wait for him to reach our seats.

I sit frozen to the spot. "What's going on, Sir?"

Mr Richardson leans across. "Theo, sorry, can you follow me? Don't worry about getting your suitcase, Mrs Bosnich will take care of that."

Surely this can't be about what happened with Sam. I've heard rumours the school comes down hard on anyone talking about being gay. I've also heard rumours about a boy in the year above who people thought was gay. He put in a formal complaint after being bullied, and the school's suggestion of resolution was for *him* to move somewhere else. Well, I won't let that happen to me, that's for sure.

Why hasn't Sam been asked to come with us, too? He's as much to blame in all this as me. I grab my rucksack from the overhead compartment and follow Mr Richardson off the coach like a shadow, the eyes of my classmates fixed on me. Even the parents in the car park are statuesque.

Mrs Bosnich leads me away, silent, her arm tight around my shoulder. I realise this isn't about Sam at all.

Thirteen

End of life care. That's what everyone is calling it.

I wish people would stop sugar coating it. Mum is dying and it is a race against time to get to her.

The journey to the hospice is silent inside Mrs Bosnich's cluttered, blue Vauxhall Nova, allowing me to contemplate the cocktail of emotions being shaken inside of me. I attempt to remain stoic, but when we pull into the car park of the single storey hospice, I finally become numb.

I can't even say thank you to Mrs Bosnich as she opens the broken passenger door.

Nan is sat on the porch steps smoking a cigarette, something I've not seen her do for years. Her eyes are puffy, her hair greasy and unstyled.

I throw my bag onto the floor as my pace quickens from a walk into a run, and Nan takes me into her arms. I scan my surroundings, staring at anything to stop myself from crying. The flowers in the garden, the birds chirping on the feeder, the water slowly bubbling from a sphere in the small pond. All things I know Mum will never see again.

"It's all going to be okay, darling," Nan says, her voice shaken, broken.

Except it's not. Being okay means Mum will come

home this evening. Being okay would be her sitting on the sofa shouting at politicians on the news, or doing a wordsearch in a bumper puzzle book, not lying on a bed dying in this pebble-dashed shithole.

"When did it happen?" I ask as I'm led inside.

"Tuesday afternoon," Nan answers monotonously.

"I would've come home earlier."

"I phoned Mr Richardson and discussed the situation with him, however, your mum wanted you to enjoy your trip. He said he would keep an eye on you."

Mum always did put others first.

Does put others first.

No past tense: she's still with us.

"I would've run home for her," I say.

Inside, the hospice resembles a building on a holiday park, except the staff are in medical scrubs rather than blazers, and the chlorine smell filling the air as we stalk the corridors comes from a pool reserved for comfort and rehabilitation, rather than pleasure. There's no water slides and inflatable tyres here.

Mum's room is small and painted a pastel blue. Underneath a watercolour landscape, she lies there, her eyes open, but vacant as if they're covered with a thin sheet of glass. I move away from Nan and approach.

Mum reaches and strokes my arm. "Hey, you," she says, her voice at odds with her body, sounding no different from when she said goodbye to me four days earlier.

"How are you feeling?" It's a stupid question.

"Like shite."

"Language, mother," I reply, and she smiles widely.

She shifts, and Nan puts an extra pillow behind her back. "Honestly, though, it has been a rollercoaster. One minute I can drift asleep halfway through a sentence, the next I feel like I could stand up and walk home."

"Where are you on that scale right now?" I ask.

"Halfway between the middle and great. Do you want a cup of tea?"

"I'll sort that," says Nan, but I tell her to leave it to me. She needs rest as well.

"There is a little kitchenette along the corridor in the family room," Nan says.

Slowly walking down the hall, it is brighter, warmer, more alive than Mum's room. People are laughing, discussing the weather, typing away behind computers. There is normality rather than finality.

In the family room, I review the shelves whilst the plastic kettle boils and vibrates on the metal trolley. All the books are cast-offs and there isn't one title I recognise. On the floor below, something familiar catches my eye. I pull out the Connect 4 box, and once the tea has been made, balance three polystyrene cups on top as I walk steadily back to my family.

Each staff member I pass looks at me sympathetically, and I realise they must go through this process every hour, every day, every year. Fair play to them, I could never do it. I didn't even know what to say to Bethany when her cat died two summers ago.

"Three-all. Next game wins," says Mum as she opens the bottom of the Connect 4 grid, allowing the red and yellow counters to spill across her cotton bedsheets.

"Your turn first," I say, as I pass the yellow counters across.

Nan stands from her chair. "I need to stretch my legs. I'll be back soon, just heading to the shop."

"Don't buy any more fags," Mum says, but I know she will. "She'll end up in here next if she keeps on chaining them."

"Please don't say that."

Mum squeezes my hand in apology, and studies the empty grid, before dropping her counter into the lower right corner. "How was Germany? Any gossip for me?"

I shake my head, but I can't hold the lie in forever. It burns inside, a chemical reaction melting my heart, taking over all nerve endings, all thoughts. "Nothing interesting, nah. Was a bit boring to be honest."

"Did you remember to get Alex a present?"

My last letter to him remains in the seat pocket on the coach. The grumpy driver who moaned for the whole three days will have thrown it into a rubbish bag by now, the face of Aachen Cathedral deep in a Biffa Bin covered with food waste and used nappies. Pretty great metaphor for the remnants of mine and Alex's relationship, I guess.

My hand hovers, a red counter in my fingertips, but I don't make my move. I can't do it.

"What's wrong, love?" Mum asks.

I clutch my knees to my chest, resting my chin on my arms. "Mum, can I tell you something?"

Her brow furrows, and she reaches out to gently tug my sock. "What is it, what have you done? What's happened?"

I close my eyes and speak before I can overthink it. "The world looks different."

"Different? What are you on about? You haven't eaten anything hallucinogenic, have you?"

I chuckle at her ability to make any situation upbeat. "No. Look, since writing to Alex, my world looks different."

"In what way?"

I throw the counter to the bed, taking her hand in mine. "I might be gay. Sorry."

"What makes you say that?" she replies, sitting up a little more, squeezing my fingers tight.

"At school, I guess. I don't feel the same as the other

boys in my year. I've never had a crush on any of the girls, even the popular ones like Pamela Anderson, but I think I do, sorry, know I do with Alex. I started caring more for him ages ago, in a way that seems odd. Kinda of like how we love the budgies. Does that make sense?"

She laughs, which catches me off-guard. "I assume you don't mean you want to send him a cuttlefish and make him crap on a newspaper."

"Alex doesn't like fish." She moves the game to the side and I perch on the side of her bed. "I'm sorry, Mum. You're not angry, are you?"

"Look, people are very different to pets, but I understand. If you're that way, then so be it. You're being very brave."

I shake my head as I bring her hand to my face. It's as cold as ice. "I don't know if I ever would've told you, but if I am, and I never said anything, I'd regret it for the rest of my life. And if I didn't tell you now…' I tail off, tears beginning to fall, unable to finish my sentence.

Her eyes glisten and she pulls me towards her until we are cheek to cheek. "You're a silly sausage, do you know that? Even if I'm not here physically, I'll still be with you here," she says, pushing two fingers onto my chest. "I'm so proud of you."

"I was so close to telling Alex, Mum. I wish I'd told him, even if he doesn't feel the same way back. He cares about me, and therefore he deserved to know. I wrote a letter but I can't send it now. It's gone, and it's too late."

"Theo?" says Mum stroking my hair as I sit on the edge of the bed. "I love you. I know someone else will take my role when I'm not here anymore, but you can't live life wondering about the 'what ifs?'. Every fork in the road leads to the right destination, even if you take a route across the fields rather than the motorway. I'm sure one day you'll get the chance to let him know. That might not be now, but in your future."

She takes a yellow counter and drops it in the grid, a line of four resting diagonally.

"Well done, as always," I say.

"Reigning champion!" she says, louder than anything else this afternoon. "Maybe you'll win tomorrow."

The evening is spent with me and Nan doing relays to the shop. We both know we aren't really 'going for some fresh air'. Reality is that it's a break from the increasingly frequent visits of nurses. The high Mum had been on during the afternoon declined rapidly.

As she sleeps, her breathing laboured, I keep talking to her, telling her all the trivial gossip she wanted. I just hope she can hear me. Her eyes are moving, but the lids close off her view of the world.

"I'm going for a…" Nan says, miming the smoking of a cigarette. When she has stepped out the patio doors onto the courtyard, I lean and kiss mum on the head.. It feels like I'm watching a scene play out, disconnected from my emotions.

I stroke her hair, tucking thin strands behind her ears. "I love you."

The gentlest squeeze on my hand lets me know she's still with me.

It was at 9.40pm when it happened.

Her grip on my hand loosened, the flicker in her eyes gone. She simply looked asleep. Nan brushed her cheek with a palm, before taking a seat next to me.

The radio continued playing, and the birds still chatted as the Summer sunlight faded towards night. The world surrounding us kept moving, but as we spent our last moment as a trio, everything froze within our bubble.

No words were spoken. They didn't need to be. Our

final game of Connect 4 lay motionless on the side table.
Mum was at peace.
Forever my reigning champion.

Fourteen

September 1996

If you'd asked me two months ago, I would've told you there'd be no way I'd return to Stokewood Secondary. The pain of the funeral and the sorting through the endless sacks of Mum's belongings became unbearable on multiple occasions.

Often, it's the strangest of occurrences which bring you back to the present and snap you out of a slump.

"Why is there a Charles and Diana tea towel hanging in your front room window?" Bethany asks as she bundles herself into Nan's bungalow.

I've been living here seven weeks now, and slowly getting used to the smell (of lavender air fresheners, not Nan).

"You know what old people are like when it comes to the royal family," I tell her. "She has more pictures of William and Harry than me. I certainly don't have my face plastered on mugs and decorative plates, that's for sure."

"What do you think of Prince William?" she asks.

"I know you're asking that to make me not think about Mum, but I ain't gonna answer regardless."

Bethany pulls out a crease on the tea towel and it falls behind the sofa.

"Pick that up, quickly. She'll be back from the shop in a minute and will only moan. She believes it possesses some magical powers."

"They won't get back together, I bet you." As she climbs on the arm of the sofa to rehang it, she stops. "Did you hear that Katie Barlow saw Mr Teale holding hands with a man?"

"And?"

"It's not a problem, honest!"

"Then why bring it up?"

She shrugs and tacks the towel back to the glass. "Just, people are weird about gay people, yet straight people are worse. Like, most end up divorced and hating each other. I dunno why everyone's obsessed just because it's Charles and Diana. They're no different than the couple who run the chip shop."

"The chippies are getting divorced?"

"It was just an example." Bethany jumps back to the floor. "Its weird people are crying over a couple because they're famous."

"Tell me about it." The only television in the bungalow has been showing interview after interview about the royal break up. I'm strangely glad to be going back at school. Bethany has been saying for two weeks that I need my routine back.

After the funeral, Nan's bingo friends tried to comfort us by leaving lasagnes on the doorstep. I can only assume they thought Nan wasn't eating. Despite heading to the bingo hall together for at least a decade, they don't know her well enough to remember her tomato allergy.

Every day there would be a new one, steaming under tin foil on the mat next to empty milk bottles and the cat litter tray. (She doesn't have a cat, but hopes it deters the neighbours ginger tom from defecating on her drive. (It doesn't.) We nearly have enough lasagne in the fridge to open our own Italian restaurant. I've eaten so much pasta that I'm almost missing the greasy £1 pizza from the tuck shop. Almost.

The first morning back at school is difficult. My brain is trying to shut out the sympathy from everyone in the year. I know they're being kind, but every question is a reminder of that evening in the hospice.

Now, though, as I sit in Mr Richardson's new Head of Upper School office at lunch, coming back was the best move. Mum would've wanted me here.

"How are you getting on?" Mr Richardson asks as he takes a seat behind a large oak desk. I'd hazard a guess that, unlike the ones we sit at, there is no rainbow of hardened chewing gum on the underside. I bet he hasn't even scratched his initials onto it yet.

"So far, so good," I reply as I nervously twiddle with Mum's emerald ring, which I've taken to wearing since she passed. It's too big for my left index finger, and I need to take care not to lose it, but wearing it means she's close. "We had practical studies with Bosnich this morning."

"*Mrs* Bosnich," he says.

"Sorry, with Mrs Bosnich. We watched another video on knife crime."

"And how was that?"

He's sat opposite me, stroking his moustache. Last year, I wouldn't have liked chatting to a teacher instead of hanging in the tennis courts with Sam, however Mr Richardson came to the funeral, and has been supportive to both me and Nan. He even drove Nan to and from bingo the other week after her clapped out Metro finally succumbed to the great scrapheap in the sky during its MOT.

"The only knives I have access to are the blunt ones in the Home Ec block, Sir," I reply.

He nods slowly, leaving a long silence in the air. If we continue at this pace I might miss Maths. I've been placed in Set Four, so missing it wouldn't be the end of the world. I should be higher but missed the grading test due to authorised bereavement leave. My aim is Set Two by Christmas.

"You're probably wondering why I have asked you here," Mr Richardson says.

"To make sure I'm okay?" I answer.

"Well, yes, of course, that is always the main thing. Today, though, I want to share with you an opportunity which has become available. It is right up your street." He stands, and pulls at the cord on the blinds, trying to shut out the sun beaming through the dirty panes. After unsuccessfully getting the blinds level, he comes back to the desk. "Speaking of streets, any news on the sale of your house?"

"It's getting closer," I reply quietly. The house I shared with Mum was too big for just me and Nan, and with her dodgy hip, me moving into her large bungalow on the other side of Stokewood was the most sensible option. Our old house on Oak Tree Crescent holds far too many memories. Every time I sat at the kitchen table, I expected Mum to walk through the door, or for the theme tunes of her favourite programmes to drift through the house.

Of course, they never did. It's amazing what reminds me of her. Her favourite NASA mug in the cupboard, the smell of Imperial Leather soap in the bathroom cabinet, the oranging leaves on the small beech tree by the garden wall, falling onto the grass and not being raked like previous autumns.

Despite discovering Mum was a bit of a hoarder, I've

done a lot of clearing, with the help of Bethany, Sam, and Matt, to clear the less sentimental possessions. All that remains is a shell, bare lightbulbs hanging in the now cell-like rooms. The last of Mum's possessions are in cardboard boxes, stored until a sale is agreed, in the old front room. It seems impossible that it is the same front room where so much laughter happened.

It does catch me off guard when I see one of Mum's old jumpers on a mannequin in the window of Oxfam, or some of her books on the charity stand in the precinct. We buried her in her favourite dress, the one she barely filled as she watched my performance in *Oliver!*

There are some items we can't ever dispose of. In the back room of Nan's bungalow, boxes of photo albums and jewellery are stacked like a giant homemade Jenga. I don't know what we'll do with them, but at least they're safe. I can't bring myself to look through the albums, instead focussing on one photo of Mum laid back in a deckchair on Bournemouth beach. It has the honour of being on top of the telly.

The black phone on the office desk rings, and Mr Richardson laughs two seconds after answering. "Yes, of course. Yes, he is in here now with me. Yes, send him through."

The conversation continues for a couple of minutes, and I sit on my hands feeling like a spare chair at a wedding. Mr Richardson's shelves are filled with box files, a few generic sporting trophies, and a picture of a young Mr Richardson at his graduation, the colour faded due to the thirty or so years between today and the ceremonial day on which it was captured.

"Who's coming?" I ask as he replaces the receiver.

"We have some new staff members and I would like to introduce you to one in particular. He will be here in any second." He stands and drags another solid chair over. "Want any water?"

"Um, I'm fine, thanks."

"Shame. I have a new water cooler." It's amazing what gets a teacher excited. He pours himself a plastic cup full and drinks it in two gulps. "Remember to get to school on time tomorrow. I have the keys to the new Year Ten lockers and will be distributing these during registration."

"Will you have spares?" I ask, knowing I'll lose mine by the coming Friday. Before he can answer, the door clunks behind me.

A man in a shirt two sizes too large creeps in, his medium dark brown hair pulled back into a ponytail.

"Come in, come in, take a seat," Mr Richardson says. The man closes the door and studies me silently, as if scared to approach.

"Hi," I say. "I'm Theo."

He smiles again, but still doesn't speak, instead eyeing me suspiciously. I subconsciously straighten my shirt collar and run my hands down my torso to get the creases out my now slightly faded jumper.

"'Ello." His voiced is soaked with a northern accent.

"Theo," says Mr Richardson, "I think you'll like this." He gestures at the man, who clears his throat, and straightens his diamond-patterned blue tie.

"Hi, Theo, I'm Mr Le Bon. No relation."

I frown. "No relation to who?"

"Simon Le Bon." I stare at him blankly. "From *Duran Duran*?" I've no idea who that is. "Anyway, it's nice to meet you. I'm the new Head of English, and I wanted to meet with you as soon as possible. I heard you excelled last year in English?"

"Yes, that's correct," I reply.

"And your pen pal project went well."

I smile as I think of Alex, wondering if his first day is

more standard than mine. I only miss him a little bit and hope he and Melody are getting on well.

Actually, that's a lie, I think about him all the time and I hate Melody and I hope they've split and are having an awful day. I know this is unfair, but life is unfair. I'm due some good karma after such an horrendous summer.

Mr Le Bon straightens his tie again. "At my old school, I oversaw the school newspaper, and during my interview it was an idea I raised when discussing improving student morale and engagement."

"And a very good idea it was, too," says Mr Richardson as he looks at his computer screen, clicking the mouse randomly.

Mr Le Bon grins. "Thank you. With the new year, it is a great time to introduce a paper to Stokewood Secondary. Mr Richardson has explained your situation to me and suggested you would be a suitable candidate to help get the paper off the ground. It is a project which, I believe, would ensure your success and commitment to English is maintained. Would you be interested in that?"

Yes, is the short answer. I don't want to be too eager, though. I can already picture after school writing clubs, me in the office as phones are buzzing around as breaking news flies in from across the town. On the other hand, if I play my cards right I could guarantee a stack of form points would come my way. I need to beat last year's measly total of twenty-six.

"Um, yeah, I dunno. Maybe? What does it involve?"

"I will be helping," says Mr Le Bon. "I will be a mentor. We can meet once a week, or fortnight, depending on exams and other commitments, and discuss potential articles." I nod at him in all the seemingly relevant places. "As editor, the final say on any content will be your responsibility, and your responsibility alone."

Editor! I've never been in charge of anything. "Okay, I'm in," I say. "Do I get to recruit anyone?"

He pulls a lime green folder from his satchel and passes it across. "Yes, of course. You will find the full details in here." I flick through the plastic covered pages of the information pack. "As you can see," he continues, "we need a photographer, a sub-editor, plus a few others to help badger some pupils for articles. I want you to read through this thoroughly and have a think about a few potential ideas. Let's say we meet on Friday lunchtime to discuss ideas. How does that sound?"

"Perfect!" I confirm. The paper will be a welcome distraction from the dark thoughts which have plagued me for the previous eight weeks.

Having escaped from the office, I make it to the tuck shop with five minutes to spare before the shutters are slammed shut by the ever-angry dinner team. When I enter, Sam gets up from the table and moves away without looking. He's done this a few times today.

"You should do an article on Matt's hair," Bethany says as she flicks through Mr Le Bon's folder.

"What's wrong with it?" I reply, lowering myself onto the unsteady metal bench, leaning forward carefully on my elbows without resting them in the pool of spilt blackcurrant juice coating the tabletop.

Matt is leant against the window, deep in conversation with the football lads. "Theo, you have eyes. I mean, look at him."

His floppy blonde curtains have been reduced to shortened spikes, frosted tips glowing on the ends of each, and haven't gone down well. "He looks like he's in a boy band."

She nods. "Yeah, the Twatstreet Boys."

I realise we've gone off on a tangent. "I'm not sure

hairstyles of our mates would make the most fascinating piece," I say as I roll a Wham Bar small enough to fit into my mouth whole.

"Not Matt's hair on its own, but you have Katie Barlow and her Rachel cut. She keeps flicking it every time she tries to flirt, even though the trend went out of fashion like eighteen months ago."

I chew until I'm able to speak without dribbling. "You can pitch that article to Le Bon on Friday."

"Wait, I have to come too?"

"If you want to be on the team, then yeah."

She rolls her eyes. "Fine. What's Le Bon like?"

I shrug. "Alright, I guess? He seems eager to take me under his wing."

"I heard he got suspended from his last school for fraud."

"What a load of bollocks. Who told you that?"

"Just a rumour I heard at break."

I stand and put my bag on my shoulder. "Like the rumour the new kid in the year below has eight nipples?"

"Like a human pig," she responds as she gathers her stuff before we head to Maths. I shake my head at the ridiculousness of it all and follow her out the tuck shop.

The Friday meeting with Mr Le Bon went well, and a plan of action was drawn up. The first edition will hopefully go out in November, and in the six weeks until the article deadline, I need to advocate for student support. With no rush to get home after the final school bell of the week, I head to the IT department to create a poster to display in the corridors.

"Hey, Sir," I say to Mr Teale as I poke my head around his classroom door. He's had a haircut too since I last saw him, and the short style makes him look much younger. Losing the messy beard has helped.

"Hey, Theo, are you okay?"

"Yeah, just wondered if I can print something for the paper. Le Bon said it should be alright."

"Of course."

I take a seat at the desk with the best view out the windows, and Mr Teale follows, leaning over to enter the password. As he types, a gold band on his ring finger catches the light. "Sir, can I ask you something?"

He sits on the desk. "Go on."

I suddenly lose my confidence. I don't want to interrogate him. He probably would rather not discuss his boyfriend with a pupil. "Um, what design should I do for my poster?"

Mr Teale lets out a chuckle. "Something bright and bold should do the trick."

"Would you like to do an article, Sir?"

"I'd rather not, but thanks for asking." He turns his attention back to the screen. "Right, if you open this one you can do a few edits, play around with the colours, that kind of thing."

After a few clicks of his mouse, he goes back to his desk and sighs from behind a large pile of marking. I get to work, and things take a step in the right direction when I realise there's a WordArt option allowing me to do some crazy text. The poster isn't the best thing ever, but it's certainly eye-catching. "How many can I print?"

"Colour ink is expensive, so do ten. You can photocopy some afterwards if you need more." He takes a swig from his *World's Best Teacher* mug. They must've had another clearance sale down *Woolworths*. Or maybe every teacher gets given one as a welcome back gift.

I collect my printing, light drizzle now falling on the windows. "Do you have a plastic wallet, please?"

"I do. One second." I stand behind him as he rummages around in his stationary cupboard, balancing carefully on a wobbly stall. "Ah, here we are. Is it big enough?"

"Perfect." As I put my posters inside, I catch myself wanting to show them to Alex. I need to get used to the fact he's gone, however much I don't want him to be. "Thanks so much, Sir."

"Take care, Theo."

As I'm halfway into the corridor, I come to a stop. Mr Teale is back at his desk, pen in hand and hovering over another test paper. I have an Alex shaped hole burning through me and need advice. But letting on I know might do more harm than good. I'd hate to open any similar wounds for him.

"Is everything, okay?" he asks, having watched me stare in standby mode across his room for a few seconds.

I panic, hopeful he can't mind read. "Sorry, yeah, it's nothing."

"Are you sure?"

"Promise."

He gives me a nod, and I finally drag myself away from his room.

Seven days later, I've tasked Matt with making a post box outside the canteen ready for next week, where students from any year can write suggestions and post them for us to review for inclusion. After convincing Bethany not to write about hair, it would improve on the grand total of zero articles we currently have for issue one.

I display posters in the main reception and meet Sam after his rugby training to walk home. Halfway back, we stop at the dairy on the hill to grab a pint of strawberry milkshake. We have found a loophole in their payment system. A pint of milkshake is forty-five pence, but you can get two pence off if you return a bottle.

The dairy stack their clean bottles in crates in the car

park behind the floats, through the side entrance gate. If you spread your hands wide enough, you can get a bottle on the end of each finger, meaning you can con them out of twenty pence. We haven't paid full price for a milkshake since April.

"Sorry if I was a bit weird today," Sam says as we enter his street.

Walking past his is a longer route to Nan's bungalow, but I enjoy spending the time with him. It's rare to get moments alone at school, partly because he runs away so much since Germany.

I've got used to him ignoring me and know why he does it. The incident in Aachen has fogged his brain as much as it has mine. Those feelings hit out of nowhere, that's the problem. You can be having a great day and then BAM! You're flooded with worry, thinking you're eight different levels of messed up.

"You weren't weird," I say. He's even being a bit weird now, though, to be honest. He hasn't made eye contact for five minutes, and he hasn't finished his milkshake or spoken about football.

"I got a letter a couple of days ago," he says, wiping a strawberry moustache from his top lip.

"From Barnaby?"

"What? No. I still haven't written to him." He takes his bag off and rests it on the garden wall. I wait whilst he digs his arm inside, like a vet birthing a cow, before eventually he retrieves a slightly crumpled envelope. "It's from Alex."

I snatch it from him and get a buzz of excitement as soon as I see his familiar loopy writing again.

"He must've got my address off of Barnaby. He wrote to me last week, asking to pass it on if I thought you would want to see it."

"Of course I'd want to see it," I reply, wondering

why Alex didn't send it to the school like normal.

"Sorry it took so long, just there never seemed to be a good time, y'know?" He shuffles on his feet a little and plays with the button on his cuff.

I grab his arm. "I'm scared to open it, Sam."

"Why?"

"He probably hates me. After all he did to make sure I went on the school trip, ignoring him as soon as I go on it isn't the best, is it? I did write a letter, but left it on the bus, but if I tell him that it'll sound like an excuse. I wouldn't be surprised if it tells me to piss off. He has every right to do that."

"Oh, shut up, Theo. Of course it won't be that. He forces a half smile. "I've got another confession."

I stare at him. He looks vulnerable and a little scared. "Go on."

"When we got back from Germany, when y'know, you got taken off the coach, Bethany found your letter to Alex in the seat pocket."

"You didn't read it, did you?" This would be worse than them reading my diary (if I ever wrote one).

"No, course not. I took the letter though as thought you might want it. When Mr Richardson told us where you'd gone, I decided to post it for you. Sorry."

All the times I've worried about Alex not getting it could've been avoided if Sam had told me this two months ago, but there is not a chance I'll be angry at him. He could easily have thrown it away after what happened between us. "Sam, you're officially amazing."

"I thought it was best he got it, that's all."

I check along the road to make sure the coast is clear and give him a quick hug. His body tenses straight away, his arms rigid against his sides.

He brushes me off. "Not here."

"Sorry."

"Look, I've gotta go as I've got a meal with my parents tonight at a new Italian bar in town, if you fancy it?"

"I'm not going within a mile of a lasagne, but thanks anyway."

He smiles. "See you tomorrow, maybe? A few of us are going down the Rec at four for kickabout or a game of Wembley Doubles if you need to get out the house?"

"I'll be there," I reply, a needed distraction from collecting the last of Mum's belongings from the old house. "I'll knock for you at about quarter to," I add, as he waves a hand over his shoulder as he makes his way down the garden path.

I stare as he goes, wondering if the warmth inside me is due to my silly crush on Sam returning, or because the letter from Alex is burning a hole in my pocket. I can see Sam's pixelated outline through the glass window of his front door. A part of me wants to go and knock so I can give him another hug, but I don't want to pressure him to reciprocate.

The drizzle falls again, but inside me the sun is shining.

Fifteen

Alexander Beauchamp
10 Tolkien
Saint Martin's
Rutherford-On-Thames
Oxfordshire

08/09/96

Hi Theo,

I have been deciding whether to write this letter for over a month now. This is the third time I have tried to put into words all the things I have been thinking about over the summer. The first two attempts were put through the shredder in our dorm master's office before convincing myself to go to the post room. I couldn't even bare to write your address on the envelope because it was eating at me inside.

After your last letter, I wasn't ready to say goodbye to you. It's that simple. I know the *Great British Pen Pal Project* was for one year only, but why should it end? I want to keep in contact with you, and I hope you feel the same.

There, I've said it.

Hearing all about your school trip made me realise I

need you in my life. Your letters are a window into the normal world, away from all of this private school rubbish I go through. No hierarchy, no infighting. Just me and you telling each other about our lives. Also, the keyring is proper cool, thank you!

Felicity has been looking after me a lot over the summer as Dad is still away, and Mum flew out to America to see him. His trip keeps getting extended, so I have not seen him for months. It is draining for Mum, and she keeps cancelling engagements because of exhaustion, I think. She is back tomorrow so I will plan something nice at the weekend with me and Isabelle.

Whilst she has been looking after us, I decided to tell Felicity about you. She kept wondering why I was being 'moany and miserable'. She thought the trip to Valencia would help (and to be fair it was good!), but she did something else too. When I arrived home, she surprised me with a few copies of the *Stokewood Gazette*.

It was in one of those papers I saw your mum's obituary. I honestly don't know what to say, and I am worried discussing this may bring back bad memories for you, but please know this is not my intention.

I am so sorry. I can't begin to imagine the pain you have been going through and I have had you and your Nan in my thoughts. At school this week, I lit a candle for her in the Chapel. If there is anything I can do, please don't be afraid to ask.

You would be there for me if I had trouble at home, and I want you to know I will always be here for you, pen pal project or no pen pal project. You're genuinely one of my closest friends and I cannot let opportunities to speak to you slip by so carelessly.

I have been back at Saint Martin's for three days and nothing has changed at all since Year Nine. I am even in the same dorm room with the same group of boys. Yours will be different I'm sure. It must be nice knowing you're not the new kid anymore, and there are hundreds of tiny Year Sevens who know nothing of the school like you do. Are you going to try for the football team again?

I have my Grade 5 piano exam next month, and I am already worrying about it. They usually hold them later in the year, but with GCSE Mock's in May already being talked about, everything has been shifted. I'm so unprepared! I will leave any further gradings for after Year Eleven. Trying to do music, alongside the rowing, is too much to take on.

I am currently staring out over the school courtyard. The rain is literally flying sideways past me and the replacement window allows a slight breeze to come through. I am certain my bunk catches the worst of it, hence me being wrapped in my dressing gown! We have been warned further damage to dorm rooms will be paid for by our parents, so we, especially Barnaby, are on our final warnings to behave during free time. I wish I was back in Spain, laying on the beach in the roasting sunshine!

Speaking of Barnaby, he has said Sam has gone quiet. He hasn't sent a letter since before leaving for Aachen. Barnaby is worried about him, so please keep an eye out to make sure he is okay.

I wish I had a lot more news to tell you from the summer, but sadly it was all pretty mundane. Isabelle went to see *Oasis* at Knebworth last month, which sounded great fun but I was apparently too young. Boo.

I am keeping my fingers crossed Sam has passed this letter on to you, and if you do wish to reply, I will be sat by the letterbox waiting for an envelope to fall through.

Yours,
Alex.

Sixteen

October 1996

I sit at the table surrounded by empty spaces. I thought photocopying twenty guides to journalism was optimistic, but at least one other person could've bothered to join the first afterschool newspaper planning group.

If the first edition is due to hit the proverbial shelves in less than three weeks, the amount of work would be far too much for me alone. Mr Le Bon being here would be helpful, too. Admittedly, after an initial bit of interest, attendance at the lunchtime sessions has been on the slide. Maybe me and Matt need to print more posters.

Out the lower school windows, I watch the last few pupils as they walk across the school field on their way home. Not wanting to be locked in the school over the weekend, I collect the guides and take them to my locker in the communal space of the English block.

"Better late than never," says Bethany from behind.

"I've been here ten minutes already," I reply as I slip my key into my pocket.

"We've been waiting for you in E10."

"Why? I put E18 on the poster."

"It definitely says E10. I blame your handwriting. Just bring your stuff through," she says as she heads into the classroom opposite.

The attendance in E10 proves it was me who got the wrong room. It may only be Bethany, Sam, and Matt, but it will reduce my workload by seventy-five percent, if they're armed with article ideas. We need a better front-page story than leading with Miss Houghton getting a new caravan. I appreciate her submitting the overly in-depth article about chemical toilets and differing types of butane canisters, but it won't exactly set the world alight.

I take two Jaffa Cakes from the box being passed around and wait until Mr Le Bon has the chalk in his hand. "So then, big ideas," he says as he draws a cloud on the board. "Let's brainstorm."

"I could do an article on the Caribbean?" says Bethany.

"Excellent start," says Mr Le Bon, adding this to the board, albeit spelling Caribbean with two R's and one B. I make a mental note to find a better proofreader before publication day, and it doesn't bode well for the English department's future. "Theo, what would interest our audience about the Caribbean?"

I shuffle a little. "I'm not sure."

"As editor, it is your job to help plan the content for these articles," Mr Le Bon says.

"Maybe the food?" I remember Bethany saying her Aunt's Jerk Chicken was better than the school's grisly drumsticks. That's not difficult when the ones at Stokewood look like they've been cooked by holding the meat near a low-wattage lightbulb for thirty seconds.

Mr Le Bon nods enthusiastically. "Superb. Bethany, did you dine on different dishes on your holiday?"

I eat my Jaffa Cakes as Bethany rattles off around thirty dishes in the space of sixty seconds.

"What about the big bananas?" asks Matt.

"Bananas?" she asks.

"Yeah, you have a picture of you and some big

bananas pinned in your bedroom?"

"They're called plantains," she replies.

"Same thing."

Bethany gives him a look sharper than the spikes in his hair.

"How about sport?" says Sam. "I don't mind speaking to the PE teachers and doing a roundup of school matches from the month?"

Mr Le Bon moves into the centre. "Now that," he says whilst pointing at Sam with a cracked shatterproof ruler, "is exactly what we need. Theo, in agreement?"

"Sounds great." It's easier to agree.

"Okay, so Sam is on sport, Bethany is on Caribbean food. That leaves Matt and yourself, Theo."

"Hey, Theo," says Matt. "Why not write about life at a private school?"

Mr Le Bon folds his left arm across his body and scratches his chin with his right hand in thought. "Are you still in contact with your friend, Theo?" he asks.

How does he know about Alex? "Um, yeah, but I'm not sure if it'd make a good article."

I was so happy to read Alex's letter, and him finding out about Mums' death through the papers meant I didn't have to awkwardly drop the news on him another way. Whilst it's good to speak to him, I have suggested to keep the same routine as last year. Allowing ourselves to write on alternate months will mean our studies aren't interrupted, and each letter will have a build-up of news we can share. Him not replying in the two weeks since my reply hopefully shows he has agreed to this arrangement.

When we first got to know each other, I was jealous of his life, but as time has moved on, I realise, outside of anything that can be fixed with money, many parts of his world aren't great either. His dad being away for such long periods seems to be putting a lot of pressure on his family, and if Isabelle is travelling for her sport, he only has his granddad close to him, which I know is not a perfect solution when you're our age. At the bare bones, we aren't that different.

After finishing the Jaffa Cakes and not coming up with anything further, we leave with a plan to hassle others in our year to do something, anything, to help fill the pages. We need to fill the space so Katie Barlow doesn't follow through on her threat to get involved.

"Can I borrow you for a moment, Theo?" Mr Le Bon asks as we file out the door.

"I'll meet you downstairs, Sam," I say and hang back whilst Mr Le Bon puts his satchel on his back and his bicycle clips around his ankles. "How can I help?"

Mr Le Bon pulls a thin newspaper from his bag. "Here is an example of one from my previous school. This is what I feel you can achieve this year."

I look at the front cover, the name *The Barnsley Star* shouting out from the top. The main article is an in-depth report on problems with the ozone layer, and there is a column discussing results from research pupils have undertaken regarding how they wish to transform the town centre. "These are way better than our ideas, Sir."

"It's early days yet, it will all come together." He smiles at me, but then looks to my hands. "Where did you get that ring?"

"It was Mum's," I say, as I move it about on my finger.

"I appreciate that, however, the rule regarding jewellery applies to both male students as well as female. Can I remind you to leave it at home in future?"

"But, Sir—"

"No buts, I'm afraid. I don't wish to see you wearing it here again, okay? People might ask questions about you, and we don't want that, do we?"

In the front room of the bungalow, I sit on the sofa with a small knife in my hand, waiting for Nan to finish peeling the spuds. She's sat with rollers in her hair, engrossed in watching the news rather than attacking the skins. The peeler hovers mid-air in her hand. As a reporter presents a news piece on council homes in Skelmersdale, she drops her hand back into her lap.

"We had a phone call from the estate agents this afternoon," she says quietly as she throws a potato across to me. "There has been an offer put in for the house." Jason and Kylie chirp loudly, sharing my sadness at the news.

I fall back into the cushions. I know the sale has to happen, and I thought I was prepared for it, but it doesn't make it any easier. My earliest memory took place there, and all my favourite memories of Mum still live between the four walls. It doesn't seem fair someone else can take all of those away from me, changing it into a home of their own, any lingering connections to Mum being wallpapered over. The flower beds she cared so much for could be hidden under decking if the new owners are that way inclined. I'm not even used to talking about her in the past tense yet. "Do you think they will buy it?"

Nan removes the mixing bowl of peels off her lap and moves towards me as fast as her hip allows, slumping onto the other end of the sofa. "I would be surprised if they didn't." She wraps an arm around me, stroking my bicep with a damp hand. "They are a lovely young couple who are moving to the area. I said to you last week I met them at the viewing. He is the one in the navy, and she is looking for a new job locally."

"But what about Mum?"

"Darling, I know it is difficult, but time moves on. This is your home now."

I look around, wondering if my presence in the bungalow may encourage Nan to modernise it. The shelves on the walls in nearly every room contain porcelain dolls which wouldn't look out of place in a horror film. In the kitchen, instead of a door, there are plastic strips which Matt says resemble the back of a porn shop, however I'm not certain how he knows this.

Something else needing to change is the phone. I'm probably the only pupil who lives somewhere that doesn't have a cordless phone. The one in the hall has buttons that can be seen from space, they're so big. I've no idea why Nan chose it as her eyesight is fine. Every time Bethany calls, I have to sit on the Yellow Pages by the front door, the maximum distance the stupid curly cord allows.

"Are we still visiting the old house this weekend?" I ask.

Nan hugs me tighter. "Yes, of course. I spoke to Alan, you know, the man who works in the butchers. He is bringing his van around on Saturday evening and we will load the remaining boxes."

"And then that's it?"

"Theo, darling, it is equally as hard for me."

I often forget, selfishly, this is someone who has recently lost their only daughter. "Sorry, Nan," I say. "Maybe I need to admit things are different now."

"And they always will be. But don't forget your mum will always be a part of you. I have made sure we have kept the most important items."

The boxes of photographs were stashed on top of Mum's wardrobe for years. One day I promise I'll go through them. If I get enough courage before the end of the year I could even ask Mr Teale to scan some onto the school computers.

"Speaking of Mum, Mr Le Bon asked me not to wear her ring to school."

Nan takes my hand and looks at it. "Your mum wore that for the last eighteen years," she says. "Maybe I can take it to the shop in town and see if they can turn it into a pendant for you?"

"Would Mum want that?"

"It's more if you want it," she replies. "It might keep it safer." She takes a tissue from her sleeve and wipes a tear from her eye. "Look at us, sat here moping about and being silly sausages. We need to be strong." She stands and straightens her floral pinny. "C'mon you, these potatoes won't prepare themselves."

Three days before the nearest weekend to Halloween, Katie Barlow strides into the form room and hands out invites to a party at her home for Saturday evening. "Fancy dress is encouraged," she squeals. "Everyone welcome!"

Bethany sighs. "I don't even have a good excuse to get out of this."

"We can say we can't be bothered," I say.

Sam taps me on the shoulder, and I spin to face him. "Don't you want to see her house?"

"I'm kinda intrigued," says Bethany. "Matt, fancy a couples costume?"

"Absolutely not, but I assume I have no choice," he says, his hair flat on his head after PE. It did look better in curtains for sure.

Sam leans back, arms above his head, revealing a Liverpool kit only partially hidden by his thin white shirt. "We can do the cinema before the party if you guys wanna come?"

"The new *Romeo & Juliet* film is out," says Bethany.

"Not more Shakespeare already," I complain. "I'm already bored of Ms Fenton making us do *Macbeth* monologues in drama each week."

"It's the DiCaprio one," says Bethany.

That does change things. "I'm in."

Matt leans forwards towards us. "I look a bit like him, don't you think?"

Bethany lets out a long laugh. "You wish. He's way hotter, ain't he?"

"No offence Matt, but she's right," I say.

"Gay," he responds. If only he knew the truth.

"Do we have to bring anything?" Sam asks Katie as she bounces back past us.

"Feel free to bring some snacks or something. Mum says she will get everything else we need for the games."

"There's games?" I ask.

"Yes, obviously. Have you never been to a party before?"

I haven't, except for the ice skating, and I'm not sure if that counts considering I was in A&E longer than I was at the rink.

Katie looks around the room, before putting her hands on Bethany's shoulders. Bethany looks at me, her face grimacing at having her personal space invaded. "Hey, Sam," says Katie brightly, "maybe you will kiss someone again like you did on the school trip."

My heart pounds in my chest and the hair on my neck prickles. Bethany's eyes are open as wide as possible.

Sam sits on his hands and his cheeks glow like a beacon. "I… I didn't kiss anyone."

I know Katie knows, and I know Sam knows she knows. Him asking her not to mention it after we'd been caught obviously hasn't worked. I beg internally for her not to mention my name next.

"I promise I didn't," Sam says facing our group, his voice breaking so half the sentence comes across high pitched.

"He was with me for the whole trip," I add, trying to help convince anyone else in earshot that nothing happened.

She cocks her head to the side and gives a sarcastic grin. "Oh, Theo, whilst I'm here, I've decided on my contribution for your little newspaper."

There it is. I want to say no, but with a distinct lack of anything exciting coming through, I sadly need her. I grit my teeth. "Yes, that would be excellent. What are you thinking?"

"Have you read those agony aunt pages in *Just Seventeen*?"

"I've never seen a copy in my life," I reply. Technically, this is sort of true as I've never read a full copy, but I do know what it is. I have a page from it hidden underneath my mattress. A few weeks ago, Bethany tore out a full-page picture of David Beckham lounging by a swimming pool in a pair of red Speedos. During personal time in my new bedroom, it has helped me focus my attention away from the staring eyes of Nan's haunted doll collection. The fact Mum's ashes are in an urn on the shelf at the foot of my bed doesn't help either, although I hope she'd find it amusing that she's sat next to my old Winnie the Pooh money box.

Bethany brushes Katie's hands away. "What makes you the authority figure for answering problems? It took you two months to get over your last break up."

"Colin was a cheater," she says.

"You reap what you sow," Bethany snaps back.

At least Katie's idea took the heat away from Sam for a few minutes, although his face is still flushed as Katie moves to another group to receive the next injection of attention she clearly needs to survive.

"What she said about Sam isn't true," I say, feeling him kick my foot gently under the table.

"When have I ever believed anything she has said anyway?" asks Bethany.

We have got away with it, but for how long?

Seventeen

Alexander Beauchamp
10 Tolkien
Saint Martin's
Rutherford-On-Thames
Oxfordshire

15/11/96

Hi Theo,

You don't understand how happy I am we are back in contact. I forgot the level of excitement I get when the Postmaster delivers something from you. I was literally like a dog waiting to go outside as I sat patiently watching him work his way towards our dorm block with the bag of mail on his back.

Thinking back to last year made me aware I never sent a mixtape of music we listen to in our dorm like I had promised. Therefore, please find enclosed ninety minutes of the best music ever (providing it was released within the last eighteen months). You have a bit of everything, taken from the CD's we have on the wall rack, including *Pulp, Oasis, Blur, The Lightning Seeds* (but not *Three Lions* - I couldn't do that to you after that bus journey to Germany) and a few others. You might like track number five!

Felix said I should put the *Friends* theme tune on there too, but I thought it was too cheesy, so I left it off. He's obsessed with watching that at the moment, and keeps greeting everyone by saying "How you doin'?" He doesn't understand the nature of the phrase, bless him.

Also, okay, you win. On the way to school on Monday I made Felicity stop the car as we passed *Our Price* and I dashed in to buy the *Spice Girls* album. I have played it in the dorm a few times, and despite Barnaby's initial protests, it's not bad at all. In fact, we are planning to dress as them for a talent show we are holding at Christmas.

The talent show has replaced the annual Christmas Concert due to there currently being no band leader. Mr McClair, who had held that position for around thirty years disappeared under mysterious circumstances, by which I mean we heard a lot of rumours about things he had got up to. Of course, we didn't believe them, but a couple of weeks back it was mentioned in assembly he would not be returning. No reason was given and there was no mention of any farewell celebration for him. It's all very strange! I am going to do some digging.

Sam hasn't been in touch with Barnaby still. Did you manage to speak to him? Barnaby isn't too bothered about the letters, but he has asked me a couple of times so perhaps wants to know he is well.

Mum came back from Chicago after spending two weeks with Dad. Between me and you, I am not sure everything is okay. Mum doesn't seem to want to discuss him or his work around the house and tends to snap when I ask how he is. I have spoken to him on the phone a few times, but the conversations are short. He is always thinking about other things when I tell him about school. He still doesn't know when he will return to the UK either.

I have asked Isabelle to speak to Mum to see if she can get more information. She thinks it is due to him having a high workload. Joanna, who I mentioned was pregnant in spring, had her baby earlier this month, so is now on maternity leave. Her home is in Chicago and Isabelle suspects Dad has been visiting her regularly to help her out. I've no idea where her own husband is. It's all a bit peculiar. No wonder Dad is stressed when he is trying to work long hours and having to help with someone's newborn baby!

School have scheduled a set of mock exams for the New Year. Well, *mock* mock exams I guess they are. They say the timing will be right for us, as it gives us three months after results are returned to work on improving our weaker areas before the real mocks. I cannot wait to escape the pressure they are putting us under. As long as the school looks good in the statistics, then they are happy. I don't think they actually care for our wellbeing. It means our Christmas holidays will be overtaken by revision rather than relaxing. I was hoping we would go on a ski trip at some point, however this is looking increasingly unlikely.

One piece of good news is I passed my Grade 5 piano exam. I chose a piece by Ralph Vaughan Williams. I was so nervous I could feel the sweat on the keys, but once I got going, the music seemed to flow out of me like I was watching someone else perform. I promised no classical on your mixtape, but I have included it at the end. Felix helped me with a tape recorder from the music department, and he put the microphone near me as I played the grand piano in the school ballroom (yes, don't judge, we have one of those…)

If you feel like things are too much, sit back and listen to me play piano and I hope it will ease the tension.

How is the planning going for your newspaper? Did many others come forward with articles in the end? You will have to send me a copy of the first edition. I will start a scrapbook of everything so I can keep track of what is happening. I was reading the *Stokewood Gazette* again the other day. It's quite funny hearing about all the news in your town. Did you hear about the man who grew some large and obscenely shaped vegetables? I am not saying nothing much happens in Stokewood, but that was the main story.

The bell has rung for our evening meal so I need to run to the dining hall. They now have themed dinners on Friday nights, and tonight is Asian cuisine. In this morning's cookery class, we were making our own sushi. The bamboo mats are quite difficult to use when rolling the seaweed and rice. It does make a nice change from sloppy cottage pie, though.

Looking forward to hearing from you soon, and don't forget to let me know what you think of the songs I have chosen.

Yours,
Alex x

Eighteen

December 1996

Alex officially has good taste in music. Of the twenty-three songs included on his mixtape, all but three are enjoyable. There's one called *Breakfast at Tiffany's* I can't listen to having missed the fashion exhibition this summer.

Although December, Nan is wearing some brighter clothes for the first time in a while. Over the Summer, when Mum was slowly fading, all her energy was channelled into providing support, and it was rare to see Nan out of big jumpers and beige slack trousers.

When you live through grief, it can be hard to see the effect it is having on you. Her hair is back to its old bouffant style, but she's struggling to sleep. The bags under her eyes are nearly as large as the two she's placed on the chair next to me after her Saturday morning visit to the market.

"This music is lovely," she says, leaning back against the work top with her eyes closed, the light from the sun casting a rainbow across her face as it passes through the stained-glass panes of the back door.

"It's composed by Vaughan Williams," I tell her. She looks at me and raises her brows. "You're shocked I know that, aren't you?"

"Pleasantly surprised."

"I only know because it's Alex playing."

"As in your friend Alex?" she says, studying the cassette box.

"Yep."

"He is very good. I wouldn't mind listening to more of this." I wait as she scans the track listing to confirm I am not lying. "I've not heard of any of these other bands."

Having raided the CD collection in the rack by the telly, the most recent artist she has is ABBA, and they're ancient. If Alex had told me just how good his skills were, I could've sorted an album full of his peaceful piano for her. Christmas is only two weeks away and I've yet to organise any presents. It has to be something special to thank her for helping me through the difficult moments this year.

I help Nan unpack the shopping, noting the cupboards are taking a festive shape despite us saying we would keep things low key. There are three packs of Jacobs crackers and two tins of sweets as part of this week's haul alone. We've agreed not to have a turkey roast this year, neither of us quite ready to celebrate it as a pair. Beans on toast on the sofa, in front of a classic film, will be our way of sliding into a new normal.

Matt and Bethany are stood in the corridor outside our form room, each holding the *Stokewood Bugle's* first edition. Despite everyone being equally against the name as me, we were already two weeks beyond the initial deadline. Mr Le Bon virtually locked us in a room after school at the end of last month until we had settled on a title.

"Hey, guys," I say as I reach them.

Bethany looks panicked. "Did you approve Katie's

agony aunt page?"

"Of course. I read through it with her on Friday lunchtime."

Matt looks at Bethany. "See, told you he would've. It's not a big deal."

I think I know what's happened. "She hasn't changed the name back to *Katie's Konfessions*, has she? I told her it was rubbish."

Bethany shakes her head. "Come with me."

She drags me to an empty room. Matt follows behind and pulls out a chair as I opt to sit on the desk.

"Did you write a letter?" Matt asks.

"No, course not. I'm the editor."

Bethany passes the paper across to me. I flick past the puzzles supplied by 10 Birch and find the problem page. The headline MY GAY CRUSH screams out from the top. "I didn't approve this headline," I tell them both. It wasn't there when I signed it off.

"It gets worse," says Matt, sitting back and cracking his knuckles.

Dear Katie,

I realised at the start of last year I might be gay. I had already been questioning myself for many months, but during a birthday party earlier this year, all my feelings suddenly made sense.

There is someone within the school who I developed a slight obsession with, but before I could build up the courage to tell them how I was feeling, I was involved in an accident and the moment was ruined.

Since that day, the person who I've got feelings for has moved on, and I have been left to continue to figure things out alone. There are people I could talk to, but I'm scared it could ruin friendships.

For a year since, I have been overwhelmed by confusion and shame. Please help advise me on a way forward.

Many thanks,

Lost & Confused

I finish reading and look to them both. "I didn't write this," I say, sweat beading on my forehead. Everyone will see it soon. "I promise."

"If it's not true then what's the problem?" asks Matt. I give him a fearful look, and the realisation washes across his expression. "Wait, you mean it is?" he says.

I bury my head in my jumper. This isn't how it was supposed to be.

"Don't give him a hard time, Matt," says Bethany quickly.

"I'm not, just he doesn't seem gay, that's all."

"He doesn't have to seem gay," Bethany replies firmly. "He's just Theo."

"Look, I promise I didn't write the letter," I say again, a sick feeling bubbling in my stomach.

"I believe you," says Bethany. "But everyone knows it was you who had an accident 'cos you moaned for weeks."

"Cos it hurt like shit!"

"Who do you think wrote it?" she asks.

Katie saw the kiss. That's how she knows, but I can't tell Bethany this. And I can't accuse Katie without outing myself either. "If it's Katie, then maybe she's trying to undermine me so she can become editor. I know how she craves being the centre of attention."

"I'll quit if she does," says Bethany.

"Same here," adds Matt, which is kind, even though he has only submitted a crossword so far, and even that was torn out from a copy of *The Sun*.

The school bell rings and I prepare to answer all the questions that will undoubtedly come my way. "When we get to class, please don't go accusing anyone, it might make it worse." I fold the paper and hide it deep inside my backpack. "I'll tell you everything later, Matt."

"You don't have to."

"I want to. I should've said before, sorry."

"You don't owe him anything," says Bethany. "Please keep quiet, Matt."

"I'm fine, honestly," he says. "My uncle was gay and he's normal."

"Theo *is* normal!" spits Bethany, punching him hard on his arm.

"Can we drop it?" I say. I know they're trying to be supportive in their own way, but it isn't helping.

As we get to the door, Mr Le Bon walks through, a plate of toast with Marmite in his hands. "Why are you all in here and not in your form?"

"Just thinking of more ideas for the paper, Sir," says Bethany causally.

"Very well." He tosses his satchel onto the back of his chair and sits. "I shall be here Friday lunchtime as always, so we can discuss them when everyone is present. If Mr Richardson finds out you're prioritising the paper over registration, though, he may question your priorities. Speaking of newspapers, the school has been offered some tickets for an England Under-21's match in Bristol in February. It will be a nice reward for your hard work on getting the articles together. Would you be interested in attending?"

"Absolutely," says Matt.

"Count us in, too," I add.

"I shall bring some permission slips in this week. Perhaps Sam would like to do a report on the trip for the next edition."

"We will mention it to him," says Matt.

"Where is he, anyway?" I ask.

"He's off ill today," Bethany replies.

"His mum says it's been coming out of both ends,"

adds Matt.

Mr Le Bon puts his toast on his desk and nudges the plate towards the wall. "Let Katie know about the football, too." I don't want to after what has come to light this morning, but I know he will find out if I don't. Mr Le Bon waves a hand to shoo us from the room. "Off you lot go or you'll be even later."

We file past him as he stands and holds the door open with his left hand. His crisp shirt is slightly too short, and when his arm is raised, it reveals a small, faded tattoo of a shark on his wrist.

"Did your tattoo hurt, sir?" asks Bethany.

He quickly pulls his sleeve down. "Just get on your way."

"I'll never get a tattoo," I say. "I'm far too scared of needles."

"I'd love one, but not a crappy one like Mr Le Bon's," Bethany says.

"Here, Theo, do you fancy me?" Matt asks as we cross the wide corridor back towards our form room.

"Gay people have standards, too," I reply. "No offence, Bethany."

In the form room, we sit at our desks with a shiny book in front of us. *Your Future, Your Career.*

"Nice of you to join us," Mr Richardson says as we slink into our usual seats. "I was explaining about a change in your timetable. From Monday, Professional Studies will be replaced by Career Studies."

"I want to go into the Navy," says Bethany.

"Really? You've never mentioned that before," I reply.

"I was watching a documentary about the Titanic on Sunday and being at sea appealed to me."

Matt leans forward. "How did the Titanic make you

want to sail? It sunk."

"Ships have improved," she replies as she flicks through the pages. "Imagine looking out and seeing blue skies and blue oceans."

"Speaking of the Titanic, I heard they're making a film and Leo's gonna be in it." I ripped the article from Nan's paper and put in under my mattress with the David Beckham picture.

"Do you ever stop talking about Leo?" asks Matt, his bag on Sam's empty chair.

"No, and you'll have to get used to that now," I whisper back, before giving him a big fake grin.

Mr Richardson coughs, and we fall silent. "Next week we have a Careers Advisor joining. You will all have a one-to-one session with her to discuss your preferred work experience employer. I'd advise completing the options slip as soon as possible. Does anyone have a dream job?"

Molly immediately discusses hair styling, so I turn my attention back to the book. I discover being Mr DiCaprio's personal massage therapist sadly isn't an option, instead being shunned in favour of butchers, bakers, and trainee undertakers (sadly not like the cool wrestler).

"Page twenty-four," says Bethany. I flick through and see a double page spread on journalism. "You should go for that. It sounds amazing."

"I've only done one edition of the paper and look what happened."

"Even so. You're good at it. If you don't pick it, I bet Katie will."

I continue reading and learn there is an opportunity to work for the *Stokewood Gazette* during work experience week. It promises to teach all areas of journalism, following a story from a lead to final copy, and even the submission of an article of your own for inclusion. "I'm gonna go for it. Are there any Navy things in here?"

She spins her book around to a page about *Mr Biggins' Model Boat Emporium*. "This is as close to the Navy as it gets in this town. I'll probably have to work in a clothes shop."

I turn round to Matt, and he's already completing his option slip. "You seem keen."

He looks like an excited child. "I'm gonna be an astronaut."

"Bollocks is that in there," says Bethany.

"Page six. You're welcome."

I scramble to find the page and show Bethany, who bursts out laughing. "That place is looking for people interested in astrology, not astronomy, dickhead," she tells him.

"What's the difference?" he asks.

"Astrology is horoscopes and star charts and things."

"Like Mystic Meg on the lottery," I add, helpfully.

"And not spaceships?" he says, crestfallen. We both shake our heads.

"Didn't the name *Psychic Crystal* give it away?" I ask.

The look on his face makes it obvious it hadn't.

As we leave for Biology, Mr Richardson is stood by the door. "Theo, can you stay for a moment?"

"I'll meet you two over there," I say to Bethany and Matt. "What is it, Sir?"

"I decided to read the paper this morning over my morning coffee."

I decide to play naïve. "What did you think? I mean, it'll improve, but it's alright, ain't it?"

"Sadly not. The letters page was simply unacceptable."

"I'm gonna find out how that happened, Sir."

"Not if I do first. If parents get hold of a copy then all hell could break lose, do you understand? I've had to send every teacher out this morning asking them to confiscate all they can find."

"It's not *that* bad."

"Not that bad? You're playing a dangerous game, young man. If anything, *anything,* happens like that going forward then there will be no more newspaper, and I will withdraw my name from your approval slip for the *Stokewood Gazette.*"

"Sorry." I'm not sure what I'm apologising for, but it seems the best way forward.

"Final warning, remember. Now go on, get yourself to science."

Mr Richardson strides from the room before I can even get my bag on, his face red and forehead deeply furrowed.

Over the week, everyone in our class has questioned me about the letter at some point. It's been horrendous. I argue that it could be referring to any accident at any birthday party, but they don't seem convinced. If I were in their shoes, I'd question me, too.

Word spread across year groups rapidly. The hushed conversations as I pass by groups in the corridor, the throwing of food at our table in the canteen, people writing 'gay boy' inside my workbooks when I'm not looking. Even my locker has been defaced with Barbie stickers and derogatory language pasted all over it. I had to take Thursday off sick through nerves.

And where will it end? Will the hate seep out the school and across town? I'll be bullied relentlessly.

Bethany and Matt have helped act as firefighters, constantly by my side battling the flaming rumours being whispered my way. Even Mr Le Bon has put a call out, reminding our fellow pupils that the paper is meant to bring people together, and not an opportunity to drive a smear campaign.

When I complained about the worst bits of verbal bullying, nothing was done. At least all copies have been incinerated. All except one.

"Can we suspend Katie's page, Sir?" I ask during the Friday planning meeting.

I hear her slam her hands on the table. "You want people to read your paper, don't you?"

"I do, but not like this."

She sweeps her hair behind her ears. "If it wasn't for me, no one would be reading it."

Bethany squeezes her milkshake carton tight, causing it to fire thick chocolate shake across the tabletop. "No one is reading it now *because* of you. We can't just make stuff up."

"I didn't make it up!" she shouts.

Mr Le Bon stands between the girls. "This was a success at my last school, and it will be a success here." He stares at us all until he confirms we have understood. "Please show some respect. Although some did read it Katie, it doesn't help if we have to bin them the same day. There is no way we can do articles like that in future. Before we print the next issue, I will have the final say on content."

There are mutterings of agreement, and with a sense no more productive work would happen, Mr Le Bon sends us home.

Bethany complains about Katie on the entire walk from school through town. Sam has now been absent all week, and I've been nominated to go to his house and drop off a care package. We pool the cash together from the pockets of our backpacks, and I head into *Somerfield* with just over four pounds.

"You two are gross," I say as I return to the car park with four Kit Kats, a can of a new Lynx scent, a bottle of Lucozade and the latest copy of *Four-Four-Two* magazine. Matt and Bethany look like a pair of slugs with the amount of moisture between their lips.

I press the button on Sam's doorbell firmly. A jaunty version of *God Save the Queen* plays out from inside as an army of garden gnomes stare at me. After a third verse, the door is finally answered.

"Hi, Theo," says Sam's mum. She has a peach towel around her neck, and a plastic covering over her partly dyed highlights, the bleach sending ammonia into my nostrils. "Sam's in the front room watching *The Simpsons*. He isn't contagious, so come through."

"Thanks, Miss Baxter," I say as I kick my shoes off.

"Call me Linda, please," she replies, smiling. "I'll be in the bathroom finishing my hair. Sam's in the front room. Ignore the mess."

I push open the door and spot the patient flat out on the sofa, asleep in the darkness the curtains are casting over the room. The air is stale and warm. I gently approach and shake him on the shoulder.

"I'm not hungry," he says as he opens his eyes, before flinching when he realises it's me. "Oh, hey, Theo. What are you doing here?"

"Just checking in." I take a chocolate bar from the carrier bag and sit.

"Chuck us a finger," he says, straightening his t-shirt.

I pass him the care bag. It looks like he hasn't washed for some time. His fringe is matted and clumped on his forehead, and the back juts out at a hundred different angles. "Thought you weren't hungry."

"You'd say that too if you only had soup for four days."

"Have you stopped being sick?"

He nods. "Yeah, I'm all good now. I'll be back Monday."

"We've got you an England ticket for a game in February, by the way."

"Football?"

"Yeah," I say, trying not to spit chocolate and wafer onto the thick white carpet. I run my feet through it, feeling its softness on my big toe, which protrudes through the end of my black socks. "Well, under-21's anyway. Mr Le Bon is taking us."

"Why?"

"For the newspaper work, that's all.."

Sam shifts uncomfortably. "Fair enough."

I leave a short silence, pretending to watch what's going on in Springfield. "You don't look ill."

"I'm feeling better, I just said."

"Good. I need you at school. We had to throw all the papers away." I wrap my arms around my knees and don't make eye contact. "There was a letter telling people I was gay."

"How did that happen?"

"Katie's problem page. I've had to deny it all week and it's been awful. She kept saying she didn't write it, but I'm tired of her bullshit. I've asked Mr Le Bon to ban her page for a while, but he won't. I had to tell Matt I was gay, though, so at least I don't have to be secretive around him anymore."

Sam leans forward. "Was he cool?"

"Yeah, he was fine, in his weird Matt way, anyway."

Sam smiles and rubs at his hair before focussing on the television. "Theo, I know you didn't write the letter."

"Thanks, I appreciate it. We've managed to get through the worst."

"Cool. We have to let Katie continue her column,

though," he says. He takes another swig of drink. "She's telling the truth. She didn't write the letter. I did."

I stand and tower over him. "You? What the hell, Sam? I thought we were cool."

"We are."

"So why did you tell everyone I was gay?"

He sinks into the sofa and presses his palms onto his eyes. "Gah, Theo, no. You don't understand. The letter was about *me*. It seemed a good idea at the time. I put the letter in the school post-box last week. That's why I've been off. I'm feeling like a million different people every day. Over the weekend I realised everyone would know I was the one questioning myself. I've been so scared that I made myself sick with worry. I didn't realise it would make people accuse you, sorry."

"Well it did."

"I know, and I'm sorry, alright?"

I pace the room to blow off some steam, and then kneel near him. "Are you sure you're, y'know?"

His whole demeanour changes. He curls into a ball on the sofa and stares at the window. "No. Well, maybe. That's the problem. I dunno. I had to tell someone. I was thinking of maybe telling Barnaby, but I haven't written to him in yonks."

"Do you want me to speak to Alex about it? He can pass the message on."

He shakes his head. "Can we keep it between us?"

"Fine. Did me kissing you in Aachen make things worse?"

"I kissed you back. I mean, Katie seeing it didn't help, but I sort of thought my letter might take the shine off the secret and make her less likely to say something."

I take another chocolate bar out of his care package. I deserve it. "I think it might have had the opposite effect."

"You're mad at me, aren't you?"

I let out a sigh. "No, course not. I guess I'm just constantly on edge. We can pretend it was a tasteless joke."

Sam's mum brings me a cup of tea, placing a new Lucozade near Sam. When she leaves, he pours its contents into the base of her yucca plant. His thighs push against the seams of his shorts causing something to flicker inside me.

"Sam, you know your letter?"

"Are we still on that?"

"Listen, you mentioned you were obsessed with someone. That was me, wasn't it?"

"You like to bet on yourself, eh." He gives me a shove and I topple onto my back. "I was actually on about Matt."

"Ha! Really?"

"Yeah, why?" he replies whilst frowning.

"Just surprised, that's all. Anyway, you don't have to be sorry. And before you ask, no I won't tell him. As for me, I have Alex anyway."

"But he has Melody?"

"It's a mess, isn't it?"

"Do you think it'll be okay when I come back to school?" he asks.

"Yeah. Richardson and Le Bon both lost their minds a bit, but they'll have calmed by Monday."

A car backfiring echoes from the bay windows and Sam pulls back the net curtain. "Dad's home. He's gonna take me to the chemist."

"You should shower first. You stink."

"Football this weekend?" he asks as he sprays a cloud of deodorant over himself so thick it looks like he's about to disappear through the doors on *Stars in their Eyes*.

"I'll knock for you at twelve tomorrow."

Nineteen

Alexander Beauchamp
10 Tolkien
Saint Martin's
Rutherford-On-Thames
Oxfordshire

15/01/97

Hi Theo,

My world seems to be crumbling a little. Sorry for starting on a low note, but it is nearly all I can think about. Grab yourself a cup of tea as it is a lot.

Firstly, before story time, I want to thank you for your Christmas card and WH Smith's voucher. I have bought a couple of new notepads with it. One for school, and one for adding my rowing schedule to. Brian and I have worked hard over the last month in the training facilities here, and we believe we are stronger than we were this time last year.

At the recent regatta, our school won the team silver. The gap between us and the winners, Darwin Academy, was only six points this time. There is a new rowing coach joining us soon, and we hope with their help it might push us to the top. In the coxless pairs, we snuck a bronze medal. It is great to know our hard work is paying off, and when the County Trials come round in two months, we will have done everything we possibly can do to force our way into selection. I have included a picture of my medals :)

Now, this is where things get weird, sorry. It all happened during the Christmas break. I knew something was different at the end of the talent show. For the first time ever, Mum was not in the audience. She never misses a performance or a sports match for me or Isabelle. In her place was Felicity. She isn't employed to take care of us in the evenings, especially the end of term.

When we returned home, she asked us to take a seat at the kitchen table and broke the news Mum had flown to America again to be with my Dad. Isabelle had heard our parents arguing over a phone call, however I assumed this was down to him extending his contract for working overseas. What I didn't realise was the problems run much deeper.

As mentioned in my previous letter, Dad's business partner Joanne was living in his rented accommodation with her new baby. Derek, who is a colleague of his from London, thought the situation was strange so raised it with his wife. The wife, Helena, is close with Mum, mainly due to their own job roles leading them to attend the same parties. Anyway, Helena discussed her husband's thoughts with Mum and, although Mum did not think it could be true, she set about finding the truth.

From what Felicity has told us, it is suspected Dad has been having an affair with Joanna for some time, and her new child is my half-brother. I guess it is now a waiting game for when Mum arrives back home.

I don't know what to think or do. I've got this weird hollow feeling inside, like I have been betrayed, which I suppose I have. Isabelle has been brilliant, and is always checking on me, but school is unaware. Felicity offered to set up a meeting with the Dean but, for now, I have asked her to hold off until I have more facts. Why is life like this?

Apologies again for this letter being a bit of a downer. If you need some light relief, remember I was told all of this whilst dressed as Ginger Spice, complete with eyeliner and lipstick. You are not getting a photo of THAT yet, though!

For what it's worth, the talent show was a nice change from the usual Christmas Concert. It was quite funny being the *Spice Girls* for ten minutes. Felix (Posh) and Barnaby (Sporty) really got into their roles. It was won by a group of students who performed a mash-up of West End songs. They were pretty good, to be honest.

In hindsight, I should have performed on the piano. I am so pleased you enjoyed the Grade 5 piece I included on your mixtape. Say thank you to your Nan for her kind words as well. I would be honoured to do a whole cassette for her to listen to, especially now we know how to record it properly. If you can subtly ask her for her favourite classical artists, we can get it ready for you ahead of her birthday.

Did you manage to find out how Sam was? Hopefully, he is back at school now. I will be keeping an eye on the papers next month for the England scores. It will be amazing to go and see them play! I've never been to Bristol but we did study the suspension bridge there in a science lesson last term. Mr Le Bon sounds like such an amazing teacher who cares about you all.

I read the school newspaper you sent through. You make quite the journalist! You will definitely get that work placement. Your way of writing is factual and entertaining, even if not everyone appreciates the puns.

Thanks for sparing me from having to read Katie's advice page. From what you said, her advice definitely sounds bizarre! It made me curious to see it so please include it in the next copy. I am so tempted to send you a letter to include about my parents. Her stupid answer might actually cheer me up again.

I'm going with Melody to see *Romeo & Juliet* soon. School approves as they think it will give us a better understanding of Shakespeare. Felix thinks we should put a staged version of the film forward for the summer performances at the amphitheatre.

Thank you for asking about Melody, she says hello. I think you would like her. We hang out on weekends as her family live nearby. We do that rather than spend time together after school because the teasing got too annoying.

Literally EVERYONE here assumes we are dating, including some of her teachers(!), and I want everyone to shut up! Melody even had 'the talk' from her parents. Whilst I found it hilarious, she was angry. I had to tell them we were just friends but it didn't make a difference. Her dad is proper scary.

I was around her house last weekend before the cinema, and every five minutes her Dad came to see us to make sure the bedroom door was open. I only wanted to listen to some of her CDs. If it was me and you, no one would check the door was open. It's crazy.

This has been a therapeutic hour of writing today. I am in the library studying for a History mock exam, which is at 8am tomorrow morning. I have mentioned before how much the teaching staff value these mock exams. If we receive a low grade we are required to attend additional learning after school. I am confident I will do enough to pass, though, yet I do not want to be complacent. So, there we have it, you find me sat here learning fun things about the Russian Revolution!

Here's to an amazing 1997!

Yours,

Alex x

Twenty

February 1997

I tap my fingers on my knees. "Will Smith?"

"No," Sam whispers as we sit at the back of the room. He is pretending to focus on anything except my questions and the sex education video Mrs Bosnich has decided to show us all, without irony, on Valentine's Day.

"What about Jim Carrey?"

"Ew, no. He's funny, but not hot. Theo, this isn't helping."

I rack my brains for more potential celebrity boyfriends. So far, Sam has answered no to everyone, except for DiCaprio, obviously. I'm trying to work out how we can get hold of the latest copy of *Just Seventeen* with him on the cover without anyone's suspicions being raised. My current thinking is Sam seeing shirtless pictures of Leo might help him find his true self. He isn't convinced.

"Are they all that hairy?" Sam asks, nodding towards the screen.

I was not prepared to see a close-up image of a vagina before lunch. It's put me right off my tuna sandwiches. "Not quite sure why you're asking me," I reply, and he bursts out laughing.

The *Stokewood Bugle's* second edition was completed

yesterday, and it was a definite improvement on our debut. Sam did a great article on the football this week and seems to have a deeper knowledge of the national team than I realised.

The trip to Bristol was a good bonding experience and beating Italy in a narrow victory was the perfect result. Even Katie was less annoying than normal. I think there's a kind person inside somewhere, she just needs to not try too hard to be popular. Her problem page was replaced by 'Konfessions of Love'. There were some bizarre anonymous letters, and I vetoed one suggesting dodgy activity occurs behind the Sixth Form block.

Even though the pressure is off Sam and I slightly, it doesn't make school less nervy, and being unfocussed has led to me underperforming. My recent mock results didn't impress Nan.

My old home tutor, Maggie, is back in England to see family, and I overheard Nan asking her on the phone if she could give me extra tutoring during her stay. Even my geography result was poor after realising I left too little time to answer the essay question. The two paragraphs I hastily scribbled didn't set the world alight.

Valentines at school when you're gay, closeted, and single is the worst. As we bundle out of Period 3 Physics, I know I'm not the only one hating hearing about love.

"Matt completely forgot to get me a present," Bethany says as we file down the science block staircase.

"He got you a card."

"Yeah, one saying *Happy Birthday to a special aunt* on the front that he nicked from you on the way to school."

"It was either that or wishing you a happy retirement."

"Urgh. I HATE him."

I know that's a lie, but once again, their relationship is off. Sam has taken Matt for a big game of football on the hockey pitches to do his duty in keeping them apart for an hour.

"Also," continues Bethany, "the chocolates he says he's got for me will be the Milk Tray left over from Christmas. They went out of date a month ago. I saw them in a cupboard in his kitchen and he thinks I won't notice."

I allow her to continue ranting all the way through lunch, switching off to think about my own relationship where possible. I did buy a Valentine's card for Alex, but the nerves pulsed too much, so I slipped it into a bin rather than the post. Knowing the dates with Melody were as friends is enough for now. With his parents fighting, I wouldn't blame him for being anti-love currently, so sending a card wouldn't have been wise.

Mr Teale is on duty in the canteen, and he approaches me as I take my plate to the hatch.

"How are things at home?" he asks.

"Yeah fine, thanks."

He nods in thought. "And the newspaper?"

"Well, better than it was. Did you hear about the first edition?"

"I did. It was a shame. Did you take a copy for your Nan?"

"Didn't get chance," I tell him. The only copy I kept was for Alex.

I like Mr Teale. He always means well. Hopefully one day he will get to meet Nan. The only chance he has had so far was at the most recent parents evening, but our meeting with him was cancelled after he was signed off with flu symptoms during the afternoon. Even though seven months have passed, I am grateful the teaching staff still care.

"Do you have family, sir?" I ask.

"My parents live in Scotland," he replies, before

making himself look busy by sweeping crisp packets from a nearby table. "Have you remembered to put in your work experience request?"

"I did mine ages ago, Sir. I'm hoping to go to the *Stokewood Gazette.*"

"Of course, Mr Le Bon did say. Think how good the next paper will be once you have learnt from the masters."

"It's not guaranteed yet. Also, calling them masters is giving them a lot of credit. Have you read a copy recently?"

"Leave it with me, it'll be fine," he says, giving me a wink.

"Do you know someone there?"

"I might do. I will put in a good word for you."

"Thanks, Sir."

"No worries. I've enjoyed your work so far. What happened with the letters page made me so angry. If you ever want to discuss it, you know where my room is."

There is something in his smile letting me know it's an invitation rather than a suggestion.

As soon as I close my front door, the telephone trills from the hall. I sit on the floor by the pile of shoes and listen to Bethany as she continues to chew my ear off about Matt. I only left her ten minutes ago. There's no escape.

"I told you they would be the Christmas ones," she says. "The packet even has holly on it for Christ's sake. I threw them straight in the bin."

I think there is a five-minute period where I don't get a word in edgeways, instead rolling my eyes to Nan when she steps over me as I lay across the entrance hall.

"Don't get that jumper dirty," Nan says as she puts her slippers on next to my head, the vinegary smell from them falling over me.

"Look, Bethany, I need to go," I tell her, replacing the handset quickly.

In the kitchen, Nan puts two frozen pies onto a tray and slides them into the oven. "Your grandad loved steak and kidney."

"What was he like?" Grandad died when I was young, the only knowledge I have being from a couple of black and white photographs, and his oak leaf medal he was honoured with during the war.

"He was just like you," she says, a satsuma half-peeled in her hand. "He was kind, caring, and did anything to help others. I saw a lot of him in your mum. You and her both have his eyes."

Mum never spoke about his death. I wonder if she reacted in the same way I had to her own passing. Despite her hoarding, I haven't seen anything at all in the boxes relating to him. Maybe Nan dealt with them whilst I was boxing the VHSs for the charity shop. I cried so much when I was putting her musical videos into cardboard boxes. Hopefully now, though, another family are getting pleasure from them. Thinking they went to a good home helps me cope with my own loss.

"Are there any more photos of Grandad I could see, please?" I ask Nan.

She shifts uncomfortably. "There might be some in the albums your mum left."

"Maybe one weekend we can go through them," I say. "It could make a nice article for my newspaper, too."

"That is best left for me. There are so many, and it will be too painful for you."

For once, I think Nan is wrong. Confronting the past full on is what I need to fully come to terms with how life is. Putting the best in an album would mean Mum's life can be celebrated properly, and not just leave me with memories to picture her. Even the photograph Nan chose for the front of Mum's order of service was the one we keep on the telly.

When I have chance, I'll rip the plaster off and look. If Nan is right, then so be it, but I'm too curious not to give myself the chance to see Mum in a new light. I want to move on, but there is no way I can do so only knowing half of her story.

Mentioning the photographs sets a strange atmosphere over dinner. The conversation is stunted, and maybe the memories hidden within those photo albums are too painful for Nan, but that doesn't mean I should be denied the right to see them. There is, however, another burning question I need the answer to.

"Can you tell me more about my Dad?" I ask.

Nan drops her knife to the plate with a clatter, and points her fork in my direction, a chip dripping with mayonnaise hanging from the end. "We do not talk about that arsehole in this house, okay?"

"We don't seem to talk about anything from my past," I tell her.

"Some things are best left unsaid."

"For you maybe," I say as I stand, "but I want to know who I am."

"It's not that easy. Your father wasn't nice, and I don't want to open those wounds again, okay? You are far better off not knowing."

"How do you know that? Everything I've done is because of what you and Mum thought best. I'm nearly fifteen now and want to know."

"I'll tell you everything one day."

"Yeah. Mum said that once." I put my plate on the side and storm to Bethany's.

I didn't speak to Nan yesterday evening. Bethany took

her side but I'm sick of being kept in the dark. It's been the most miserable day of the month by far, even including seeing Valentine vaginas.

"Sometimes, knowing things is worse," Bethany says as she pulls a box of Maltesers out her bag on the walk home. "What if you found out something big?"

"Such as?"

She shrugs. "I dunno, like, what if your Dad is a really famous rockstar?"

"Do you think he could be?"

"No, of course he isn't."

"Well, I want to know even more now, just in case."

She hands the Maltesers across. "I'm sure one day you'll find out the truth but falling out with her isn't gonna help. Take her some chocolates and apologise."

"Where are they from?"

"Matt," she says as she folds her arms. "He thinks getting me a new box makes up for Valentine's Day." She says it loudly enough for him to hear as he walks in front of us with Sam. She looks away when he attempts to make eye contact.

I put the half-box of chocolates in my bag and plan potential ways of getting the four of us back together as a gang. Sam has been stressed for a few days now trying to act as a barrier between the pair.

"I wrote to Barnaby," Sam says when we're alone. He's gone quiet again and is concentrating on kicking a tennis ball along the dirt path. "Thought it was best to apologise for not being in contact. I didn't tell him about you know what, though. Do you think he'll write back?"

"I hope so. Me and Alex still write and I'm pretty sure they get bored of their own friends in the dorm."

"I should have asked him for more information about Melody for you."

I shake my head. "God, don't do that. They're just

friends and things are cool as they are. I don't want to come across as needy."

"We should go and visit them."

I stop and let the ball roll into the ditch to my left. "Really?"

"I dunno. I think it could be fun."

"Maybe next year. What if he's disappointing in real life?"

"He won't be. Probably just a bit posh."

"Nah, I don't wanna risk it. He's the best thing currently, what with Bethany and Matt, and Nan. Let's leave it as it is."

When I get home, I put the kettle on and go to the front room. Nan is sat on the floor with her back to me. In front of her, a box containing photo albums has been opened, the contents spread across the floor. Nan's eyes are red and bloodshot when she turns to look at me.

"I'm sorry," she says, and hugs me awkwardly when I kneel next to her. "I didn't mean to snap at you last night. You were right, you do deserve to know."

Had I known how upset she'd be looking at the pictures, I wouldn't have pushed it. I pass her the chocolates. "I'm sorry, too. I got too caught up with not knowing." She turns a few photos over and moves them about on the rug. "You don't have to do this, Nan."

"I do. Hiding from the past won't solve anything, and by denying myself the chance to see these again is denying your Mum lived a wonderful and happy life for her thirty-six years." She takes a photo and hands it to me, smiling. "That was her first school photo from Stokewood."

I study it closely. It could've been taken on the same day during autumn term as my one, albeit with an outdated chocolate brown, seventies background. Her collar is big, but it doesn't detract from her smile, which is central between her two freckled cheeks. "Mum was pretty."

"Wasn't she," Nan says taking it back. "If someone who didn't know us saw this one and yours together they would swear you were sister and brother."

I look to my own photo on the mantelpiece above the three-bar fire. We even have the same slightly wonky front tooth. "We should frame this one," I tell Nan. With any luck it could replace the many Princess Diana pictures on display. Even the clock by the dining table has minute and hour hands sticking out from Diana's face.

"I haven't seen these for years," Nan says. "We should shop for frames at the weekend. There are so many photos in here I'd forgotten about. It's amazing how life cycles through the same stages. Have a look at that one there."

I follow Nan's finger to a larger photo which has been placed near the back.

Deborah Barker. Drama Rehearsals. June 1974.

I flip it over in disbelief. There she is, Mum at fourteen years old, dressed up on-stage playing Nancy in a Stokewood Secondary production of *Oliver!*

Twenty-One

Alexander Beauchamp
10 Tolkien
Saint Martin's
Rutherford-On-Thames
Oxfordshire

29/03/97

Hi Theo,

That photograph of your mum on stage was beautiful. Thank you so much for showing me. She looks like such a wonderful person, and it is no wonder you discovered your acting genes, even if you were unaware you had them. I compared it to the photo of you as the urchin, and the family resemblance is strong. I am sorry I never got the chance to meet her.

Crikey, Bethany and Matt are on again and off again more than Ross and Rachel! It sounds way more exciting than it is on the television, though. Have they managed to make peace yet? Hopefully, it is not putting too much pressure on your group, especially with Easter coming! I don't want you to juggle your time between the both of them. Tell them to get each other an egg and get over it!

I've been meaning to ask, and sorry if I shouldn't -

How are you feeling yourself? I know last year you were a bit mixed inside, but I want to make sure you are alright. Your news is always often about other people, and I love that, but I want you to know I am still here to listen to you should you ever wish to tell me anything. I promise whatever you say will not change anything between us.

Speaking of which, what did you think of *Romeo & Juliet?* Leo was <u>SO</u> hot in it, wasn't he? Especially in armour. He makes me feel very <u>very</u> fuzzy. Now I know how Mum felt when she used to kiss the photograph of Donny Osmond displayed in the kitchen.

On the way out, I asked the cinema if I could have one of their posters when they don't need it anymore so I can sneakily have him staring at me next to my bunk. He would be my perfect boyfriend. The soundtrack is good, too. We have added *Radiohead* and *The Cardigans* to our latest mixtapes.

Things are okay at home, for now. Dad flew back to England with Mum. By all accounts, it was a bit of a frosty journey. Of course, my parents must think I am too young to understand what is happening, as they have been putting on such an obvious front whenever I have been around. I want to know more about Joanna and her baby. Dad and I had a row when I tried discussing it over Sunday lunch.

At the weekend, every time I came downstairs they made a show of being in the same room, both taking it in turns to ask me questions about the rowing and school. It is so fake. They never have this much interest in me. They keep hugging each other, and it makes me hate being there.

They are clearly lying. Isabelle said Dad denied the baby was his, but that is not a surprise. I am waiting for the truth to come out, however long it takes. Mum apparently told her the baby looks like I did when I was a month old, but all babies look the same to me so maybe Dad is telling the truth, and Mum is being delusional.

Either way, Mum has forbidden Dad from staying in the same house as Joanna again, which is fair. She demanded he spends more time in England. I'm not sure if he will agree to this, but for the next month at least he will be here. I did note though he hasn't cleaned the patio and barbecue area like every other Spring. He either has too much on his plate, or he is not planning on being here for Summer.

Is it bad I don't care too much? Dad has never been there for me or Isabelle anyway, not unless it's paying for holidays and things like that. He is more interested in shipping us off to school and letting someone else look after us. It is much better being somewhere with friends who are funny and kind, rather than hiding in my room whilst another argument plays out in the kitchen.

I have asked if I can spend the summer in France this year with my aunt. Having a month in Bordeaux would be wonderful. I could cycle around the vineyards and might even be allowed to taste some wine without having to sneak it out the bottom of the bottles in the recycling box. Cambes exudes such a laid-back environment, and the days never seem to end.

It is Isabelle I worry most for. She has her A-Level's in two months and has been trying to juggle all this with visits to universities. She has her heart set on Sports Science at Durham. Their facilities are apparently amazing and being able to continue with hockey is something which is non-negotiable. With that focus, I know she will excel. She is a lot more committed than I. I'd like to row without having to study for a degree at the same time. More on rowing in a moment…

Barnaby has said Sam has been in touch. It was his birthday last week, and I spotted a nice card pinned to the board in the dorm. Thank you for whatever you said to him, it clearly worked. Barnaby loves getting letters from him and is even thinking of inviting him to a rugby match in the Autumn. I was offered a ticket, but I have declined. I could watch and play rugby for fifty years and still not understand the rules. Every time we play, I spend most matches laying on the floor with a bundle of students on top of me.

Barnaby got an N64 for his birthday so this has replaced the PS1 we have. We've only got Mario 64 and WWF Warzone, but it's such a good console! Everyone from other dorms keep trying to be extra friendly so they can come and have a go. It is making us look popular!

Finally, I've been saving the best news until last.

I GOT ONTO THE COUNTY TEAM!!!!!!

The regatta could not have gone better. Brian and I aced our heats, winning the first by one of the biggest margins ever recorded for our age group. There were three hours before the final, and rather than overthink it, we took ourselves away from the venue and walked into Windsor. It allowed us to ignore the occasion before we were due back on the water, and by the time the hooter went for the final, we were mentally prepared to take on the two kilometres of water standing between us and a place on the team.

Needless to say, from the first stroke we were both entirely in sync with one another and had a half-boat lead by the three-quarter point. We knew our training had been enough for our stamina to maintain position, and when we crossed the line in first place, everything hit at once and we both laid in the boat crying. Three years of hard work, and all the pain of being overlooked last year, has come together, and been forgotten. I even slept with my gold medal around my neck at night.

We have to go to the Lake District for the County

Championships in May, so will be a busy time as they start three days after our final set of mock exams. I keep daydreaming now I will one day row for the country. Can you imagine that! For now, though, I will keep celebrating our current victory.

As always, please find enclosed some photographs covering the happier points from above. This Friday we have permission to go to town, so I am buying a scrapbook to keep all of your letters and gifts in one safe place. I don't want to lose anything you have sent as they are all so special to me.

Keeping my fingers crossed you get the work experience at the newspaper!

Sending regards to you and your Nan,

Yours,
Alex x

Twenty-Two

April 1997

Bethany studies Alex's letter. A grin is permanently fixed to my face. "He says Leo is fit and he makes him feel fuzzy, Bethany." My right leg bounces involuntarily as we sit on the bench waiting for Sam and Matt.

I am ninety-nine-point-nine percent sure my instincts are correct, regardless at Bethany's insistence I keep my cool. It made looking at Alex's pictures even better, especially the one with him and Brian in their rowing outfits as they were thrown into the water by their teammates. Finding out (99.99999%) that Alex is gay two hours after getting my work experience placement at the *Stokewood Gazette* confirmed has made this the best day ever.

Like, E.V.E.R.

Finally, Bethany passes the letter back. "It does seem pretty conclusive," she tells me, as I read through it again, not believing my luck. "Don't get too excited, though. You've been wrong before."

"Don't get too excited? I wish I could remain calm, but Alex is gay, Bethany. Alex is gay, Alex is gay, Alex is gay, Alex is gay!"

Bethany stands and pushes me gently. "Jesus, shut up will you."

It's literally all I've been able to think about. During our Home Ec practical in period one, I was so distracted I forgot to put the eggs into my Victoria Sponge, meaning I spent an hour producing what looked like a sad, flat, sticky pancake.

"At least now you've stopped moping about the place," Bethany says. "I've never seen anyone so mopey in all my life as you were during the Easter break."

"Is he still moping?" asks Matt, taking Bethany's hand, their relationship again currently green lit.

"Alex is gay!" I say excitedly as I bounce around him and Sam like a kangaroo on a sugar high.

"Are you sure?" Sam asks as we move towards English.

I nod. "In his letter today, he talks about how much he fancies Leo DiCaprio."

Matt turns around from in front. "Even I fancy Leo DiCaprio."

"Yeah, but he *likes him* likes him. He wants a poster of him next to his bed and to lick his face."

"He didn't say lick," Bethany replies.

"Well, he *implied* it."

"Fair enough," says Matt, taking Bethany's hand again. "Even I wouldn't go that far."

"You don't even have a photo of me in your wallet," Bethany complains.

"I see you every day, what's the point?"

Bethany drops his hand and quickens her pace.

Sam leans across to me. "This could be the shortest 'on' period those two have had," he whispers. "I think the current record this month is two days."

Mr Le Bon hands me my article back after our English lesson. "'Have we got the idea of private school pupils wrong?' is a very good angle," he says. "I knew it'd make an interesting piece, and the thought you have put in is well rounded. It is an excellent example of critical thinking. I'm glad you have finally taken my advice. If we manage to get Katie's article on the impact of the bypass extension in time, it is looking like we could have a great edition on our hands."

Katie saw sense after the last Konfessions of Love page, finally understanding not many people cared for her column. Most gossip happening at this school is known by everyone by the time we go to print anyway, and I'm sure half the letters are faked by her friends to fill space. Sam was extremely glad to see the back of it.

"You should take a copy of the paper with you on work experience," says Mr Le Bon.

"I think ours is better than the *Stokewood Gazette*, Sir."

"Maybe don't say that to them."

"Even Nan said so."

Mr Le Bon laughs. "Unsurprising. How are things at home?"

He's still asking once a week, but I don't mind. It's nice he cares. "Everything is good," I say, which they are, especially now reminders of Mum are present in the bungalow. "When Mum died, I never thought I could get over losing her, but we're focussing on celebrating her life instead."

"That's the right way of looking at it. You've come a long way since I first met you. Admittedly, not all your studies are at the level we would like them to be, but you have found some new interests, notably with journalism, and your written work has come on leaps and bounds. You need to channel this energy into the syllabus and I will mark you as likely to receive an A grade next summer."

"The syllabus is a bit dull, though, that's the problem."

"Any parts in particular?" he asks as he takes a cloth from his desk drawer and cleans the lenses of his new glasses.

"Seamus Heaney. If I have to read any more of his poems I might have to throw myself out the window." I've tried to understand poetry, but it's not for me. Having to dissect every single word to find the hidden meanings is too much hard work. Why can't they write what they're trying to say?

"Heaney is one of the greats," Mr Le Bon says.

"You're not the one studying him."

"True, but if it wasn't his work, it would be someone else."

"I guess." I put my article into my backpack, retching at the smell. I transfer my two-day old egg sandwiches into the bin.

"We can always do extra poetry lessons when you're back from the gazette." I screw my face a little. "Think about it over the weekend. Now, I have some marking to do, so off you shoot and I'll see you Monday."

"Have a good weekend, Sir. Oh, is Teale in today?"

"I think so. He was here at lunch."

"Cool."

Mr Teale is in his usual position behind his desk. I tap on the door and he gestures for me to come in. "Hey, Theo."

"Hi, Sir. I got confirmed for the *Stokewood Gazette*," I say. "Thank you for whatever you did!"

He stands shakes my hand. It's weirdly formal. "I'm so pleased for you. You're going to be great there. You look like you could burst."

"I've had one the best days ever."

"I'm glad to hear. I always find Fridays better, too. It helps I'm off to Spain for two nights."

"Nice. What are you doing there?"

"We have friends in Catalonia. I've not seen them since Christmas so it will be nice."

I think of Alex and his summer trip. "I'd like to go to Valencia."

"Valencia is nice. Huge park in the city centre and a nice big golden beach. Quite hot in the summer, though."

"Maybe one day."

"I think you've earnt a holiday. It's been a rough ride these last few months." Yeah, and then some. "I'm sorry again for what happened with the school paper. Mr Richardson knows my thoughts on censorship. In an ideal world, people need to hear about those things."

This is my chance. If I'm going to get an ally to help me unravel the knots in my mind, it needs to be Mr Teale. Right here and right now. I pull out a chair on the desk nearest to his. "Sir, can I ask you something?" I want to ensure I'm not misreading his hints.

He leans back and links his hands above his head, staring straight towards the ceiling. He knows what's coming. I swallow the spit building in my throat and feel myself shake. "When did you first know? Like, about, y'know."

Mr Teale bites his lip and stares out the window. "We shouldn't be discussing this, Theo."

"Sorry. I was just, it doesn't matter, sorry." I push my chair back and stand.

"Sit," he says. "I said we *shouldn't* be discussing this, not that we *can't* discuss it." He keeps glancing towards the door, and the blood has drained a little from his face. "Why do you ask?"

"Do you remember the pen pal thing we did?" He nods. "Well, I'm still writing. I found out today the boy I'm writing to is gay."

He sits forward, a psychiatrist analysing me. "How

does this make you feel?"

"Happy. See, the thing is, I think I am, too."

"Wait here a moment." He walks to the door and pokes his head into the corridor, checking both directions. He leans close as he passes me. "This stays between me and you, okay?"

"Promise."

He sits close enough to allow his voice to be no louder than a whisper. "I respect you telling me, and I will be happy to advise, but it isn't simple. If people find out, then I could lose my job. It is that serious."

"Like, other teachers?" I ask.

"Other teachers, parents, anyone on the PTA. Even agreeing to help you is enough to potentially end my career."

"They can't do that."

"They can, Theo, they can. Have you heard of Section 28?" I shake my head. "Discussing homosexuality is not encouraged in this school. In fact, it is happening across the country as we speak, and teachers like myself are terrified."

"Why? I've done nothing wrong."

"I know it's ridiculous, you know it's ridiculous, but that doesn't change anything. We have been forced into the shadows, like an underground moral mafia."

"I promise I won't say a word, Sir, but you're scaring me a little."

"That wasn't my intention, sorry. I needed to make myself clear. Do you have your IT workbook with you?"

"It's in my locker. I can go and grab it if you want?"

"No, it's okay. Bear with me." Mr Teale goes to his cupboard, bringing back a thick book on something technical. It has a picture on the front of two bearded men with large glasses hunched over a big box-like computer. It must be at least twenty years old.

"Why do I need this?"

"You don't. But if anyone comes in then we can pretend I was talking to you about computers. Now, where do you want me to begin?"

My main intention was to see if Mr Teale had the same feelings as I did when he was my age, and how he coped with it, but there is obviously something darker playing a part here. The secrecy around our meeting, the whispering voices. "Has it always been like this?"

"No, is the short answer."

"What's the long version?" I ask, knowing the more I learn, the harder things may be.

"I'll keep it brief. I would give you some tips for research, but good luck trying to find a book in the library as they will have been pulled from the shelf."

"Shit, seriously?"

He thankfully glosses over my impulsive language. "Seriously. Being homosexual has always meant putting up a fight. Even after homosexuality was legalised, we have feared for our lives. I don't just mean physical violence, either."

"Oh, like verbal bullying? My friend Matt calls things gay a lot. Well, he did until he found out about me anyway. He's been slightly better since."

"Yeah, in one way, I do mean that, but it gets worse. Verbal bullying and physical violence are obvious ways for people to belittle us, but there's the neglect too. For years, our community has suffered the consequences of being left to suffer by those who have the power to help. Even today, the idiocy reigns supreme. I'm gay, I've been with my boyfriend since my first year of university, yet the teachers here do not know."

"But if you tell them, wouldn't they be on your side?"

"Do you feel everyone in your year would be on your side, Theo?"

Mr Teale gets it. Like his IT lessons, he knows how to allow students to relate to more complex issues that, from the outset, seem impossible challenges. Teachers like him are so valuable, which makes the fact they go through this even worse.

Sweat forms on my forehead, drips down my temples, trickles along my spine. "I guess when the newspaper came out, that week was tough. Everyone was questioning me about it, and it got so bad I acted up, not concentrating in class. It's why my grades have suffered, but I can't exactly tell Nan."

"And that is my point. It's the same in the staff room. Some teachers have been in the profession for forty years plus. They have seen it all, and yet still do not understand the psychological damage they are doing in schools, to people like you and me both. Every single one of them is complicit in the damage being done to young gay people in this country, and it makes me sick."

"Don't they ask about your wedding ring, sir?"

He nods. "I tell them my wife works away. There is a whole backstory about how this ring belonged to my late father, and I inherited it when he passed away."

"But you didn't?"

"My father is still very much alive. My parents live in Edinburgh so the chance of any staff running into him are slim to none, thankfully." Mr Teale checks his watch and moves quickly. "Sorry, Theo, I have a plane to catch this evening. I said to my other half I would be home by four and the traffic is going to be a nightmare. I could sit here and talk for hours and, trust me, I want to. I have kept this bottled up for long enough."

"I appreciate it, Sir, thank you. Can I come by again?"

"We will sort something. Remember, not a word to anyone, not even your Nan."

Possessions gathered, I follow Mr Teale towards the

main reception. I only know a small percentage of his story, and the fact no lessons have been learned since he was my age makes me fearful. Fearful for myself, fearful for Alex. We're the mis-shapes, the misfits, the broken biscuits. If there is a way for two boys to come through this unscathed in this day and age, I'd love to know how. The more I learn, the more I realise being called gay in the classroom is the tip of a hellish iceberg.

Nan is in the kitchen when I get home, which spoils my plan of passing off the Tesco Victoria Sponge I have in my bag as my own. "Let's say I did not score well in the practical."

She rolls her eyes as I put it in on top of the cereal selection boxes. I grab a mug from the top cupboard, trying not to drop the carefully balanced crockery onto the floor. "Do you need all of these cups?" I ask. Considering there are only two of us, the amount we have is a little excessive.

Nan shuffles closer. The limp from her dodgy hip is becoming much more noticeable, but she refuses to use a cane. The last thing I need is to spend more time sat waiting in hospitals. She opens a few cupboards, studying their contents carefully.

"Perhaps we don't need quite so many."

This is an understatement. We even have three different gravy boats. I bet Charles and Diana, who stare at me from a commemorative wedding mug, had less tableware at their reception. It's clear where Mum got her love of hoarding from. I better not inherit their habit, although my clothes scattered across all furniture in my bedroom shows the trait is creeping in.

"We can box more at the weekend and take them to the charity. There's bubble wrap in the box room near the Christmas paper in your room. Go bring it through."

Seeing her desk when I enter reminds me I was going to send a congratulations card to Alex (for his rowing, not his coming out). It's then the idea hits. Alex's Mum knows Princess Diana. If I can get her autograph, Nan would be over the moon. Her card drawer is another example of hoarding but, despite the many rammed in the space, the closest appropriate one I can find is a square card with a cartoon blue car on the front, the words *Congratulations on Passing your Driving Test* emblazoned across the top.

I grab my pencil case and masterfully edit it with any of my felt tip pens still with ink in. I wish I lived closer to the Lake District so I could cheer him on from the stands. "Can I borrow a stamp?" I shout once done.

Nan comes through and passes me one from her purse. She looks around my bedroom. "What you said about the crockery was correct. Maybe we should do something with this room, too?"

"Can we lose the dolls?"

She takes one from the shelf and strokes its fake hair. "Yes, we can lose some of them. We can see if we can get you a new bed, too."

"Can I have a double please?"

"I'm not sure if there is space, darling."

There definitely isn't space, especially if I have to keep her bureau to do homework on. I've got used to the metal framed bed, but it's ancient and creaks like an old ship. Bethany said my room looks like the one we saw at the Past Lives Museum. I'm not sure if the waxworks there were better or worse than the dolls.

"I've been thinking," Nan says as I finish writing Alex's address on the envelope.

"About?"

"Your mum."

"What about her?"

Nan sits gently on the end of my bed, the springs groaning, and looks to the shelves. She stretches and takes Mum's urn into her arms, as if cradling a baby.

"How would you feel about scattering her ashes? It doesn't feel right leaving her on the shelf."

"Where would we take her?"

"We should take her back to Bournemouth. She loved it there. We could do with a weekend away, too."

I think of Mum in the deckchair. "That sounds perfect."

Having her in my room with me has been nice, and I'll miss telling her urn my good news each evening, but she deserves to be at peace somewhere more aesthetically pleasing.

I sit in the Editor's office of the *Stokewood Gazette*, close to the end of my work experience week. The editor, who prefers to be called only by his surname, Clargo, enters with a coffee, its contents dripping from the plastic cup and falling onto the carpet tiles.

"So, four days down, one to go," he says as he takes a seat on the other side. "How have you found it?"

"It's been great, thank you."

I was so nervous on Monday, and the excitement was missing after an incredibly boring morning. I spent the day sorting through paperwork in multiple filing cabinets, but the office improved when the lead community reporter, Janice, arrived. Fresh out of university, she went against the grain of the stuffy reporters. She was like a rainbow in a sea of beige. She took me out in her car to interview a couple celebrating their diamond wedding anniversary. They supplied us with unlimited custard creams which may be why it was such a highlight.

"I'm sorry it isn't exactly thrilling here," Clargo says. "Stokewood is not the biggest place, and often the only thing to report on is potholes or new wheelie bins."

"I've had some great fun, honestly. All my friends were jealous I got to visit the opening of Funtangutan!"

Clargo smiles. "Not every day is as exciting as that, young man. Last week there were three separate stories sent in about faulty sewers."

"People still buy the paper, though," I say, trying to be optimistic. "This job has been more interesting than what other people are doing. Two of my mates wanted to do something with sport and they're litter picking in the rain at the Lakes golf club."

"I'd much rather be stuck in the office than in the rain. And yes, people do still buy the paper, but circulation numbers are decreasing. We need to appeal to a younger audience."

"I guess older people think we're useless."

"What do you mean?" Clargo says, as he takes out his notepad from the top pocket of his shirt, before licking the nib of his pen.

"Um, I mean there isn't anything in your paper which tells people about all the good things young people do. Like, I've got a friend who rows for his county. The paper normally puts things in about vandalism and loitering."

"Is this friend local?" asks Clargo.

"Nah, but I think there must be plenty of young people in Stokewood who are doing amazing things. We don't just hang around at school. Well, we do, but not always."

"Can you give me some examples?"

I sit for a few moments, draining my coffee to give myself some time. "I guess, even with me, I'm the school paper's editor. Last year we did a production of a musical and went to Germany. Then you have all the sports teams, like Stokewood Vikings, and the scouts must do some interesting stuff."

"We've reported on them a lot," he says.

"Yeah, but no offence, it's written *by* adults *for* adults. Our paper at school has been good because we're writing it for people our age. Things they care about. Things that affect *them*."

"I'm going to take a risk," he says, leaning forward, the light bristles of his goatee resting on steepled fingers. "How would you feel about being the new youth reporter for the *Stokewood Gazette*?"

"Seriously?"

"Deadly. You said we need younger voices talking about younger successes. I'm willing to give you the chance. I can ask Janice to mentor you. Maybe an article once every month or two, and then if people connect, we can make it regular."

I can barely believe what Clargo is saying. "I'd love to, thank you."

"Excellent. You will be reimbursed for your time of course. I'll speak to the HR team and ask them to look into creating a short-term contract."

That evening, I sprint across town as fast as my shiny school shoes will allow to tell Nan the news. I cooked the dinner whilst she rang everyone in her phone book to spread the word.

"You'll be the talk of our bingo group." She squeezes my cheeks as I scoop baked beans into an old microwavable Christmas pudding pot. "That's an idea, you can do a report on us if you like."

"I'm covering things for young people. They wouldn't want to hear about bingo."

"I still feel thirty," she says.

"Thirty is ancient."

I feel like a celebrity at school. Mr Le Bon proudly

pinned my GCSE stress article from the latest *Bugle* edition onto the main noticeboard outside the headmaster's office, and some the Year Elevens I mentioned by name are now saying hello to me in the corridor. I've never felt so cool.

"Are you planning anything for your birthday?" asks Bethany as we walk home, freshly cut grass sticking to the front of our shoes.

"Nah. I don't feel like celebrating much at the moment. Anyway, I'll be away in Bournemouth with Nan."

"Wow, rock and roll," says Matt.

"Yeah, I'm scattering Mum's ashes."

Matt's face goes white. "Shit, sorry."

"It's alright. You're right, though, it won't be the best birthday, will it?"

"You'll have to make next years' even better," says Sam, as he throws his arm around my shoulders.

"Such as?"

"Have a party," says Matt.

"Maybe. It's ages away anyway."

Sam tightens his arm, squeezing the air from my lungs. "Your birthday will be perfect timing, though. It will be right at the end of our exams."

"Have you all been planning this?"

There is a short silence. "It was their idea," says Bethany.

"So, you're in on this too?"

"We need someone to do something better than Katie's," says Matt.

Despite not wanting to make a big deal out of turning sixteen, it probably will need to be a little bit special. Katie Barlow has already sent out invites to her 'Christmas inspired masked ball', whatever that means. Her fancy dress party last year was so saccharine and unbearable that we walked out after ten minutes and sat in the park.

"Fine," I say eventually.

Bethany shrugs Sam away so she can hug me. "We'll make next year your best birthday ever."

Twenty-Three

Alexander Beauchamp
10 Tolkien
Saint Martin's
Rutherford-On-Thames
Oxfordshire

29/05/97

Hi Theo,

Hope all is cool!

I've spent most of this month on the river to prepare for this weekend's county championships. I have checked I have packed everything around fifty times today alone. I'm so nervous. It helps having Brian with me. It would have been awful sharing a dorm with people I didn't know.

I am sorry your birthday card is a little bit late. The mock exams were quite intense. I was thinking of you, as always, especially this year. I hope your Mum got the send-off she deserved. Things like this are never easy, and when I say I hope it went well, I trust you understand what I mean. I lit another candle for her on the day.

Your request for Nan's present wasn't strange at all,

so no need to apologise. I called Mum and asked if there was anything which could be arranged. I am so excited for her to see it, but she mustn't open it until her birthday! Make sure you hide it somewhere <u>very</u> safe.

Mum has been busy at work with the Summer royal arrangements, so I have spent the last couple of weekends with Dad. He is trying to put things right, especially with Isabelle and I, however, I am unsure if my parents' relationship will survive. He is due to fly to Chicago next month and has promised this will be the last time he will be there for an extended period.

Due to my parents once again being more involved with work than they are with me, it has been agreed a summer in Bordeaux will be going ahead! I am flying out in July and will be lodging in my aunt's farmhouse until Mid-August. She lives in a place called Cambes, which sits on a river, surrounded by wonderful, rolling countryside. I am going to have the most blissful few weeks. I wish you were able to be there to make it even better. I would send you a postcard, however I only have your school address (hint, hint!).

At the end of August, Mum will be in Paris for work, so she has invited me to stay with her in a hotel for the last weekend of the month. I have never been to Paris so it will hopefully be a lovely trip. I will be travelling there through the Channel Tunnel, which is much better than having to get a ferry. Ironically, even though I am a rower, I get terribly seasick. I was once ill on a ferry before it had left the harbour.

Isabelle will be travelling to Asia with friends to 'celebrate life', as they put it, before she heads off to university. I think they are planning on seeing Vietnam, so Felix is so jealous and has been complaining they have stolen his idea of going there. I have had to promise him I will visit with him when we are eighteen.

I appreciated your honesty in your last letter. Knowing yourself is always so difficult, and for you to be completely open to me meant a lot. Your questions regarding my admiration for Leo DiCaprio made me chuckle, mainly as I was using the same approach in my last letter to you.

Yes. I am gay. Obviously.

Wow. That is the first time I have written it down. It feels strange, but I have this sudden wave of calmness in me. Like, everything feels right when I read those words back to myself.

I believe I told you before I had slight feelings for Felix in the past, and I guess since that moment I always suspected I was gay. I have tried so hard to figure things out for myself, including hanging around with girls like Melody more, yet it isn't something we should have to figure out alone, is it?

Without you, I wouldn't have known for sure. You mean everything to me, and knowing you are going through the same emotions makes me realise I will never be alone. Wherever I am in life, I know I need to reach out and someone will be there.

There are often certain types of incidents here between boys, mainly under the umbrella term 'initiations', but I have never taken part in any of that kind of activity. I wouldn't want to, either. I am happy with who I am, and where I want to be in the future. You will always be a part of that.

I have come back to writing this letter. I needed to take myself for a walk around the fields outside to keep myself focused. Part of me wanted to run and tell everyone who I was, but that will be a task for another day!

At the lower end of the fields, we have some allotment space, so I have helped the chefs bring vegetables from the gardens back to the kitchens in wheelbarrows. There seems to be an abundance of onions so I imagine it will be on the menu a lot over the next few days. I'm glad I won't be here, not that I am expecting the food in the Lake District hostel to be much better.

The chefs are lovely, and I think they like me asking about their job. So many boys feel the kitchen staff are below them, but I think they are great. It would be nice to work with them sometime.

We held a pizza party two weeks ago. We had Eurovision playing on the television, and the night was made better when the UK actually won. With all the Britpop music and a new Labour government, living in this country feels pretty good right now. It's a shame things at home aren't better.

I am so glad the mock exams are over. I think I did well, although got a little confused for the History exam. To prepare us for next year, they are releasing our results on the GCSE results day. We have been told the school will have something special planned for the day. Barnaby says the new *Oasis* album is out the same day too, so should be great fun.

Don't forget to watch the new Jurassic Park film soon. We are going at the end of next week and I want to know what you think of it!

Brian has come through in a panic as he cannot find his knee support. I bet you any money it is already in his sports bag.

I hope you like the cards, and I look forward to speaking to you soon.

Theo Barker-Hall, thank you for being amazing,

Yours,
Alex x

Twenty-Four

June 1997

My birthday was the most difficult day we have had since the day Mum died. I helped Nan recreate one of Mum's childhood holidays, doing all the activities they used to do together.

We had jacket potatoes from a mobile van in the pleasure gardens, spent an afternoon in the amusements hiding from the rain, and in the late afternoon sat with ice creams on the low wall separating the promenade and the endless golden beach.

We even stayed in their favourite hotel, The Royal Bournemouth, located on the approach to the pier. I woke at 6am on the day, and Nan was already dressed, sat in the window seat looking at the small sailing boats bobbing on the sea. We walked in silence down the hill, and along to the end of the pier.

Despite being a Bank Holiday weekend, the town was still asleep, allowing us to say goodbye in peace. As we waited for the wind to settle, the sun broke through the clouds and illuminated the Isle of Wight's polar bear cliffs a couple of miles east.

Nan closed her eyes and whispered some final words, before tipping the urn. I rested my head on the wooden fence and watched as Mum floated away, riding the waves towards the horizon.

"Bethany, squeeze in a bit more," Mr Richardson says as he tries to take a photograph of the team behind the school newspaper.

We've been asked to do a report on the newspaper for the school prospectus, and I've brought in a disposable camera so I can use a picture to surprise the team by including it in my proposed article for the *Stokewood Gazette*.

Mr Richardson clicks and winds the camera multiple times, and I'm hopeful at least one will be usable. The Friday meetings have become structured, and after our photo op, we cram as much planning into the last five minutes as possible.

"Theo, I have some more information regarding the potential sale of the youth centre," says Katie Barlow, my new sub-editor.

"Fantastic. The deadline is this time next week, so would you be able to have something together for then?"

"Absolutely!" she replies and gives me a high-five. Over the last few weeks, Katie has turned a corner, and is no longer putting herself front and centre. Since ditching the *Konfessions* idea, she has got stuck in and has worked hard to help me bring the paper to standard. It's been a remarkable change, and one Bethany doesn't trust.

"She's defo up to something," she tells me.

"Ah, let it go, it's better than how she was. Sam, how is your sport article coming along?"

He gives me a thumbs up. "Very nearly there. We have the inter-form athletics competition on Thursday, so I'll get the results ready that afternoon."

"Sweet, you're amazing."

"I am. Oh, also, a sixth former has come back from the north after a rowing thing so I put a note in his pigeonhole asking for an interview."

"Cool. Matt, what are you working on?"

He doesn't answer. Bethany leans across until she's right by my ear. "He looks like he's doing newspaper stuff, but I know he's doing his chemistry homework for fifth period. He keeps asking to borrow mine."

"How are things between you?"

"They're great, actually. What about you and Alex?"

"We aren't dating. There's a difference."

"Yet," Bethany says, poking a finger onto my nose firmly.

I push her away, keeping hold of her wrist. "Oh my god."

"What?"

"Sam, y'know the sixth-former you mentioned?"

"What about him?"

"He rowed up north recently."

"Yes, and?" he replies, head down, focussing on his column.

"Was it for the county?"

"Yeah, something like that."

"Do you think he'll be able to get the results?"

Sam pokes out his bottom lip. "I can ask."

On the Monday afternoon, my legs shake as we head across the playing field. Sam kept to his word and came up trumps. In my bag I have an envelope containing the results of the County Championships, telling the others there is no way I'd open it in front of them. If Alex has won, his dream of rowing for Britain could become a reality.

The next school paper is all but signed off, and my report on its progress should appear in Wednesday's *Stokewood Gazette*. Nan seeing me in the paper on her birthday will make it an even more special day. I can't wait for everyone to see it.

Small buttercups form a polka dot blanket over the cricket outfield, and the temperature is comfortable enough for Matt to have removed his shirt, showing off a slight hint of pectoral muscle, which in his mind are bigger.

"Do you want to come round for Nan's birthday this week?" I ask.

"Will there be cake?" Sam replies.

"Yep. It's her first birthday since Mum passed so want to make it fun."

"I've got footy training but can sack that off for a week," says Matt.

"You can't use a twisted ankle excuse this time," Sam replies.

"I'll think of something. Your Nan is cool, so I'd rather be there. I think we're playing the bottom team this weekend so training ain't important."

"You say this like you're the top scorer," says Bethany.

"It's not only goals that win games. Anyway, I'm a defender. Think of me as Stokewood Viking's equivalent of Stuart Pearce."

"You wish," says Sam. "I'll be about any time after school."

"Cool. I think some of her bingo friends are coming over in the evening so we can do our bits before then."

As we approach the dairy, me and Sam split off to get our usual milkshake. We collect the empties from the crates, get our discounted drinks, and sit back against the wall in the sunshine.

"I never said thank you," says Sam as he focuses on the trees opposite.

"For what?"

"After the letter got into the paper. It took me a

while to realise, but you were great and I never thanked you for it."

I wipe the milkshake from my top lip and sit. "I didn't do it for any thanks."

"You didn't have to do it at all. But you came round, you didn't get angry, and you've generally been decent."

"I guess it helps when I was going through the same myself."

He nods. "I think I'm ready to talk about it." He closes his eyes and lifts his head to the sky so the sun catches his cheekbones. "I'm definitely a little bit gay."

"Was it Matt being shirtless that did it?" I ask, hoping the joke might ease the tension a little. The side-eye and smile he gives lets me know I've gotten away with it.

"You know when you know, don't you?"

I nod along. "Yep. It's weird how it creeps up on you. You spend more time denying it yourself than you do having to deny it in front of other people. Sorry again for Aachen, for what it's worth."

"I've already told you not to apologise for that. It happened, and no one needs to know."

I think of Katie, praying she will never discuss it. "Do any others know about you?"

He shakes his head and downs half his drink. "I'm not ready to tell them yet, but think Matt is suspicious. How do you manage to keep everyone from asking?"

"I dunno. I guess no one cares."

"I bet they would if they knew."

He has a point. Matt has got better at not calling things he disagrees with gay, but I still hear it on a daily basis in the classroom. As far as I'm aware, there are no gay people at school other than Mr Teale and the two of us.

"We should go to prom together next year," I say, only half serious.

"Yeah, even as a buddy, I don't think I'm ready for that."

"Can you imagine? It could be the worst idea ever."

He leans his head onto my shoulder. "I do love you as a friend, though."

I gently kick his foot with mine. "I love you too, *buddy*."

At home I slink off to my room and quickly tear open the county championship results. My heart is pulsing around my ribcage, and I furiously flick through the pages until I find Alex's race. I'm not religious, but I find myself praying to anything and everything hoping he's done well.

Under-16 Coxless Pairs, sponsored by *Flora*.

1. R. THOMPSON / V. SINGH (Cumbria) 07:05:24
2. B. SMITH-COXLEY / D. SMITH-COXLEY (Berkshire) 07:06:16
3. B. JACKS / A. BEAUCHAMP (Oxfordshire) 07:09:04

National bronze. What a bloody superstar! I want to send another congratulations card, but I know he'll be dying to tell me the news himself. I take a pair of Nan's scissors from her bureau and cut the page out, sticking it to the side of my wardrobe with Blu-Tac. I've never felt prouder.

I take Nan's shoulders and guide her gently towards the kitchen. "Keep your eyes closed."

"They *are* closed, you daft git," she replies, her arms stretched out in front like a geriatric mummy expecting to be shoved headfirst into a wall.

We slip through the plastic strips into the kitchen.

Matt, Sam, and Bethany stand to attention, waiting to see what's in the envelope Alex has sent to her. I've been so tempted to open it using the steam on the kettle but knowing my luck I'd destroy it.

"Have you got the fire extinguisher out?" Nan asks.

"I like how you think I can afford that many candles, Nan," I say, and I feel her elbow in my ribs. "Right, we're gonna count you down. Five, Four…"

I look to the others and encourage them to join in. "Three, Two, One, OPEN!" She stands for a moment and looks around the kitchen. "It's the envelope," I say to give her a hint.

"Oh, I was expecting a cake."

"You don't have to sound too thrilled," I reply.

She pulls out a chair and takes a seat, studying the envelope closely. "This is lovely paper," she says. She turns it over and notices the crown stamp across the seal. She looks to me in shock.

"Please open it," I say, unable to take the tension.

She does as she's told, putting a hand to her mouth when she realises where it's come from. "Oh, Theo, come here," she says, standing and pulling me in tightly until I can feel her tears on my cheeks.

"What does it say?" asks Sam.

"Oh, it is simply wonderful." We wait until she has dried her eyes with a tissue. "It's from Princess Diana."

"Seriously?" says Matt.

"Alex's mum has contacts," I reply.

Nan holds the letter at arm's length and clears her throat.

"Dear Mrs Barker-Hall, I am writing to you to congratulate you on your sixty-eighth birthday. I understand you have had a difficult year, however you have provided such love and support for your grandson, Theodore, and that is a testament to the strong lady that you are. It is true when they say time can heal pain, however it

is important to not allow time to dampen the love you hold for those no longer with us. Your daughter will remain part of both you and Theodore, and I shall keep you all in my thoughts."

"That's lovely," says Bethany, who's also crying.

I wish Alex was here. I need to give him the biggest hug possible right now. In fact, I wish Alex was here all the time. I owe him so much. Not just for the letter, but for letting me be myself, and for supporting me at times when he didn't have to.

"You should frame it, Nan," I say.

"We could hang it in the front room next to your Mum's picture."

Sam moves and takes a seat next to Nan, handing over a gift that has been terribly wrapped, more sticky tape visible than red paper. "Happy birthday."

Nan takes it from him, and rips it open, revealing a gold frame. She looks at me, and I look at Sam.

"Barnaby told me Alex had arranged the letter," he says. "I thought it'd look good in a frame, too."

Nan dusts the frame for a tenth time as we stand in the front room. As Matt is the tallest, we allow him to hammer a nail into the wall. When the letter is hung, Nan stands in awe, clutching her royal tea towel between closed fists.

Whilst she's occupied, I slice a large tray bake into pieces, carefully placing them into a Quality Street tin under the watchful eye of Bethany.

"Does your Nan know you're gay?" she whispers.

I nod as I lick the knife. "We haven't discussed it, but I think she's figured it out. At first I thought Mum told her when we were in the hospice. Nan has never asked about girlfriends or things like that, so doubt she will ask me outright about boyfriends, but every time someone gay is on telly she makes a habit of saying 'ooh, I like him. Isn't he lovely'. I think she's waiting for me to raise it in conversation."

"When will you do that?"

"I dunno. At the moment, it doesn't feel like it needs to be said. If I tell her I love Alex, then it might change things, and I don't want to put her in that situation."

"You love Alex?"

I freeze. "Even I wasn't expecting to say that." It's true, though. I think. "I mean, I guess, yeah. I think about him way more than most people and look at his photographs most days."

"I don't feel that with Matt."

"Maybe you will one day."

Bethany gives me a hug, and I accidentally wipe chocolate cake along her arm. "Alex probably loves you too, y'know."

In a perfect world, he probably does, but we don't live in a perfect world.

After a chaotic game of charades, Nan settles with the evening news. It isn't long before a gaggle of grannies from the bingo club descend on the bungalow.

The four of us act as crowd control as they form a lengthy and excitable queue to view the royal letter on the wall, Nan reading the words slowly and carefully aloud to each. There's so much pandemonium and tears that you'd think she'd put an announcement out that her Virgin Mary portrait near the fireplace had started crying.

"I've got something for you guys," I say to our group as we hide in the kitchen. The *Stokewood Gazette* lays flat on the table, and I open up the centre spread. The photo of our school newspaper team stares back out. "Surprise!"

"Ah, Theo!" says Bethany, snatching it for a closer look. "This is amazing!"

Sam gets close. "Good job, Theo. Like, actually cool."

"Wanna walk to the shops to get a few more copies?" I ask. I leave it open on the countertop. Having something else to show off would make Nan's birthday even more special.

We spend the remaining sunlight laying by the river on the meadows, and then buy all *Gazette's* stocked in the newsagents on Bridge Street. I know our families will want to distribute them to anyone and everyone. I take a few for the school and get back home for a tea and cake dinner.

I've promised to cook for Nan tomorrow, just me and her, and last weekend we splashed out on quality steaks from the butchers in the precinct.

"I'm home!" I call as I kick off my shoes. The house is eerily quiet. "Nan?" I can see her in the kitchen, holding a mug of coffee and staring onto the garden. I approach her slowly, and she turns round and gives me a gentle smile. "Is everything alright?"

"Come and sit," she says, taking the *Gazette* and opening my article.

"What do you think?"

"It's lovely, and I *am* proud of you." There is something odd in her voice, as though she doesn't believe her own words. "The ladies were equally impressed."

I take her hand and rub it gently. "Then what is it?"

She takes a deep breath. "This Mr Le Bon."

"What about him?"

"Has he always been good to you?"

I think of all the opportunities he has given me, all the times he has asked after Nan, the times he has pushed me to do things I'd never have done otherwise. "I think he's one of my favourite teachers."

She nods. "I see." She takes the paper and spins it so

the article is facing me. "I said one day I would tell you about your Dad. Well, there he is."

It takes two cups of tea and half a pack of party rings before I'm even a little settled. Nan has remained at the table throughout as I try to get my head around the news.

"Are you one hundred percent sure?" I ask for the tenth time.

"Wait here." She disappears into the spare room.

I stare closely at Mr Le Bon's picture. I guess we have the same colour hair but dismiss any other resemblance as chance. I could probably find similarities with most middle-aged men pictured in this week's edition.

Nan limps back to the table and slides a photograph towards me. "I found this picture in an album. I wasn't going to show you yet."

I take it in my hand, and see Mum, looking youthful, her arms wrapped around her baby bump. To her side stands a shirtless man with a cigarette in his right hand. Above his gold bracelet, a small shark tattoo can be seen on his wrist. I feel angry I've been lied to for the whole year. Even after asking Nan about my Dad, she hid the fact he was already in my life.

"I can imagine it is a bit of a shock," says Nan as she strokes my shoulder.

I brush her hand away. "Why didn't you tell me in the first place?"

"I didn't know, darling."

"Bullshit." I stand from the table and throw the newspaper in the bin. "I've always done everything you and Mum wanted. When I asked about him, why didn't you say? I'm fifteen so you can't keep hiding things forever."

"It isn't like that, Theo."

"So why did you lie?"

She takes a deep breath as she looks to the ceiling. "I haven't seen him since he left town all those years ago. When you were born, we all tried hard to adjust. Mum was living here at the time, and it was cramped. One evening, I was with you upstairs. You can't have been more than a month old. All hell broke loose. Him and your Grandad were at each other's throats."

"Over what?" I ask.

"Your Grandad thought he didn't have his priorities right. Every other day he would be at the pub playing pool or spending money on cigarettes whilst we struggled to make ends meet. We were making sure we were available to take your mum to appointments, or to look after her when she was under the weather, to babysit you and give her space. Your father came home drunk one night and Grandad finally lost his temper and told him he could not stay the night. The next thing we knew, he was gone."

I pull the paper from the bin. "Why didn't he want me?"

Nan shakes her head. "I don't think he was able to cope. Him and your mum were only in their early twenties. He'd lost his job not long before they found out your mum was pregnant. Something had to give."

I sit back, feeling guilty. "Would things have been better for Mum if she wasn't pregnant?"

"Never. And don't ever think that," Nan says quickly. She walks towards me and drags me up for a hug. "You gave us all a purpose."

"Except Dad."

"I don't think it was entirely his fault. That was the chain that broke, and if we wanted to fix it, we all left it too long, none of us wanting to admit we may have been in the wrong."

"But why did he come back? And why did he not say

anything?"

She lets go and fills the kettle. "We didn't have an address for him, only that he had gone up north somewhere."

"Surely he must've recognised my name?"

"You were called Nigel initially. After his dad. He wouldn't know that we changed it after he left."

I shuffle slightly. "And Barker-Hall?"

"You mum was just Barker then, remember. It's too common a surname for it to be linked."

"So he might not know I'm his son?" The look Nan gives me says it all. I worry about Mum, and how she'd feel if she were here now. "You said they argued. Was he ever violent towards her?"

Nan shakes her head. "Never. Regardless, once he had gone, we thought it was best if we kept him at a distance. We thought we were doing the best thing."

There it is again. 'Doing the best thing'. Making me get homeschooled, making me go back to Year Nine, and hiding me away from my own Dad. "I want him to stay in my life."

Nan stops stirring her tea. "It might not be easy."

"So? I've already lost one parent and I don't want to lose another." I know I've upset Nan as soon as I say it. She holds both her hands to her face. "I didn't mean that, sorry. It's just he has been so good to me, and I'm scared things will go wrong if I lose him again."

"You're right," she says. She leans back against the kitchen counter and picks at the remaining crumbs of her birthday tray bake. "I will phone the school and ask for a meeting."

"He's away for a couple of weeks for band camp in Oslo."

"Why is he on that? I thought he just did English."

"No idea. Probably better than teaching us, ain't it?"

She smiles and strokes her sticky hands on my cheeks. "We will sort this for you, I promise."

Twenty-Five

Alexander Beauchapt
10 Tolkien
Saint Martin's
Rutherford-On-Thames
Oxfordshire

20/07/1997

Hey, Theo!

I cannot believe your news about Mr Le Bon being your dad. How are you feeling about it? I can understand your reasoning for wanting to keep him in your life, especially since he did not know who you were during your time together on the newspaper. I read the *Stokewood Gazette* you sent and yeah, I can see a resemblance. I think you have the same hairline.

I hope you are able to reconnect fully now he is in your life. Of course, he will never replace your wonderful mum, but having a bond with a parent is so important at this stage in your life. My relationship with my Dad is slowly fading and it seems as though I am a constant afterthought for him. Twice he has been due to call, but the first occasion he sent a note (via Felicity) saying he was too busy with work, and the second time he forgot completely. I remained by the phone for an hour in case he was confused with the time zones, but it never rang.

I am unsure if he has spoken to Isabelle at all, however with her traveling around Asia, I feel it is most unlikely. Speaking of which, I have news about results day! It turns out the *Big Breakfast* will be broadcasting live from our grounds throughout the morning! It will be on the 21st of August, so please watch it! You'll see what I mean then about how ridiculous the buildings in our grounds are.

I am so glad to hear your Nan loved the letter from Princess Diana. Her framing it and hanging on your wall is so cute. Mum has promised to take me with her to work when I see her in Paris next month, and I hope to meet her. I cannot wait, and it will certainly be memorable. I reckon mum's doing this as she is majorly overcompensating for my Dad being an absolute DICK, but it will be lovely, regardless.

We are going to spend some time in Montmartre and have a meal somewhere special near the centre. Due to her work, we have been given an apartment close to the Arc de Triomphe.

Normally at this point I would give you the good news about the county championships, but I have sneaking suspicion you may already know. We were taken on a coach from our hostel to Coniston, which turned out to not be close at all. It was at least an hour in each direction, and the weather was appalling over the higher ground.

On the way back from the event, we stopped at a Pizza Hut where an area had been reserved for networking between the teams. I sat opposite a chap called James and overheard him discussing his A-Levels with a member of our crew and thought I was hearing things when he said he was from Stokewood Secondary. I asked him at the end to make sure and couldn't believe it when he said I had been correct.

I asked about you, however, he said he hadn't met you before, but he had read the school paper, so that's something. I told him he should do a report for the next issue in the new school year. I am sure he will have some photographs he could submit, too.

The next national tournament will be here before long. I am not expected to get picked for our age group as the two teams who beat us were both incredibly strong. Brian and I were ecstatic with our bronze medal, and even with additional training, it would have been difficult to find the five or six extra seconds to take gold.

If I were the national selectors, I would give the first two slots to the Smith-Coxley twins from Berkshire. There is something about them and they could reach the highest level, even if they did come second. Their strength is slightly lower than the winning team, but they have such elegance in their strokes. If they can keep on improving, then I would not be surprised to see them pushing for an Olympic place within the next decade.

Sorry for this letter being slightly short. Both my wrists are strapped from overuse on the oars, so the school nurse has said I must limit my writing to fifteen minutes at a time.

I look forward to hearing from you, and I cannot wait to tell you all about Paris.

Au revoir,
Alex x

Twenty-Six

July 1997

I stand outside Mr Richardson's office on Thursday morning, pacing up and down reception, my heart beating fast. Even with my ear pressed to the office door, I can't overhear the conversation taking place inside. Nan has been in there with Mr Le Bon and Mr Richardson for over twenty-five minutes. For once, I'd rather be sat in double maths.

I take an interest in the school photos, trying to spot if Mr Le Bon is in any of them. It's difficult to tell with all the dust settled on the glass. Thankfully, my nerves calm when Bethany comes around the corner and passes me a Diet Coke. Her skirt seems to be another inch shorter than last week and must be on the borderline of what the Head deems acceptable. She's already on a warning for messing with the length of her tie.

"How is it going?" she asks. "Any news yet?"

My head drops. "I think it's bad news."

She takes a seat and pats the cushion next to her. I join and she places her hand on my knee. "You always assume the worst. She has to do what's best for you, and if you want him to stay at the school, then that's what should happen."

"It's not just school, Bethany. It's everything in life.

What if he doesn't want me?" I ask, fighting back tears.

"Don't think like that, okay?" she says as she grabs my arm. "Who wouldn't want you?"

I sit with my head resting on her shoulder, my legs shaking, the ticking clock above the entrance soundtracking the drawn out wait. Eventually, the door to the office clicks open and Mr Richardson emerges. "Bethany, back to class, please."

Bethany stands and kisses me on the cheek. "I love you." She pulls her skirt down and disappears up the nearest staircase.

"Theo, do you want to come through?" says Mr Richardson. I take a deep breath and follow him inside. Nan is sat next to Mr Le Bon on the sturdy blue chairs under the noticeboard, they're both clutching a paper cup of water tightly. Mr Le Bon's shirt is darkened with sweat.

"Hi. How was the band trip?"

"Very lovely, thank you."

The pleasantries seem forced. We know why we are here. "Did you know?" He shakes his head. "You genuinely had no idea at all?" I'm not sure if I believe him.

He takes a sip of water and looks to Nan, and then back to me. "If I'm completely honest, something did cross my mind a while back, and I wondered if the boy I left behind could be a pupil here. I dismissed it and told myself I was being stupid. I guess somewhere inside of me there was a thought that coming back to Stokewood would lead to us reconnecting eventually, but I never tried to find you. Maybe I should have, I don't know. Things didn't end well and what if finding you made it worse?"

"When did you first think this?"

"Do you remember when I spoke to you about the

ring you used to wear? It looked similar to one your Mum used to wear when we were courting."

"Is that why you told me to take it off?" I ask.

He shakes his head. "I know the ring was special to you, but school rules are school rules. Back in the early eighties, most girls had a ring like that. I got your Mum hers from a shop in town, but it was hardly unique. I think most of my friends bought the same for their girlfriends. None of us were rich when we were younger." He scratches at his fingers and sighs deeply. "It reminded me of what I lost all those years ago, I guess. The chances of your ring being the same one I bought seemed too farfetched. It would be too much of a coincidence for me to teach the child I left behind."

"Except it happened."

Mr Le Bon shrinks, withdrawing into himself with guilt. "I'm sorry, Theo. If I knew you were my son, I would have said something. Maybe not to you, but to Mr Richardson at least."

"So what happens now?" I ask Nan.

She shrugs. "That's what we need to establish. We have to think about your schooling and if it will have any effect on your grades."

"I don't want him to leave," I reply immediately.

Nan takes my hand. "I know you said you want him in your life, but life is not straightforward. We need to look out for you, and what would be best, especially as your exams get closer."

I release my hand from hers. "Everyone has always made decisions for me. What about what I want?"

"Theo, look, there is no point in getting angry—"

"It's not that. I was told being homeschooled was the best for me. I was told coming back here was best for me. What now? What if you think it's best he leaves, or if I leave? I don't want to keep going through these changes." I pace around the room, my frustration getting to me. "I like it here, and I like Mr Le Bon. I've had the best year. The newspaper has got me engaged, and I feel settled. Everyone thinks they know what I should or shouldn't do, but I want to have a say this time."

Mr Richardson stands in the centre. "I can't make either person leave. Technically, no one has done anything wrong."

"This has come as a complete shock to me too, remember," Mr Le Bon says to Nan. "I know you are concerned for him, but he's a good kid. Even if Theo weren't my son, it has been enjoyable getting to know him as a person."

Nan plays with the cuff of her knitted jumper. We all stare at her, and she lets out a long sigh. "I guess you're right, both of you. What if we work on arranging an agreement between us all? A way where we can all move forward."

"Can we carry on as we are?" I ask.

"I wish it were that easy," says Mr Le Bon. "Things have changed, but it doesn't mean this new normal needs to be too much of a seismic shift. Maybe we take baby steps. I'd love to reconnect with Theo."

"Nan?" I ask. She's staring into space.

"Is that what you want, Theo?" she replies.

"It is. I know you want to protect me, but like I said, Mr Le Bon is cool. Well, for a teacher anyway."

She stands and pulls on her coat. "In that case, I guess I can't stand in your way. But we must take things slowly."

I've gained a parent, nearly exactly a year after losing one.

With only one more lesson between morning break and six weeks of summer, I find myself back outside Mr

Teale's classroom. He's taking posters off the walls behind his desk.

"Hey, Sir. Do you have a few minutes?"

"Hi, Theo, of course, come take a seat."

"Why are you clearing out your room?"

"No reason." He tosses the posters into the bin under the desk. "Just thought I would freshen the place up." The walls have dark squares where the posters had sat, the surrounding areas bleached by the afternoons of bright sunlight. The patchiness makes the room look dirty and in disrepair.

"Are you all set for Summer?" he asks.

"I guess. I'm kinda looking forward to being able to relax a bit. Are you off to Spain again?"

"I am. Flying out with Jeff next week."

"Is Jeff your boyfriend?"

"He is."

"Is he a teacher, too?"

Mr Teale takes off his tie and unbuttons the top of his shirt. "Used to be. He left three years ago. Well, that's a lie actually. He was relieved of his duties because of what I said to you before. That's why I'm a bit twitchy about discussing this stuff."

"What did he do wrong?"

"The head of the Parents Teacher Association put in a formal complaint regarding him promoting homosexuality in the classroom."

"Promote it how?"

"He was a religious education teacher, and during one a lesson they were studying different types of marriage. A pupil was off to a Hindu wedding, you see. One kid asked if he thought gay people would be able to marry one day, and he said he hoped so. The next day, he was called into the office and that was that. He was given the choice to walk from his job or get pushed." Mr Teale's right hand is clenched, angry at the injustice.

"Surely you can't lose a job for saying something trivial. Are you sure that's all he said?"

"One hundred per cent. He should've ignored the question. That's always the easiest thing to do."

"How about you, Sir. Do you think we might be able to marry one day?"

He scoffs at the question. "Not in our lifetime, no. There is too much work to do to even think it will be a possibility. The problems we face will snowball. Another generation will grow seeing us as second-class citizens. I feel sorry for you, Theo. I should be changing the world to make things easier for younger people, but I have failed."

"Is there anything we can do, as pupils?"

"Sadly not. You saw first-hand what happened when it was mentioned in your newspaper. If any teacher gets a sniff of you doing something like that you'll be out on your backside quicker than you can say trigonometry."

I slump back into my chair. "Why aren't people fighting against it?"

"They have been!" he says angrily. "Sorry, but it's not like we are sitting back. Lesbians have raided the BBC, there have been marches in Manchester, even protestors in parliament, but it's made no difference. We are seen as dirty and a threat to the very moral fibre of this country."

"Won't the politicians do something?"

"It's them who have caused it. I've felt shame ever since I knew I was gay. Hiding it from my parents, and then from my classmates, and now from my colleagues. If I believed in a God, I'd pray that you won't go through what I have. I can't even drink in the pub with Jeff without fear of someone spotting us together. I feel like I am being forced underground."

"There must be something we can do," I say.

"Just leave it! You messing around will make things worse." He's been waiting to get this off his chest for far too long, sat shaking in his seat, a vein popping on his forehead. "Look, Theo. I wish I could be more positive. I hope things do improve one day, for both our sakes. The truth is, well who knows? Now if you don't mind…"

His eyes are vacant as I collect my belongings. I'm terrified for my future. What if things never get better? I need the six weeks away from this place more than ever.

Twenty-Seven

Alexander Beauchamp
16 Rue Massenet
33880 Cambes
France

18/08/1997

Bonjour, Theo!

I hope you are having a wonderful summer so far. I know I shouldn't be writing yet, but after your last letter I wanted to say a quick hello, instead of a boring postcard.

The weather here today is stunning. I opened the shutters on the farmhouse and had an interrupted view of sunflowers stretching far into the distance. There was complete peace, aside from the chirping of a few birds.

This farmhouse has changed so much since my previous visit in '94, and the two rooms in the converted barn have been given over to tourists. Whilst the current occupants had breakfast, I spent the morning walking along the river.

It is like you would imagine it to be. A real chance to switch off from the stresses in life, of which there are plenty. When I am old enough (and if I have the money), then I will follow in my aunt's footsteps and spend summers here. I think you would enjoy it, so you always have an invitation to join me. It would be wonderful to walk through the forests and along the river here with you.

This may sound silly, but I have a reoccurring vision of you being here with me one day. There is one particularly quiet place by the old mill where you can lay under a willow and listen to the water bubbling past. Every time I have been there this month I have thought of you, wondering when I will get to show you it's beauty.

I have gone quite soppy there, apologies! I best leave this letter for now. I can smell the scent of bread drifting up the wooden stairs to my attic room, and I know the table will be full of cheeses and meats. You're obviously important, but nothing beats food like that!

My flight home is tomorrow evening and I only have a week before packing and heading across on the Chunnel. There is a training camp at Henley in that week too, so I'll be so shattered. Mum is going to collect me from Gare de Nord on the following Saturday lunchtime to start our Paris adventure!

I look forward to hearing from you, and I cannot wait to tell you all about my next trip!

Au revoir,
Alex x

Twenty-Eight

August 1997

I'm seeing Dad every Sunday to help with the bonding process. It has been enjoyable, however, it's difficult to call him Dad to his face. He did try and find middle-ground and suggest I call him by his first name, but he doesn't seem like a 'Clive.'

The first few visits felt like an afterschool detention, albeit with microwave meals and films on the TV at his flat, rather than being made to do additional homework.

Before school, he's heading to Barnsley for the week to visit old friends, so this afternoon we're heading to our second football match together as a treat. Stokewood Town are playing a friendly against Tenby AFC, and Dad has invited Sam and Bethany.

They've been fantastic with Dad and have helped me settle into this new way of life. When we're back at school they've agreed to keep the news under wraps. Being at the football will help Bethany get over her and Matt's latest break-up. (This time it was caused by Matt forgetting to send a postcard from Florida. He's no Alex.)

I was woken this morning by sun blasting through

the small gap I left in my bedroom curtains. It was lighting the porcelain doll directly above my feet, and in my dozed state I genuinely thought there was an evil child levitating above my head.

My ears feel on fire from the sunburn I got yesterday. As I soak them in after sun lotion, the front door opens.

"Morning," I call out over my shoulder. Nan doesn't answer, and when I turn round, she's staring at me with puffy eyes, her cheeks glistening with tears. "What's up?"

"It's Diana."

"What's happened to her?"

"I don't know how to tell you this, but the news broke this morning she's been killed in a car crash." She pulls me into a hug, her skin cold against mine.

"I'm sorry, Nan," I say. "It must be such a shock. I only saw her last week."

She lets go and gives me a strange look, before pulling a flaking tissue from the front pocket of her cardigan. "Come through to the front room."

"In a minute. I'm gonna get you a coffee. You're freezing." In the kitchen, I pull two mugs from the cupboard, adding extra sugar to her cup to give her energy. I remember how weak she was the day after Mum passed, often forgetting to eat over the following days.

As the kettle whistles away on the side, I turn on the small radio. The music which normally blasts out from Fox FM is strangely absent. In its place, a news reporter is discussing how there had yet to be a statement from the Royal Family. It was only when they mention that Prince Charles is expected to fly to Paris that the penny drops.

I leave the mugs and dash in to see Nan. She's sat on the footstool a few feet from the television. On screen, pictures of police surrounding the entrance to a French underpass play on loop, interspersed with solemn reports from the presenters. The tea towel is hanging from the curtain rail again.

"I'm sorry, Nan. I must've been half asleep. I thought you meant the woman from your bingo with the purple-rinse."

She brushes the edge of her framed letter, taking it from its hook and cradling it in her hands. "She was such a wonderful woman. I feel so sorry for her boys. I can't imagine what they are going through."

I can. Although not as public, I know the grief of losing your mother all too well. The moment you know they're gone feels like a switch being clicked off in your brain. You're no longer a child. You have to grow up immediately, be mature in the most difficult of circumstances. It's not something that goes away. The reminders of their life flashing back to your thoughts at the silliest moments. Even the sound of a fruit machine can trigger me these days since our visit to the arcades when scattering the ashes.

"I know how much she means to you, Nan. I'm so sorry." I sit between her legs and a wave of panic hits. "Nan. Alex is there."

"Your Alex?"

I nod as she strokes my hair. "His mum worked for Diana, didn't she? When he last wrote, he said he was heading to Paris to spend time with his Mum whilst she was working in the city. I'm scared he's caught up in this."

Nan leans forward and wraps her arms around me from behind. "Theo, he wouldn't have been out in the city late at night, and he definitely wouldn't have been in the car with the princess."

The constant news, the worry for Alex, and the images of Princes William and Harry on the telly bring last summer's feelings back to the foreground. My mouth is dry and my body tense. Inside I'm empty, the same as when I walked away from the hospice. I've no appetite, no desire to see anyone.

Sleep would be a welcome break, but when I drift, the flashbacks become vivid. Mum is there, in the old house sat in her favourite chair moaning she hasn't won the lottery. I'd give everything in this world for the chance to have one more game of Connect 4.

When I take Nan to the Methodist Church to sign a book of condolence, I light a candle for Mum, just like Alex has done before me.

Twenty-Nine

September 1997

I stand at my locker, trying to rearrange the items like Tetris so the door can close again. Bethany stands next to me, sporting a short new hairstyle. "My hairdressing aunt is using me as guinea pig. What d'ya think?"

She gives me a spin.

"It's nice." It's different, I'll give her that.

"From you, that's a massive compliment, so thanks. What are you doing anyway?"

I push at the end of a shoebox until it squeezes into the small remaining gap between my PE kit and cooking ingredients. "Nan is redecorating my bedroom."

"What's in the box? All your dirty magazines?"

I click the locker shut and walk to registration. "I don't have dirty magazines. It's just personal stuff."

"Such as?"

"You're so bloody nosey." She keeps staring at me. "Fine. It's the letters from Alex."

"You shouldn't bring them to school."

"They'll be safer here. Dad is gonna help put some shelves up and I'd hate for him to see them."

She nods. "So, you've put them outside his classroom? Fool proof."

"Just cos he's my Dad, it doesn't give him permission

to look through my locker. If they were at home he might accidentally knock the box over."

"Does he know you're gay?"

I shake my head. "I haven't gained enough courage." Telling him would ruin what we've built over the last two months. "Remember when Bosnich changed the subject when someone asked about specifics in sex ed last year?"

"Yeah, but that's different."

"Well thank God Dad isn't my science teacher. Can you imagine how bad discussing sex with your dad in front of all your friends would be?" I wave a hand causally across to our classmates as we enter the form room.

"Alright?" Sam and Matt say in unison as we take our seats. They both have new buzzcuts. In late summer their new cuts remained hidden under back to front baseball caps, which have somehow become popular again thanks to *Boyzone*, not that they would admit this.

"Glad to be back?" I ask.

"It's alright, I guess," says Sam.

"I'd rather be back in Florida," says Matt.

"I wish you were back in Florida," Bethany mocks.

The relationship is seemingly 'off' for good, which is probably best for both of them.

"How's your Nan?" asks Matt.

I take a bite of an apple from my lunchbox. "Yeah, alright, ta. Dad took her to London yesterday to see the memorials."

"Shouldn't he have been at inset day?"

"Probably. I'm glad to be back. It means I won't have to hear *Candle in the Wind* on loop all day. It's driving me nuts."

"Did Alex go to the funeral?" asks Bethany.

"Dunno." I watched it at home, only paying attention to those in the pews, not the service itself. Every time there was a glimpse of ginger hair, I leant close to the screen, trying to see who it was before they disappeared from view. Ninety-nine percent of the time it was Prince Harry. "He hasn't written since it happened so I'm not sure how involved he was."

"Write to him first," says Bethany.

"I should, but I sent a note to his school when she died and if I write twice in a row it breaks the rules and he might hate me."

"Theo, they're only rules you've made."

"I'm sticking to them. I don't want him to think I'm hassling him."

Mr Richardson enters as rain batters the windows, another annual academic cycle ready to begin.

"Welcome back, everybody. It's lovely to see you all. Before we start, I would like to introduce you to Joshua, who will be joining us this year."

We all stare at the new kid who slides through the rear door and shuffles to a table in the far corner. His arms are close to his side, and he looks so timid that he'd probably have a heart attack if given a Kinder Surprise, but there is no escaping the one very clear and obvious fact.

JOSHUA.

IS.

HOT.

"Close your mouth, Bethany," I say as her jaw almost hits her lap.

"Holy smokes," she says slowly, still making eye contact as she applies lip gloss suggestively.

"He's not that hot," Matt protests.

"He kinda is," says Sam.

I drop my apple with a bounce. "Literally stunning."

As soon as first break comes, we remain in our seats and

wait for Joshua to walk past. "Hey," I call out before he leaves. He smiles, revealing two rows of perfect, white teeth. His brown hair flops over his face, coming to rest on the top of his prominent cheekbones. His eyes are so bright it looks like he has natural mascara on his lashes.

"I'm Bethany," she says, leaning forward on her arms. "You can call me Betty."

"No one calls you Betty," says Matt.

"He can call me anything he wants," she whispers back.

"I'm Theo, that's Sam and Matt." They put their hands up in a semi-wave, and I offer mine out for a handshake, which he awkwardly high-fives.

"Hey guys." He hadn't spoken for the first two hours, sadly something that hid his cute American accent. "Nice to meet y'all. I gotta go on some tour." He slings his bag over his shoulder.

"Wait!" I don't know why I shouted as I've nothing to offer. "Um, wanna hang with us?"

He pulls Mr Richardson's seat from the front. "Sure. What do you do on recess?"

Bethany continues to stare, and Matt and Sam are no help. "There is a canteen which is alright, and we have an area in the tennis courts where we play football."

"Neat. I'm not great at football. It was more baseball and ice hockey at my old school."

"I broke my arm ice skating!" Not exactly the commonest of common ground, but it's a start.

"Neat." He says this a lot.

"Where did you move from?" asks Sam, who I know is as giddy as the rest of us. Well, except Matt, who's now stood waiting for us to follow him outside, jangling loose change in his hands.

"Seattle. Do you know it?"

"I've heard of it," I reply, which is about the extent

of my knowledge.

"It's in Washington? In the Northwest?"

I can see Sam using his finger to draw an invisible compass on the desk. "He means the top left," I say, trying to help him out.

"Do you want to come to the cinema this weekend?" asks Bethany.

Joshua is silent for a moment.

"We're all going," Sam adds.

"Neat. Maybe. Look, I gotta go find this tour, but catch y'all soon."

"If they don't mention it, your post gets delivered to the pigeonholes by the art rooms," I call as he walks away.

He nods at me and disappears.

We spent the next three days chasing Joshua around, trying to get him to hang out with us, however every lunchtime he'd sneak off home. His house is a large new build past the playing fields, all posh with a gated driveway.

Surprisingly, on Friday, he appears at the lunchtime newspaper planning group, something which will put everyone in a good mood, with the exception of Matt.

As Katie Barlow and Bethany lean over his desk, Matt remains stony-faced. "It's so embarrassing," he says as he watches them chatting.

"Am I detecting some jealousy?" asks Sam.

Matt grunts. "It's more everyone thinks he's the hottest person in the world."

"To be fair, he is," I tell him.

"Not you as well. I can't be bothered. I'll see you later."

Despite mine and Sam's protests, Matt leaves the room, leaving me to cover for his part in the next edition.

Dad is at the front, busy doing some marking, not paying any attention. After the success of last year, we've been given more autonomy.

"Hey, Katie," I call. She stops her conversation and joins our table. "As sub-editor, what is your thinking for the next edition."

She pushes at her bobbed haircut with both hands. "Joshua is gonna write a piece about the American schooling system, and how it's different from the UK."

"Great. Sam, you still on for sport?"

"Yeah, may as well."

"Great. I'll do a piece on Diana or something."

"Isn't everyone sick of that?" Katie asks.

"Yes, but parents will love it, so more people will hear about the paper."

She nods. "I like your thinking. When's the deadline for articles?"

"I've no idea." I turn to the front. "Hey, Dad, when do we have to get stuff done by?"

As soon as I say it, the room goes dead quiet, only broken by Katie laughing. "I've not heard anyone call a teacher Mum or Dad for about ten years."

My cheeks rush with blood.

"It's an easy mistake, Katie," says Dad. "The deadline is in a week."

"Neat," says Joshua.

"You're definitely not doing another problem page this year, are you Katie?" I ask.

She shakes her head. "No. Mr Richardson said not to. My other articles were better, anyway. The last one helped save the closure of the youth centre."

"I think that was more to do with some bloke putting in the million quid investment, but I admire your self-belief."

I help Sam to put together ideas for his sports

section, but we get interrupted when Joshua pulls a chair opposite. "Hey guys, do y'all wanna come for Thanksgiving this year?"

"Can do, yeah," I say nonchalantly, holding back the little voice inside my head which wants to scream yes. I've never been to a Thanksgiving. I bet Alex has. Guilt bubbles inside me at having improper thoughts over Joshua.

"My Grandpa does an awesome spread, and he'd love to have people there. I'm sure you can invite your families."

"Sounds neat," says Bethany. Bethany never says neat. "My Dad has got a new camcorder, so he can bring that, if your parents wouldn't mind?"

Joshua bites his lip and takes a strong interest in a paperclip on the table, bending it out of shape. "Um, I don't have parents."

"What happened to them?" asks Sam. I elbow him in the ribs hard and he splutters. I hate people asking me what happened to Mum, and I don't want Joshua to feel the same.

"I'll just say they're no longer around," Joshua says quietly. "It will be my third Thanksgiving with Grandpa. We prefer it to be busy still, so come over."

"When is it?" I ask.

"Normally at the end of November, but we're doing it at the start as Grandpa has to fly to the States for work."

"What does he do?"

"Property. He was born in England, which is why we're here now, but still has businesses there."

"What will you do when he goes?"

"I go with him. If I can't then I guess I can stay with one of you?"

I think about how quickly Dad would be able to

convert the spare room at the bungalow, but Sam gets there first. "We have a place at mine."

"Neat. Thanks. Look, I gotta head. See you next week guys." Joshua gives a salute and departs. Sam is beaming at his potential new housemate.

The jealousy is immediate, stabbing at me like a compass to the hand, and I fold my arms tight across my chest.

"You have Alex, remember," Bethany whispers.

"I know, I know."

"Anyway, Joshua is totally straight." I hope she's wrong. It's annoying everyone is, by default, straight until proven otherwise. "Theo, didn't you notice he kept checking out Katie's arse every time she bent over in front of him?"

"You would too if she shoved it in your face every five seconds."

At the vending machine in the foyer, Bethany's junk food choices clatter down the chute. "Here, eat this and cheer up. You're such a moody git."

As I chew on a Mars Bar, an idea pops into my head. "Here, that camcorder your Dad has. Can I borrow it?"

On Saturday morning, I head out with Dad as he drives to thirty garages to look at new cars. Despite sitting in twenty, and test driving at least half of them, we drive home in his Peugeot 306. I'm cramped in the front, with the back seats taken over by a selection of ferns and shrubs Nan asked us to collect from Mr Murray's farm.

We power along the single-track road which splices the cornfields of South Lew. We're the only car visible, and the countryside stretches off like a patchwork quilt into the distance. A wave of calm floods over me and I turn the volume lower on the CD player.

"Hey, I was listening to that," Dad says as he flicks

the ash from a cigarette out the window.

"I'll put it back on in a minute. This is nice."

"Running errands for your Nan?"

I let out a snort. "No, just all of this," I say, gesturing to the fields. "I like spending time with you." I never thought I'd be someone who could hang out with their Dad, zooming through the countryside, the autumn sun in the air and eighties music on the radio. It feels right.

"I am sensing you want to tell me something," Dad says. He slows as an old woman crosses in front of us, causing a spikey plant to slide forward and stab my neck.

Now feels the right time to come out, but the words lodge in my throat, stifling the air in my lungs. I fix my gaze onto the fields.

"School all okay?"

"Nothing has happened there."

"Except your detention last week."

I look across. "You know about that?"

"Karen told me," he says, smiling.

"Karen?"

"Miss Saunders. Apparently you threw a Twix out an upstairs window?"

"I was hungry."

"You could've had someone's eye out."

"That's what she said, too." It wasn't my finest moment, and the movement had been anything but subtle, however no one has ever been injured by a flying chocolate bar. Teachers can be so overdramatic.

Dad flicks the cigarette out the window, and it fizzles and dies on the tarmac. "You need to keep your head and your eyes focused. And don't eat in class."

I turn back to the front, ignoring his slip back into teacher-mode.

I increase the volume of the radio, but he cuts the engine and silence falls again. "How are things with

Alex?”

My mouth goes dry. Is he trying to get it out of me? “Alex is fine, thanks.”

He nods. “I saw you putting a box with his name on into your locker. I recognised it from your bedroom.” I remain silent. “I didn’t look in it, if that’s what you’re wondering.”

“I wanted to keep his letters safe.”

“Fair enough.” He fires the engine into life but allows it to tick over. “Theo, I know this is still new to us both, but you’re a good kid.”

“Thanks. You’re cool too.”

“Even though I’m a teacher?”

I chuckle to myself. He is, though. He’s leant back with large shades over his eyes, his denim shirt only fastened with the bottom three buttons. He looks cool without trying. Why couldn’t I have inherited that?

He takes another cigarette from the door pocket, and sparks a match, before taking a long draw. The cherry glows red, and he breathes a cloud of smoke outside. “Your mum would be proud of what you’ve achieved this year.”

“I hope so,” I reply. “I miss her a lot.”

“I can imagine.” He turns his head and gives me a slight smile. “I know I can’t fill the gap she has left, but if you ever need to talk about anything, I will listen.”

I take a deep breath, ignoring my sweaty palms and the sound of my heartbeat drumming through my ears. “Well, I guess there is something.”

He flicks ash into the ashtray, tapping the fingers of his right hand on the steering wheel. “Does it involve Alex?”

“Yeah,” I say quietly, sitting on my hands.

He nods. “Understood. Say no more. It doesn’t change anything between us.”

"Thanks."

"Is this what you've been discussing with Mr Teale?"

My blood runs cold, my stomach knotting. "I…no."

"Mr Richardson saw you in his room. Told me to keep an eye out. I asked Mr Teale what you were talking about and he made something up. He was quick, I'll give him that."

"Don't tell anyone, please. I don't want him to get into trouble."

"And neither do I. It's safe with me." He leans across and slaps me on the knee gently. "I will never let anyone hurt you, okay?"

Birdsong fills the minute of silence that hangs heavy in the air. He knows he can't guarantee what he is promising.

"You were right," he says.

"About?"

"This. It is nice. Let's enjoy it and not worry about the future for now, yeah? It'll be okay." He finds first gear and revs the car, the engine roaring through the still country air.

Let's not worry about the future. Easy for a hetero to say.

They aren't the ones who stare at their ceilings at three in the morning wondering if they'll be discarded for who they love.

They don't need to make excuses to leave a room when the homophobia starts.

The television channels are never changed when straight people are on.

They aren't the ones being called immoral by all corners of society.

They aren't the butt of everyone's jokes.

They aren't the ones who will be alone.

They aren't the ones who are taboo.

They are the ones who are going to be okay.

Thirty

Alexander Beauchamp
11 Tolkien
Saint Martin's
Rutherford-On-Thames
Oxfordshire

18/10/97

Hi Theo,

You. Are. Officially. Amazing. I was so intrigued by the size of the gift you sent for my birthday. Annoyingly, I had to wait for six hours before I was alone and I could put the tape in the video player.

When your face came on screen I virtually danced around the room. You are even cuter than I thought, and your accent is wonderful! I don't think it is like a farmer at all. It is easily THE best birthday message I have ever got. I am embarrassed to tell you how many times I have watched it. My favourite bit was the end where you were waiting for Bethany to stop the recording, and you sat there grinning at the lens. I really loved it.

Mum has asked me to pass on her thanks regarding your kind words about recent events. It was an incredibly difficult time for all of us. We visited Montmartre and had our meal. I tried snails for the first time and they are quite nice. They have the texture of snot, but the masses of garlic oil countered that.

We were meant to go to The Louvre on the Sunday before returning. Sadly, as you know, everything changed.

I was first aware something had happened when someone banged on our hotel door at 3am. Obviously, anyone waking you at that time of day is enough to cause panic, and this was heightened when a man in a dark suit entered. Mum was ushered into the bathroom and my immediate thought was that Isabelle was in trouble. After results day, she travelled to Morocco for a week and I know she hadn't been in contact for a couple of days.

When Mum came back in, I was told to dress quickly and put everything I owned on the bed. We were ushered down the fire escape and bundled into a waiting car outside the hotel. Minutes later I was at the embassy, still unclear what was happening. The embassy is a grand building in central Paris, but I was taken to a windowless room, whilst Mum disappeared.

Around half an hour later, Mum told me the news of the crash. I thought back to the police vehicles on the ten-minute drive, realising we had passed close to where the accident occurred. With Mum's job, she had to communicate with royal households in the UK, and I was to be put on the next train to London. It was as we came out the channel tunnel that the minder I had been given received the call breaking the news the Princess had died. It was such a shock.

Felicity collected me from the station and I stayed around her house for the next four days. As always, Dad wasn't present. I wasn't at the funeral, hence why you didn't see me, but I watched on television. Although Mum is so closely linked to the Royal Family, I was kept at a distance, with the only interaction being when I laid flowers at Kensington Palace.

As soon as the funeral was over, I was shipped back to school. I am even here at weekends for the foreseeable future. The loneliness is unbearable. Isabelle is in Durham and our regular phone calls are the only family interactions left.

To keep myself occupied, I am working with the kitchen team, tending the allotment, and preparing vegetables for meals. A pastry chef, Madison, has promised to train me in the kitchen next week. She said there are apprenticeships available locally and I am considering doing one. Do you think I would be good at it? It would take some pressure off going to university, and after being abandoned by my family, it feels right I should do something for myself.

I am sorry you did not get to see my school on the *Big Breakfast*. Luckily for you though, Felix's sister recorded it, hence the VHS tape included with this letter. I got to meet Denise Van Outen and Richard Orford! Barnaby and Felix have told me Denise is 'even fitter in the flesh' and they have not shut up about her since. They have put a picture of her from a magazine on the wall, replacing Geri Halliwell, so they must be serious about liking her. My Leo poster is better than theirs, of course.

How have things been going with your Dad? My Dad didn't even send me a card or call me this birthday. He thinks putting some money into my account is an example of good parenting. Mum was furious with him, but what's new?

Maybe I will use the money to go travelling next summer. Isabelle really recommends Vietnam.

Your new Joshua friend sounds interesting. How hot is he? Not that I am jealous! (Well, maybe a tiny little bit). I enjoyed his article in your paper about American schools. He must find it weird being over here now. It seems so different. Thanksgiving will be great fun. Think of all pumpkin pie and tater tots! Have you found out what happened with his parents yet?

The school talent contest will be returning for a second year at Christmas. I will NOT be on stage this year but playing piano in the foyer when guests arrive. I was put forward by our new band leader, Master Sharpe. He made me audition and everything! Luckily, it all went well and I am therefore the new lead pianist for the school band. There is talk of us doing a national youth performance at the Royal Albert Hall in July. You and Nan have to come!

I have to head to rowing practice now. I hope you have a wonderful thanksgiving, and I look forward to hearing all about it. Say hi to your friends for me!

I am off to watch your video again :)

Yours,
Alex x

Thirty-One

November 1997

Joshua's house is gigantic. It's taken five minutes to walk up the driveway, and with swimwear packed, I reckon he has more than one pool.

It is so posh there isn't a doorbell, instead a large brass lion's head knocker on a solid oak door. Nan passes me her homemade pecan pie and loudly knocks three times. The noise echoes like gunshots off neighbouring buildings.

Footsteps patter the floor inside and the door swings open. Joshua is stood in lime green sunglasses and knee length boardshorts… and nothing else. If I didn't know I was gay before, I definitely would now. He has an athletic body, and knowing I get to spend the today watching his pecs and abs, this party will definitely be more successful than ice skating was.

"Hey, guys, come on through," he says.

"Nan, this is Joshua from school. Joshua, this is Nan."

"Hey, Nan," he says, flashing a smile, and leads us into a wide, bright hallway. "Grandpa is with Jolene but should be out soon."

"I've bought pecan pie, Joshua," Nan says proudly, holding the foiled offering in outstretched arms.

"Neat!" He places the dish onto the breakfast bar next to another pecan pie. "I didn't know you Brits made that kinda thing."

"A lady from bingo tore a recipe out of *Woman's Weekly*," Nan says proudly.

"It sounds de-vine. I'll give y'all a tour when the others arrive. So far it's me and Katie. We're in the pool, come through."

Each room seems to get bigger, until we reach a glass door at the end of a second reception room. The scent of chlorine seeps out, and my mind is pulled into the evening at the hospice. Not now. I shake the thought from my head. Mum would've loved to live somewhere like this.

The indoor pool is small, but grander than the plastic paddler I had when I was young. Katie is at the far end, laying back on a sun lounger, a colourful drink in her hand. She raises it in the air when she sees us.

"Take a seat," says Joshua. "I'll get you some drinks. Cocktail?"

"I'll have a gin please," says Nan.

"Cocktail is great for me, thanks," I add.

"Virgin, right?" asks Joshua, staring at me wide-eyed.

I immediately go red. "What?"

He takes a look at my panicked face. "As in no alcohol?"

"Oh, yeah, please, cheers."

"Coming right up!"

He scuttles to a wooden bar, and I watch every step. As he brings the drinks, there is a knock at the door and he disappears. I strip, putting my towel around my shoulders, and sit at a table.

"This is all very fancy, isn't it?" whispers Nan.

"Quite impressive."

"It's a bit better than the bungalow, isn't it? I wonder

if it's too late to build a property portfolio."

I look at her. "I know you said you want live freely, but even you wouldn't be able to upgrade to this."

She takes a long sip of her gin and tonic. "A girl can dream."

Sam, Bethany, and Matt enter the pool house with their parents, and Joshua furnishes them with a drink. It isn't long before all the younger people are in the pool, leaving the adults to gossip on the sides.

"This house is ace," screams Katie as she punches a beach ball into the air. It lands with a wet thud on the side and bounces towards the back door. Sam jumps out to retrieve it.

"Yeah, I love this house. It's slightly smaller than our one in the States, but I can't complain," Joshua replies.

This must be the kind of house Alex lives in when not at school. He hasn't mentioned a pool, but with his family's money, it wouldn't surprise me. I wish he was here. It'd make today perfect, and we haven't even got to the food yet.

Sam bombs back into the pool. "There is a sauna at the back!" he says excitedly, shaking his head to disperse the water from his hair.

Joshua nods. "Only a small one. Grandpa has a swim and a sauna every morning. He says it's something about toxins. I barely use it. You guys go ahead if you like."

"Is your Grandpa coming in?" I ask.

"He won't be long. He always loses track of time when he's with Jolene."

I bet he does. Every time I look at Joshua's body another five minutes seem to have passed. I have Alex, what am I doing? Would he be jealous? Maybe. Urgh, we aren't even dating. I need to play it cool.

After another round of drinks, an older gentleman clatters through the door. His shorts are emblazoned with the American flag, and a bushy grey moustache rests on his top lip. His leather sandals slap the wet ground as he makes his way along the outskirts of the pool.

"Hey, guys, y'all having fun?" he says offering a long wide wave of his arm. His voice is raspy, almost gravel like, his vowels drawn out in a southern state style.

"That's Grandpa Jon," says Joshua. We each wave in turn as we're introduced. He pours himself a green drink in a tall glass, places an umbrella against the rim, and takes a seat opposite Nan. He kisses her on the back of her hand as she offers it to be shaken.

"Fancy a sauna?" asks Sam.

I snap my eyes away from Nan and follow Sam up the metal steps out the pool, trying to avert my eyes away from his red shorts.

I've never had a sauna before, and the heat is making it difficult to breathe. The pine benches smell the same as the woodwork block at school after an hour-long sanding lesson.

"This is a nice house," says Sam.

"You don't say," I reply, taking a sip from a bottle of water.

He shuffles slightly on the bench until he's sat right beside me. "Hey, Theo. I've been doing some thinking," he whispers, despite us being alone.

"About what?"

"Just life."

"Vague."

He punches my arm gently, before taking a deep interest in the sand timer on the wall near his head. He spins it around gently. "I guess I'm trying to come out."

"Genuinely?" I thought I'd be able to spot the signs of someone confiding in me about this subject, and I kick myself for not realising how much Sam must've been building up to this conversation. "I'd say well done, but I don't want to patronise you."

He nods, before leaning back and staring into space. "Don't tell anyone else."

"I wouldn't, you know that. I appreciate you telling me."

"I knew you'd understand. I've been trying to say something for a few weeks now, but I kept bottling it." His voice is restrained, holding back all emotion.

"Is it Joshua and his annoyingly hot body that's made you tell me?" I ask, trying to lighten the mood.

Luckily, he laughs. "I think even Matt would say he was gay himself after seeing those abs." We stare out the glass door at Joshua in the pool, the overhead spotlights making him glow. Sam takes another swig of water. "I guess I knew back in September but kept lying to myself. I wish I had your confidence."

"Oh, I'm *not* confident," I say. "I got lucky with Alex. He made me understand myself, especially as he was feeling the same way."

"Bethany said you love him. Is that true?"

I let out a long sigh. "In a way, I do. Having never been in love, I dunno if I do or if it's a silly crush, but I do think about him all the time. I was obsessed trying to spot him on the *Big Breakfast* the other day, but after watching it three times, including pausing on any crowd shots, I didn't spot him."

"Does he feel the same way back?"

I shrug. "Who knows. He came out to me, too, but don't tell Barnaby I told you that. We're just good at being us, I guess."

Sam gives me a sweaty hug. "I'm jealous of you, y'know."

"Oh, piss off," I say laughing, pushing him away. I don't want there to be any danger of a repeat of Aachen. "You're amazing so there is nothing to be jealous of. If you've come to me for advice, though, no luck. I'm kinda winging it."

"We can wing it together." Sam's shoulders have relaxed, the offloading of concerns more beneficial than the steam in the sauna.

"You're still speaking to Barnaby, aren't you?"

"On and off. I need to write again really. It's different for us, though."

"How come?"

"He's straight for starters. And I don't fancy him. In a way, he's like an imaginary friend. I'm comfortable telling him things because I know whatever I say won't come back to our school."

"Does he know you're gay?"

Sam bites his lip and hugs his knees. "Not yet. I mainly talk about exam stress, stuff like that. It's quite therapeutic."

"Maybe we *should* go and visit like you suggested."

"One day, maybe." He reaches towards his feet and takes his water bottle. "Cheers!"

I clunk mine into his. "We best get back out there."

"Or people like Katie will talk?"

"No, I'll pass out if I sit in here any longer."

"Not great, especially with your reputation for dramatic party exits."

As we reach the pool, Grandpa Jon is still sat with Nan. She's leaning with her elbows on the table, gazing as he animatedly tells her an anecdote.

Joshua swims to me as I bob in the shallow end. "Hey, I think Nan and Grandpa are getting on like a house on fire," he says, nodding across to where they're sat.

It's getting to the point where I might need to hide the gin. She's already on her third glass. "It's nice Nan has a new friend," I say.

"I bet you any dollar they sit next to each other at the meal. I reckon we're watching their relationship blossom."

"Get out," I reply. "He has Jolene."

"What difference does that make?"

He is standing in the chest deep water, his nipples glaring at me. I can't look away, they're homosexually hypnotic. "I don't think Nan would want to interfere between him and Jolene. She hates drama."

"Nonsense. By Christmas they'll have planned a trip away together. Grandpa is a sucker for a road trip, and the more the merrier."

I want to vomit at the thought. "Nan is a good Christian woman," I tell him. "She even has a picture of the Virgin Mary in the front room."

"What does that have to do with anything?"

I'm not sure how different the culture is in America, but things like this don't happen in Stokewood. "What does Jolene think about all of his trips with other women?"

"Not much considering she's a motorbike." I stare at him blankly (in the eyes this time). He scrunches his face a little. "Who did you think Jolene was?"

I give him some side-eye and come over all hot. "His wife," I say quietly.

Joshua laughs loudly and splashes water at me as I cling on to the side, my laughter stopping my ability to paddle.

"Grandma died an age ago. The way he goes on, though, you do sometimes wonder if he's married to his bike." He laughs again. "Can you imagine if I didn't tell you? You'd have thought Grandma was being kept in the shed whilst we had a feast in the dining room."

I look across to them both, still deep in conversation. Nan is taking in Grandpa Jon's every word. For the first time in months, she looks at ease, her smile genuine, and not one of pity. In fact, I'd say she looks younger, more like Mum before the illness came.

Nan and Grandpa Jon did indeed sit at the table together, and I walked home alone whilst he showed her Jolene. In the two weeks since, they've met twice and he's promised to take her on a road trip when he's back from the States.

On the day he flew to Seattle, Joshua moved into Sam's. Sam's mum agreed to the deal, albeit reluctantly. However, as she drove us into school this morning, me and Sam remained silent as she and Joshua chatted non-stop. It wasn't the usual conversations I have with Sam's mum, either. They discussed American Politics, the state of policing in both countries, and even agreed to go to a baseball game together, should the opportunity arise.

In the canteen, Joshua and Sam are next to each other as I wait for Bethany. When she arrives, she has a face like thunder. I try to engage, but all she can do is watch Katie in the queue with Matt. Katie keeps brushing his short curtains from his forehead and laughing. When he sees us looking, he crouches a little.

"I think they're dating," says Bethany as she bites into a Scotch Egg, brushing the crumbs onto the already sticky floor.

I want to disagree, but all the signs are there. "Sorry."

"I'm fine with it," she spits, in a manner that hints she is, indeed, not fine with it at all. To be fair, Bethany and Matt have been 'off' for over two months now and were never actually great together in the first place.

"Ask Katie what's going on in a second," I say.

"No way."

I take an interest in a leaflet for a Christmas Carol concert on the table. "If you don't want to know, that's cool."

"What if she says they are?" Bethany says, pulling the leaflet away.

"Well then you'll know. You should ask Joshua out. And I don't mean to make Matt jealous."

Bethany rolls her eyes. "Joshua would never say yes."

"Why not? He likes you."

"Has he said that?" She tilts her drinks bottle back and forth as she thinks.

"Well, no. But I know you like him. Joshua is hot and you're only human, and he obviously already likes you as a friend."

"He likes *you* as a friend."

"Listen, it's clear he ain't gay. The universe would never be *that* kind. Anyway, I have Alex. Joshua always involves you in things, like Thanksgiving, and he never does that with other girls in our year."

"Katie was there."

"Oh my god, you're obsessed with Katie. Did Joshua sit next to her for the meal? No. He made sure he sat next to you and he constantly wants to talk to you. '*Hey Bethany, tell me more about your holiday in the Caribbean,*'" I say, mimicking inverted commas with my fingers. Bethany grabs my hand and pulls it to the table. "All I'm saying," I continue, "is that you're obviously attractive and interesting and funny and Matt should've realised how lucky he was to have been with you."

"Are you sure *you* aren't asking me out here?" she asks, leaning closer to my face.

"No offence, but you aren't my type."

She giggles and accidentally spits a chunk of egg at me. "Do you genuinely think Joshua would say yes?"

"There's a good chance. Want me to ask him?"

"We ain't seven. I'm quite capable of doing it myself."

"So, you *do* want to ask him out!"

"I'll ask him after Christmas, I promise."

"That's ages."

"Well, I wanna focus on my mocks. Speaking of, have you done those test papers Staunton gave us?"

"Nah, I've been busy with the newspaper." I plunge a straw into my Capri-Sun and squeeze juice into my mouth. "I've been thinking of giving the paper up."

"All of it?"

"Just the school one."

"Why? You're doing well."

It's nice to be recognised, but I'm running out of ideas and will be too busy with my GCSE's. I've hinted to Dad about moving on, but I need to tell him outright. "I'll keep on doing the *Stokewood Gazette* pieces."

"Maybe you could do a piece on love triangles."

I slap her arm and gesture with my eyes in Matt and Katie's direction as they walk towards us. As they sit, I stand, grating the bench along the floor. "Matt, can I show you something?"

"Can it wait?"

I look at Bethany. "Um, no. Follow me." I grab hold of his bag strap and drag him out.

The corridor is full of younger kids, some playing cricket with a tennis ball in the hallways, the outdoor areas too full of puddles. Mr Daley is acting as umpire, ignoring his actual lunchtime duties.

"This best be important," Matt says as we get to the corridor. "My chilli is going cold and it cost me two quid."

"Are you dating Katie?" He doesn't say anything, instead looking embarrassed. "It's cool if you are. She actually seems normal."

"As opposed to?"

"Sorry, I didn't word that right. I meant she isn't as annoying as she used to be."

"Come in here." He kicks open the toilet door. The rain is belting against the windows and it stinks. Proper stinks. I tuck my nose into my jumper, trying not to vomit an orange juice and pizza cocktail onto the cold tiled floor. "Yes, we're dating. Kind of."

"Cool. That's all I wanted to know."

"Did Bethany make you ask?"

I start to answer, but he stops me mid-sentence and pulls my jumper down. "I can't understand a word you're saying."

"Sorry." I take a deep breath and think nice thoughts. Even Nan's lavender air fresheners at home smells better than this. "Bethany didn't put me up to it. I wanted to know. And anyway, Bethany will be fine."

"We met in town at the weekend. I think a lot of people have got Katie wrong."

"That's what I said a minute ago. I thought she was annoying as hell when I joined, but she's alright."

"She's fun."

We're interrupted by a chain flushing. A kid from the year below walks out the cubicle, tucking in his shirt with one hand and eating a sandwich from the other. "You stink," Matt says. The kid stares at the floor and leaves quickly.

"Bit harsh." He's right though. The kid stinks like a wet flannel.

"Don't tell anyone about us, will you," Matt says.

"I won't. You're not being very discreet, though."

"It's all very new. We haven't kissed yet if that's what you're wondering."

"I honestly don't care."

He nods. "Mind if I go eat now?"

Wondering if I'll soon pass out from the toxic fumes, I follow Matt out and take a deep breath of fresh, corridor air.

Thirty-Two

Alexander Beauchamp
11 Tolkien
Saint Martin's
Rutherford-On-Thames
Oxfordshire

19/12/97

Hi Theo,

So, Mum and Dad are getting a divorce. Isabelle called me a minute ago to break the news. They couldn't even be bothered to tell me themselves. Isabelle was distraught on the call, but I think I have already accepted it.

Mum flew to America again to meet with Dad at his HQ, and Joanna came into the office with the baby. It was the kid's first birthday recently and Dad had bought him a lot of new clothes and toys. It was the first time Mum had met the kid in person, and now he has a full head of deep red hair, identical to me.

Dad finally admitted to having an affair, and that was it. It couldn't be saved. I guess it is good it has finally happened, rather than everything remaining in limbo. So, yeah, I have a half-brother in America now. He's called

Bryson after some author. When Mum returned home, she sold one of Dad's BMWs without his knowledge and then flew out to Cambes to spend time at the farmhouse. Here's to <u>another</u> three weekends of being stuck at school.

Isabelle came to the talent show last week. It was nice to have her here. She has cut her hair short since being at university and has four piercings on the side of her right ear. She used to always be prim and proper!

Last weekend I spent the day with Madison in the kitchens. When she banged on my dorm door at 5am, I thought about chucking it all in there and then. After a coffee, we went to the allotment and collected some broccoli, and then made batches of broccoli and goats cheese tarts. I had to roll the pastry, and Madison guided me on making the filling. My first batch wasn't great, but I improved throughout the morning.

For the afternoon, we made fruit scones, whipped cream, and damson jam. I have basically been living off them since. They are so good! Please find enclosed three jars of spare jam for you and Nan to have over Christmas. It'll only go to waste otherwise.

When I see Mum I will let her know I wish to do an apprenticeship instead of university. Isabelle was unsure on the idea, but I know what I want. In fact, I have never been so certain. Madison is going to take me to college open days in the new year. She is so great!

With your other Christmas present, please don't open it until the day itself. It is something which I know you will love, and I am so excited to hear what you think of it. I will benefit from it as well. I have stored the present you sent underneath the tree in the corner. I have shaken it a few times to guess what it is. I thought it was a book at first, but it is far too light. We have received a number of gifts to our dorm this year, which is unusual. I have spotted one to Barnaby which I am certain is from Sam!

I am glad you enjoyed Thanksgiving at Joshua's. The picture was great and his house IS massive! It is way bigger than mine, that's for sure. I'd kill to have a pool AND sauna! I guess mine will seem bigger if Dad stays in America. Think of me over Christmas with all that going on, won't you.

Speaking of Joshua, can we take a moment to appreciate his looks haha! I know you said he was hot, but Jesus Christ. Maybe I should do baseball rather than rowing.

St Martin's got a silver again for the third year in a row. Darwin Academy snuck the win in the final race, but the gap is getting closer. Brian and I achieved first place in our event so a repeat of last year at the County Championship is on!

Are you all set for your final mocks? I can understand your hatred of Maths, especially trigonometry. Were you taught the SOHCAHTOA method for remembering the different functions? If not, look it up.

How is your Nan getting along with Grandpa Jon? From what you have said, she seems to be enjoying her new lifestyle! I cannot believe you came home and saw her in a pair of leather trousers! It must have been a shock after all the knitwear and aprons. I think it a road trip on Jolene is the least she deserves. Now your Dad is in your lives, the pressure seems to be off slightly, and it will do her the world of good. Why did Jon call the bike Jolene anyway? Was that his wife's name?

You have both come so far since your Mum passed, and she will be looking down on you both and loving everything you are doing. I'm proud of you both, too.

Next time I write it will be 1998, which is crazy. That will be the fourth different year we have known each other, and it has been the best time. I am excited to see what our futures hold. Once the GCSEs are out the way, life can truly start. I am in the kitchen again tomorrow morning before Felicity collects me for Christmas. We are heading to London for late night shopping in Bond Street. I don't have many gifts to buy, but I want to get Isabelle something special. After that, two weeks of relaxation!

Wishing you and your Nan a wonderful Christmas.

Yours,
Alex x

Thirty-Three

January 1998

I stand in the kitchen, losing patience at Nan's slow progress. Every time I think she's ready, she turns around and heads to check her bags again. It's her hairbrush she's lost this time, even though I've told her it's definitely in the front pocket of her holdall.

"Jon will be here soon," I call down the hall.

Dad enters and swoons over my new polaroid camera, spinning it in his palms like an archaeologist who has discovered King Arthur's sword in our rockery. "Lovely bit of machinery, this is," he says, the same thing he says every time he sets eyes on it. "How much film do you have left?"

"I've got a box upstairs but don't waste it."

"I won't. Are you sending these pictures to Alex?"

I jump and sit on the countertop. "Yeah. I'm gonna put pictures of us into my next letter. I'll take it to Sam's birthday next week, too."

Nan's leather trousers squeak from the hall, her new fashion passion making her audible before visible. She's taken this new lease of life by the horns. With a denim jacket and a dyed haircut, she looks at least a decade younger than this time last year. "Right then, are we going to have this photograph or not?"

"We were waiting for you," I tell her.

She pulls out a kitchen chair and leans on its back.

"Theo, you sit there," says Dad. I position myself in front of Nan, and Dad stands back, pushed against the cooker, squinting into the viewfinder. After a quick click, the polaroid whirrs out the front.

"Let's have a look," says Nan.

"You have to wait a few minutes." I do laps around the kitchen, shaking the polaroid to produce the image quicker. I'm not sure if it helps, but slowly it comes into view. We both look happy, and it would've been the perfect image if Nan's knickers weren't hanging like bunting from the door handle. Nan looks on aghast. "I'm still gonna send it."

The music from the radio is drowned out from the roar of Jolene pulling up outside, a petrol scent creeping through the letterbox. Nan skips to the front door. I was worried at first when Nan told me she'd agreed to a two-week holiday around central Wales with Jon, especially in winter, but when she went through a detailed itinerary, I wished I was going too. I've never seen the Brecon Beacons but loved studying them in Geography.

The fact she'll be in the sidecar and not riding pillion helps put my mind at ease. The fortnight will give me and Dad time to bond, and I'm looking forward to moving into his flat. They say a change is as good as a rest, after all. Now Joshua is sixteen, he's being allowed to stay home alone, so we have planned food around his before seeing Titanic at the Odeon.

"Theo, have you seen my travel iron?" asks Nan.

I roll my eyes. "You're staying in hotels, Nan. They have irons there these days. They have kettles there as well, in case you've taken that, too. If you had your way you'd need a trailer for that bike."

"I like to be prepared."

That's an understatement. I've already removed two packs of hangers from her bags. Joshua is more nervous about their trip than I am. I'm happy Nan has found someone, and the way she talks about Jon is similar to me discussing Alex. She hasn't said they're a couple yet, but it's clear they're enjoying their time together. She even described Jon as 'dishy' in conversation the other day.

"Come on, let's get you strapped in," says Dad, stood on the doormat with her holdall in his hands. He steps onto the driveway and checks Jolene from all angles. "Beautiful piece of machinery."

Jon lifts his goggles and opens up the storage compartment, allowing Dad to ram Nan's belongings into whatever space remains. "Brought her over with me from the States," he says. "She's my pride and joy."

Every inch of the black bike glistens in the low Winter sunshine. I thought Joshua was overexaggerating when he said Jon spent hours each day polishing the bodywork, but Jolene has been buffed within an inch of her life.

"Have a great time, Nan," I say. She holds Dad's hand as she lowers herself into the cramped sidecar. Jon passes her a teal helmet, furnished with a red stripe and the image of a bald eagle, and she pulls her goggles over her eyes.

"I'll see you soon, darling," she says, giving me a hug. "Enjoy your time with Dad, and don't do anything I wouldn't do."

"Likewise." I give her a kiss on the cheek. She already smells of fumes. "Let me get a quick picture before you go!" I run to the kitchen and grab my camera.

She grins widely at Jon as he sits above her, revving the engine, and I catch a shot without their knowledge, hoping I can transfer their pure happiness to film.

Dad shakes Jon's hand and taps Nan on her helmet.

"Safe travels, Gromit."

Jon revs Jolene to the max, and I wave them off as they leave the cul-de-sac. Nan continues to wave until she disappears from view. I look at the polaroid in my hand and know it deserves to be framed. She's a different woman these days.

"Are you all packed?" asks Dad, puffing his cheeks as he drags the overflowing wheelie bins up from the side gate.

"Yep. I'll go get my suitcase."

In the distance, I'm certain I can hear Jolene speeding towards the edge of town.

After what has seemed like a lifetime wait for the cinematic event of the decade, I arrive at the Odeon, desperate to raid the popcorn counter and get the best seats.

I hide in the foyer and lean on a radiator to get some heat into my body as snow creates a white carpet outside. The sliding doors open, and Katie strides through, with Matt trailing a few feet behind. "Hey guys."

"Heya," says Katie, whose hairstyle isn't too dissimilar to Kate Winslet's on the giant poster hanging to our right. "Matt's being miserable."

"I'm fine," he says. "I just didn't realise it was over three bloody hours long."

"Not long enough if you ask me," Katie replies. "I'm gonna get a Coke."

At the counter I spot Bethany collecting nachos. Joshua is stood next to her and they're so deep in conversation that they don't notice us. I stalk behind them and stick my head between theirs. "HI!" Joshua throws his family bag of Quavers into the air. "Sorry."

"Hey. Are the others here?" asks Bethany.

"Just Sam missing. He better be on time. I have a hot

date with Leo."

"It's his birthday so he'll be here, don't worry."

We take a seat on the large red sofas and send Katie and Matt to collect the tickets from the box office. "Are you both alright?" I ask.

Bethany and Joshua look at each other. "All good. We met earlier and had a drink at the diner."

"And?" I push.

She furrows her brow. "And what?"

I've known her long enough to understand her trademark 'look' telling me to be quiet. Her lips purse and her eyes narrow.

I sink into the cushions, stirring my drink with a limited-edition curly straw. I went against having ice (not just because it's cold enough in here already, but it didn't seem right when it was the factor that caused the real Titanic's downfall). "Hey, Joshua, can you remind them not to book rows near the front please?"

His hand hovers near his mouth, a mound of popcorn inches from his lips. "Why me?"

"Please?"

He stares at me oddly but agrees regardless. Once out of earshot, I lean into Bethany. "Why haven't you asked him out yet?"

"I didn't find the right moment."

"You've been with him all afternoon! You said you would ask after Christmas."

"I'll do it later." She stands and stares towards the front doors, her mouth wide open. "Oh my God."

I turn in my chair and see Sam walking towards us. He isn't alone. He'd been coy about the cinema trip when I phoned him to see what the dress code vibe was, and now I realise why.

His companion is stocky. His deep blue blazer is paired with cream chinos which have creases in the correct places. Although we've never met, I know precisely who he is. That uniform has been displayed in photographs on my wardrobe door for two years. I put my drink down and run across. "Barnaby?"

"Hey," he says. "Nice to meet you, Theo." I look over his shoulder and into the bustling market square. He catches my gaze. "Alex isn't with me, sorry."

"Barnaby was randomly passing through town this morning," says Sam.

Barnaby nods. "We were just down the road. When I remembered it was Sam's birthday, I asked mum to run by his estate so I could post a card through his door."

"He forgot in his last letter," says Sam.

"I forgot in my last letter. Anyway, when we got there, Sam was in his front garden, so thought I would say hello properly."

"How come you're still here? I mean, it's cool, but isn't your mum sat in the car waiting?"

Sam shakes his head. "Turns out our parents both wanted to go to the pantomime in North Lee, so they're there, and we're here."

I nod. "Cool." I want to ask about Alex, but I know Barnaby wouldn't want to be bombarded with bizarre, hormone-driven questions this early into the evening.

When we'd originally planned Sam's birthday, everyone (aside from Bethany) said Titanic would be a waste of time, but now our group has extended even further with the arrival of Katie's closest friends Laura and Jenny.

I sit between Sam and Joshua and lay back in the chair with my feet on the top of Matt's seat in front. Barnaby opens a bag of Maltesers and offers them around.

As I reach in to take a handful, Barnaby leans forward from the seat behind. "How are you getting on living at your Dad's place?"

Everyone goes quiet, yet I realise there's no point in hiding it anymore. Keeping one secret at school exerts enough pressure as it is, let alone two. Passing Dad in the corridor ten times a day never helps, either. "It's been great, thank you. I've only moved in whilst Nan is away on a trip."

Katie almost gets whiplash with the speed her neck snaps around. "I thought you didn't have a Dad?"

"We found each other last summer," I tell her.

"What's he like?"

"It's Mr Le Bon."

"I knew it!" she screams, causing everyone in the cinema to turn and look at us instead of the trailers. "I was saying to Laura I saw you and him shopping for plants together in a garden centre recently. It was weird."

"It'd be weirder if he was in the garden centre with him and he weren't his dad, though," says Matt.

"True. I don't know what to say," she replies.

"You don't have to say anything. I'm cool with it, and so are this lot," I say, gesturing my hand along my row. Thankfully, the lights dim, and the greatest film ever stops further questioning.

The coal-coloured streets are illuminated by the moon as it peeks from behind the high-rise flats at the end of Sam's road.

I shake Barnaby's hand. His rugby grip is firm. "It's been great to meet you, finally."

"You too," he replies.

"D'you both wanna come in for cake?" asks Sam.

I said to Dad I would be home by nine, but he'll understand.

"It'll be great to speak to you more," says Barnaby.

We enter Sam's house and pitch up in his

conservatory as he grabs drinks from the kitchen. Hopefully he has something chilled for me. I'm yet to recover from seeing Leo splashing around looking so hot.

It's surreal to be sat opposite someone who's been a supporting character in the background of your life for so long. Barnaby looks identical to his appearances in Alex's photos, which sounds obvious, but I always imagine people to be different in real life. He's taller than I thought, I guess, but only just.

"So, how is Saint Martin's?"

"Like hell," he replies flatly. "Well, I mean it's okay, but we have so much work ahead of our mocks. Most evenings in the dorm are spent with heads in books rather than in front of the television. It's all rather dull."

"It's the same here. We've only been back a couple of weeks but it's exams this, exams that."

"Tedious, isn't it?"

"Extremely. What do you do to relax? You're not a rower, are you?"

He laughs. "Can you imagine someone my size in a boat? We would capsize or sink. Or both. I play rugby, but in the summer I do field events in athletics. I have the school record for discus."

"That's well cool. I'd suggest our schools should have some kind of competition together, but you'd trounce us!"

"I wouldn't say that. A lot of boys are useless. They only get places because of you know what." He rubs his fingers together to mimic flicking through a wad of money. "I think we have the most normal group in our dorm. Felix is a bit odd sometimes, but overall, we're cool."

"What's Alex like?"

Barnaby looks out to the garden, and his pause makes me nervous. "I don't know how much he has told you."

"About?"

"Anything."

"We've discussed everything. He talks a lot about his family and the rowing, and he told me you were Baby Spice at the talent contest."

He laughs again. "We should have won. Did you see the photos?"

I shake my head. "He wouldn't let me. It seems you get on well, though."

"We do. Alex is great, but I do worry about him. His home life isn't stable, especially currently."

"His last letter said his parents were divorcing, which sucks."

Sam comes through and hands out plates of chocolate cake. "Sorry for the delay. I was roped into helping Barnaby's mum open the boot of her car, but it wouldn't budge."

"I told her it was knackered. I'll make her take it into the garage tomorrow. I was telling Theo about Alex. His parents are getting divorced and she's flown out to France."

"Is she not back yet? That was before Christmas."

"She came back briefly, but then disappeared again. From what Alex was saying, she has bought a property near her sister's place, and plans to move the family over there in May. Don't tell him I told you, though. Just, you know, keep an eye out."

I sit and put my half-eaten cake onto the table. "You mean Alex is moving to France *with* her?"

Barnaby shrugs. "I guess he has to."

My world has been shattered. I know the idea to meet in Trafalgar Square in two years' time was not a concrete plan, but Alex leaving England will extinguish any hope of it ever becoming a reality. There has long been something deep inside of me that believed I'd meet him at those fountains. With us both studying right up until summer, that chance could be gone forever.

Thirty-Four

Alexander Beauchamp
11 Tolkien
Saint Martin's
Rutherford-On-Thames
Oxfordshire

22/02/1998

Hi Theo,

Before I begin, can we discuss your Christmas present? You don't realise how excited everyone in the dorm was when I showed them the copy of Goldeneye for the N64! We have literally been playing that non-stop in all our spare time. I can't thank you enough! The multiplayer mode is such good fun. When I have been here on my own at the weekends, I have been working through the story mode and have nearly completed all levels on Secret Agent difficulty!!

I knew you'd like the polaroid camera! An added benefit is getting to see all the snapshots you have taken. The photo of you and Barnaby together was so surreal!!!

I loved the picture of you and your Nan before she went on her adventure! I completely agree she looks like a different person now she is with Jon. Maybe if they get together properly you can move in with Joshua and get to use his pool and sauna every morning. That would be amazing!

I've just got back from a walk with Barnaby as I needed to clear my head during our revision hour.

Everything he told you is true.

I'm so sorry you didn't find out from me. I was going to tell you, I promise. I am struggling to process the situation and cannot believe I am being put through it.

A fortnight ago, I went back to my family home for the first time in two months. Isabelle has passed her driving test so collected me in one of Dad's cars he has reluctantly given to her. She barely spoke on the journey, and when we pulled into the driveway, the estate agent's sign was nailed to the wall. Mum didn't even have the decency to tell us herself. It was a real kick in the teeth.

All weekend she kept saying about how the move will be a "fresh start", but I cannot bring myself to be happy. It may be a "fresh start" for her, but not for me. I don't want a frigging "fresh start"!

Every day is a revolving nightmare, like I am trapped on a carousel of abandonment. Mum will only allow me to stay in the UK if I am to continue to A-Levels, and then potentially university. She does not support my interest in working the kitchens and said that it is beneath me. How did I come from two parents who are so morally bankrupt?

When I leave here, I will lose everything. I will be leaving behind the rowing team, the opportunities with music, and most importantly, my friends. That includes you as well. Even though we have never met, I always believed we would and that thought has been keeping me motivated for a long time now.

If I did not go to France, it would have been

Chicago. Dad has bought an apartment in the West Town area. I have seen some photographs and it has stunning views, but he is there with Joanna and Bryson so, no thank you.

I thought life was working itself out, but it has been cruelly snatched away. God, I am sorry for being so miserable. I must be a burden on you as well.

How did you find Barnaby when you met him? He was being truthful when he said it was all a last-minute plan. He told me you were lovely, but I knew that anyway.

The results of our mock exams came back this week. I achieved some great results but have been given extra study for English and History as, apparently, I should be aiming towards an A Grade. The C's I achieved have been viewed as something of a failure. If anyone else had to juggle education, rowing, and being abandoned by their family, they would find revision equally as difficult.

With the rowing, Brian and I are preparing for the County Championships next month. We easily won our latest competition but that was to be expected as it was only against one other school. It means I have another gold medal added to my collection. It is a shame they aren't solid gold. I could sell them off and buy my own house near you.

How good was Titanic?!?!! I bet you didn't love it as much as me and go to the cinema FIVE times to watch haha! Leo was once again excellent. It might be my favourite film of his so far, but I still prefer the *Romeo & Juliet* soundtrack. I cannot wait for it to come out on VHS. I will watch it every day. Some parts were a bit stupid, but I knew it would not be entirely historically accurate. I think it is up there with Jurassic Park for my favourite film ever.

Have you listened to much new music recently? We

had the latest *Oasis* album on, but the Britpop bands have dipped a little in recent months. It feels like the whole Cool Britannia period is over. I am not sure if it was Princess Diana's death which kickstarted the change but, since then, the mood in the country seems ever so negative, like a bubble has burst. Even Felix has moved away from guitar music, instead preferring The Prodigy.

Last month I decided to join a school committee. The Deans are insisting we host a grand dinner between the end of our formal lessons and the first exam. My role is to help decide on a menu, which has allowed me to do taste-testing on potential dishes. We have chosen a feta, black garlic, and sundried tomato soup (trust me, it is exquisite). I am thinking maybe a pâté starter, and a lemon and thyme chicken main.

Madison has taught me so many new techniques, and my current forte is cream horns. They have fresh whipped cream on top, but it is the layer of homemade blackberry jam which brings them up a level. I have included a recipe for you so you can make some of your own. You'll need the stainless-steel moulds, so have included two for you (I stole them from the kitchen but don't tell anyone!) Let me know how you get on. You can buy the jam and pastry if that is easier.

Having the meal means not having one of those American themed proms that seem to be popular lately. If we were to have one of those, we would need to do it jointly with St Agatha's, and the teachers at both schools were allegedly not keen. Melody told me that their school are planning a marquee event in Henley instead.

Have you confirmed plans for your birthday? Asking Joshua to host is a great idea. With your nan and Jon spending so much time together, it would work well.

I only have one letter to write to you whilst at school. It feels like an end of an era. Please promise me, that

wherever in the world I land, we can continue this.
I can't imagine a life without you.

Yours,
Alex x

Thirty-Five

March 1998

Dad's flat is freezing. His insistence at keeping the window open at all hours to stop condensation causes heat to escape immediately. The word about him being my Dad spread rapidly after Katie found out, but two months later, no one seems to care. Even Katie herself agrees he's cool, for a teacher.

Sam's been spending a lot of time here over the last two weeks, and he was insistent on coming for dinner tonight. As Dad finishes cooking in the kitchen, the chain flushes in the bathroom, and Sam wanders into the living room.

"What did you want to see me about?" I ask as he slumps next to me on the sofa. He's been acting *very* odd the last couple of days. I thought it was because he won't be accepted onto Geography A-Level with poor grades. It'd be great to have him on the course with me, so I've promised to help him with his revision before we sit our GCSE's. "What's wrong?" I ask again.

Sweat pours onto his temples from under his Nike cap. "I think I might tell people I'm gay."

"Really?"

"I feel I need to tell people." He shuffles across so he's closer, cradling a cushion to his chest as he rests his head on my shoulders.

"You don't have to. No one is entitled to know."

"But no one cared when you came out."

"Technically, I've never told anyone," I reply. I take a bite out of a misshapen cream horn from the plate balancing on the sofa's arm. "It's never come up outside our group."

"People know," he says flatly. I look across to him. "There have been rumours, like, in the changing rooms and things."

"Well, that's great." It's my turn to sweat. What if they're planning to bully me?

"Sorry, I didn't mean to panic you. I'm sure it's fine."

I think of all the times Matt used gay as an insult. Even though he never does it anymore, others do. If I tell people the rumours are true, then who knows what would follow. I've heard about people being beaten in the toilets, and it'd only take one person to destroy me.

"We should both keep quiet for now." I can tell this isn't what Sam wants to hear, but we have enough to worry about already.

"Can you imagine if one day we never had to come out?" he asks.

I chuckle at how ridiculous that is. "Yeah, maybe one day. Don't hold your breath, though. I was talking to Mr Teale about it recently. We were talking about one day being able to get married."

"You and Mr Teale?"

"You know what I mean. Why don't you chat to him? He's been helpful. Just have to be quiet about it. He can get in a lot of shit if anyone finds out he's talking to pupils about, y'know."

"Why?

I shrug. "They can sack you for mentioning it."

After plenty of swearing in the kitchen, Dad comes

out and passes us beans on toast. "Should've been some sausages too, but I cremated them. It's the gas oven's fault. Unreliable. Terrible piece of machinery. What time are you guys heading out?"

"In about half an hour," I reply. "Joshua and Bethany are coming here and then we're gonna watch a film at his."

"And what classic will you be watching tonight?"

I wish I could think of a cool answer. I scan my eyes around his living room. Posters for the greatest films (in his opinion) of all time cover the four walls. *The Magnificent Seven, Dirty Harry, North by Northwest.* "We're watching *Spice World*," I mumble.

He smiles. "It's not a bad film."

"You've seen it, Mr Le Bon?" says Sam.

"Saw it at the cinema. A few of us teachers went for a social."

"Really?" I ask.

"Well, I wouldn't say it's up there with *The Godfather*, but I've seen worse."

"You always say that."

He shrugs. "It passed a couple of hours. You'll probably enjoy it. Surprised you didn't see it at the cinema yourselves."

"We watched *Titanic* instead," says Sam.

"That's hardly *The Godfather*," I mock.

"I'll take you to see a proper film one day," says Dad. "It can be one of your birthday presents. There's a film festival in Barnsley over the late May bank holiday. We can travel there and you can see where I was raised."

"Do you miss the North?" asks Sam.

Dad shifts awkwardly in his armchair. "I do, but I get to go back regularly. Actually, Theo, when I went for Easter, I told people about you." He puts his plate on the side and grabs his coat from the rack, pulling a photograph from inside his wallet. "That's your grandad."

The man in the picture doesn't look old enough to be my grandad. He doesn't look much older than Dad, who's next to him on the pub bench in the picture. I pass it across to Sam.

"He looks cool," says Sam. "His beard is huge."

Dad chuckles. "He made a promise to grow it until Barnsley won the FA Cup."

"And you told him about me?" I ask.

Dad nods. "He knew I had a son, but I didn't tell him until recently you were back in my life."

"How was he?" I ask.

"I needn't have worried. From the moment I told him, he automatically loved you, too. I showed him your pictures and told him about how you are getting on at school. He was impressed with your newspaper. I was thinking maybe we could meet him when we go north?"

"I'd love to, thank you."

"Can I come?" asks Sam. "My grandparents are proper boring."

"I think on this occasion it should be the two of us," replies Dad with a smile. "I'll clear it with your Nan, Theo. Maybe your next article for the school paper can be on him."

"I thought you wanted to give that up?" says Sam. Dad looks across.

"Um, I was thinking about it maybe, cos there's only two months left of school."

"There's a kid in Year Ten who is interested in it," says Dad. "He wants to be a journalist when he's older and keeps hassling me in lessons with example articles."

"Are they any good?"

"To be fair to him, yeah. They're alright. He's a bit of an oddball, but he's keen."

"He can be the new editor if he wants?"

"I wasn't saying about him to get rid of you," Dad replies.

"I know. But I've got exams and stuff coming, so why not? I don't mind, honestly."

"As long as you're sure," says Dad as he shoves a pile of baked beans into his mouth.

"I'm sure. I'll make my last article a good one."

Spice World is an excellent film, and I'll never hear a bad word against it. For the two weeks since, Sam has been shouting "*And I'm Victoria, Malcolm,*" at me on loop. He's sat on the opposite side of the school hall with his hands tucked into his sleeves as we wait for our parents evening meetings. I bet any money he'd rather be discussing the film instead.

"Who are we seeing first?" asks Nan.

I pull out my crumpled timetable from my pocket. "Science with Staunton in a few minutes. Then we have Saunders for Maths. After that we can go."

"What about English?" she asks.

"I told Bosnich there wasn't much point with Dad being the head of department."

Nan isn't listening to me, instead waving at Grandpa Jon who has arrived with Joshua. I drag a couple of chairs nearby.

"Alright?" I ask Joshua.

"All good, thanks. Could do with not being here, though." He looks around the room, nervously picking at some skin on the edge of his thumbnail. "Bet I get a roasting."

"Nah, they'll be fine. You've had to adapt. That went in my favour when I joined."

"That only covers so much," he replies. "My parents had dreams of me going to Harvard when I was younger.

They would be bamboozled I've ended up here. I might go back to America to study one day. It's harder because I won't get a sports scholarship. Being out of sport for a year is easily enough for you to fall down the picking order."

I think of Alex. "Did you enjoy all that? Like, the pressure to do what your parents wanted?"

He pokes out his bottom lip. "I guess I was used to it. In the States, it's the norm. Do well at school, head to college on a scholarship, everything falls into place."

"Stokewood isn't the worst place to be."

"Not at all. I actually like it here, man. I mean, you guys do some odd things. Like, I'll never understand everything even if I'm here for the rest of my life, but you guys are cool, and Grandpa and your Nan seem to be quite settled."

Grandpa Jon is animatedly explaining something about bikes, and Nan is taking in every single word.

"I think they're going to Ireland next," Joshua says.

"On Jolene?"

He nods. "Three weeks he wants to go for. I'm gonna ask Sam if I can stay at his again. I was so bored at home on my own when they went to Wales. Anyway, I best go. I gotta see Richardson in a second. Catch you after, yeah?"

"Yeah, I think Bethany is coming soon so could go for food?"

Joshua faces me. He checks over both shoulders and leans in so close I can smell the hotdogs on his breath. "What would Bethany say if I asked her on a date?"

"She will say yes," I reply.

"Are you sure?" His eyes light up, bigger and greener than normal.

"One hundred percent."

He nods. "Neat!"

The atmosphere has changed in Mr Teale's classroom. Sam lost his bottle as we waited outside, instead deciding to run home rather than stay and speak. And as for Mr Teale, he looks beaten and withdrawn. Dark circles have formed under his eyes, his unstyled hair and creased shirt giving the impression of a man who hasn't slept for weeks. He messes about with some paperwork, doing his best to delay sitting.

"Are you alright, Sir?" I ask.

"Yeah." He gives me a smile, before resting his head in his hands. "That's a lie, sorry. Everything is not alright." He stares into my eyes. "I am sorry for how angry I was when I spoke to you at the end of last year. It wasn't aimed at you."

"That's okay. We're allowed to be angry. You said so yourself."

He focusses on his desk, stabbing a red ballpoint on some paperwork. "I think you need to know, at the end of term, I shall be moving on."

"You can't go, Sir." If I'm here for Sixth Form, I'll need him here. I can't do this alone. "Is there anything I can do to change your mind?"

He shakes his head. "I wish there was, but sometimes you've got to admit defeat. It's been a while since I was in your shoes, Theo. Back then, I had visions of changing the world, to make life easier for those who came after me. We are stood on the shoulders of giants; the people on the picket lines, the people who acted against the corrupt governments who were saying we were sick in the head. Despite this, I have let you down. I should be fighting back against those who allowed gay people, sometimes only a few years older than me, to be lost through neglect. So many died or disappeared after they had been shunned by society. And what do we have to show for it? Nothing. You sit here now in a position which is no better than the one I had been in all those years ago. That is a failure. I am sorry, and I should have done better."

"So why are you leaving?"

"Last year, a Sixth Former came to me, much like you now. Said he'd seen me with Jeff in a pub in London."

"And he told the Head?"

"Quite the opposite. Said he wanted to talk to me about growing up gay, and if the world was as bad as it seems. Instead of supporting him, I told him he must have mistaken me with someone else, and he should not choose to be gay as that is a dangerous path to take. He never came back to school. I failed him, and the weight on my conscience is too much to bear."

"But you've helped me, Sir. You've made that change."

There it is again. The shaken head of defeat. "Even so, I should be helping everyone. Who knows where that other kid is now. Because of my actions, they may be in further danger." He moves to his desk and opens his satchel. "They've won. Again. I'm sorry. One day, it will change, but not today. And it may not be tomorrow, it may not be for decades, but you're a good kid, but you need to keep your head above the water. Here, I have this for you."

He passes me a hardback book. The cover is a black and white photo of a protest, with the title *From Legalisation to AIDS: The Battle for Gay Rights in the United Kingdom* big and bold in the centre. "This will educate you far more than I'll be able to. Look after it as you won't find another copy."

I slide it into my rucksack. "Thank you."

"Promise me one thing, Theo, whenever you get the chance, stand for what you believe in. To get change you need to be the change."

I let out a long sigh. "I don't think I can make much difference."

"Every flood starts with a single drop of rain. Be that drop of rain, Theo, please be that drop of rain."

There is nothing more that can be said. He's stood in front of me, car keys in hand, our time together over.

That night was the worst this year. I began to read the book under the light from my torch, hiding under my duvet, terrified Dad would catch me. There were so many stories of activism, but also the brutal treatment of our community. It wasn't even localised. So many countries around the world have their own tales of violence and discrimination.

For the first time in a long time, I couldn't sleep, fearful for what lay ahead for when I woke, for when I grow.

For the first time in a long time, I laid there and cried.

Thirty-Five

Alexander Beauchamp
11 Tolkien
Saint Martin's
Rutherford-On-Thames
Oxfordshire

29/04/1998

Hi Theo,

Well, I guess this is it.

I know we are going to continue writing, but it does feel like things will be different now. Dad will be staying in Chicago with Joanna and my brother. I hope Dad loves him more than he loved me. Once I became a boarder at Saint Martin's, I was out of his way. It is probably me coming to this school that made him feel as though he was free to have an affair.

Mum's decision to move to France has gone through. She has sent me photographs of the farmhouse. I recognise it as it was the one I could see from my bedroom window last summer. I know Mum will be happier. As for me, well, we will see.

Out the two options, I know life is better in Cambes

than it would in America. Mum shall be moving the week before I finish exams, so Felicity will come to the school on the Friday afternoon, and our journey will begin straight away. I won't even have the chance to say goodbye to everyone.

Mum tells me there are many bakeries in Cambes where I might be able to get some work experience. She is determined to sell the French dream to me, so feels this is meeting me halfway, provided I still study.

I'll miss being at school, which I guess is quite a sad thing to say. I have become used to my weekends here and helping Madison in the kitchens.

By having to move when I do, it does mean I will unfortunately not be able to make your birthday party. Whilst you are all together having fun, I will be in the car speeding towards the airport. I so desperately wanted to come, and I am so sorry I cannot make it. I tried to ask Mum if I could move a few days later, but the tickets for the flight have been booked, and a lot of my belongings have been boxed. Mum will be heading to Bordeaux airport to meet me on arrival. She has paid for a few days at a hotel in the town and I cannot get out of it.

I appreciated your invite, thank you. I wanted to meet you and all your friends as it feels like I know you all so well. Barnaby has shouted across the dorm for me to tell you he will still be coming. I hope you have a wonderful time, and make sure you take lots of photographs! I will be thinking of you for the entire journey to my new home.

My time in the rowing competitions has now been completed. It was the County Championships two weeks ago. We put in a strong performance, however missed out on gaining a podium finish. It was more competitive this year, and the Smith-Coxley twins dominated. We placed fifth but were only three seconds away from third.

It was a great day at the regatta, and for my final row it was perfect. I don't mind too much about not getting a medal this time. I know me and Brian have put our all into the training. We are stronger and fitter than ever.

Isabelle has been selected to represent England in the upcoming European Under-20 championships, and as they will be held in Nantes, I think I will be able to go and support her, so that is at least one positive! The football World Cup is in France this year too, so I might be able to get to some games, if tickets haven't sold out. I think Felix wants to come over in the summer so I am glad I won't be totally alone all the time.

You will have to come and visit as well. I know we have made plans like this before, but I mean it. You are so important and I cannot let you just be the boy who writes. I need to have you in my life. I am not sure how, but we can make something work.

Do you have any plans for the summer yet apart from Barnsley? It's amazing you have another grandparent. Isn't it funny how life works out? Speaking of grandparents, I hope your Nan is having a wonderful time in Ireland. I have never been there myself. I hope I am having new experiences when I am nearly seventy.

Bethany and Joshua are finally together then! It seemed like that was going to happen eventually. Fair play to her for bagging someone so hot! He seems such an amazing person as well! Barnaby said he can talk and talk, but he loved hearing about how Ice Hockey works. Barnaby was obsessed with watching it at the Winter Olympics and has been convinced to try it if he finds anywhere

e local to practice.

There is so much more I wish I could write but it feels like it is all a bit final somehow, does that make sense? If I stop now, it means I will have to write again, not that I need an excuse. I have included my new address on the attached card.

I need to take this to the post room whilst not many people are about. I keep crying and feel silly. I know we will still stay in touch but, it's just *everything*.

Thank you for giving me a purpose for the last three years. One day we will get to cycle the vineyards together. I will meet you under the willow by the old mill.

Yours, today and always,
Alex xxxx

Thirty-Six

Early May 1998

I wait on Nan's driveway, sitting on the recycling bin in the sunshine. I can't remember the last time I was alone. Dad is at a conference, and did offer to take me, but I need to keep focused before the last week of exams. The conference sounded dull as dishwater, anyway. I have a million places I'd rather be than listening to men in suits talk about 'goals' and 'targets'.

If I'd remembered to bring Nan's spare key before she left, I could be inside now, however, that would mean more Biology revision. I'll take sitting in the sunshine, instead. Revision is not a Saturday morning activity, after all.

I lay back against the porch wall and slip my headphones on, soaking up the vitamin D with the *Spice Girls* swinging, shaking, moving, and making it.

A shadow forms over my closed lids. I open one eye, and Joshua stands in front of me.

"You're ruining my tan," I say.

"You'll only burn." He squats next to me. "Grandpa Jon called half an hour ago from the service station. They should be back in a second. I've grabbed some rolls from the shop so thought I'd meet them here. We're having a barbecue at ours this evening if you wanna come."

"Sounds good, cheers." Going will mean not having my head in a textbook, which is always a bonus. "Are the others coming?"

"Bethany will be there. I think Sam and Matt are in Manchester for the soccer."

"Ah yeah, last day of the season."

"I might go with them next year. I used to go to the ice hockey, and I kinda miss it, y'know."

I think back to the England game I went to with Dad in Bristol last year. "I imagine it's bigger and better in America. The last time I went it rained for the whole match. We got soaked."

"I think it sounds cool." Joshua stands and kicks a stone around the driveway, striking it at the far wall. "Did you hear about Teale by the way?"

I think back to our conversations in his classroom. "I guess he wanted a change."

"Change? Everyone wants change but getting yourself fired is sure hell of a way to go about it."

"He wasn't fired," I tell him. "He wanted to leave teaching, that's all."

"That's not what I heard. Haven't you heard the rumours?" I don't react. My blood is boiling. "Apparently he was doing some dodgy stuff behind the scenes. Christ knows what that was."

"It's a lie, Joshua. Teale was amazing."

"Hey, I think I can hear Jolene." He stands dead still, but the only noise I can hear is the sound of a crow on a roof a few doors along, but moments later, the familiar roar of Jolene blasts round the corner and pulls onto the drive. Grandpa Jon steps off and pats her engine tank, before heaving Nan out the sidecar.

"Heya, how was it?" Joshus asks.

Nan takes my hand. "It was excellent. I think I need a bath, though. My arse is numb. Be a darling, Theo, and grab my bags, will you?"

"Good to see you, guys!" says Jon. Joshua gives him a high five and clambers into the sidecar.

"I'll call you later, doll," says Nan. I head inside whilst she waves them off, dumping the bags in the front room.

I pick at some broken biscuits as I sit on the counter. "Juice?" I ask Nan as she enters into the kitchen. She seems a little coy and doesn't answer. I pour two glasses anyway and take them to the table. There is something different but I can't put my finger on it.

"Chuck us a cushion, will you? Not sure my backside can take these wooden seats after being in a sidecar for three weeks."

"Did you have a fun trip?"

"Yes, was lovely, thank you." She says as she lowers herself gently into the seat, flicking through a women's magazine. "Jon asked me to marry him when we were in Ireland."

I hope she's joking, but with the way she is nonchalantly focussing on the magazine, I assume she isn't. I put my hand on the pages and she turns to me. "I said no."

I nod slightly. "Didn't it make the ride home awkward?"

"No, it was fine. I told him to get off the floor and stop being a silly sod."

"You mean he got on one knee and everything?"

Nan laughs. "No, he was on his knees checking the tyre pressure at a garage outside Galway. I may be enjoying myself, but I'm not ready for another marriage."

"But you will be one day?"

"Never say never. I'm glad to have Jon. He's good for us all. I think we are going through France next. He is in America for business next month, but maybe over the summer we shall find some time.”

Even the word France grates on me. I hope Alex will settle there, and one day I’ll make it there to see him.

Nan turns her head slightly, studying my face. “Are you okay? Good few weeks without me?

I shrug. “Mr Teale has been sacked.”

“Sacked? Whatever for?”

“For being gay.” The immediate silence that hangs over the kitchen is deafening. “So it’s true, then.”

“I don’t know the details, but sometimes things happen.”

“He told me he was leaving, but not because of this. He knew it’d happen. The same happened to his boyfriend, too. It makes me sick.”

She takes a deep breath. “There was a complaint, that’s all know. I’m sorry.”

I’ve had enough of sitting back and watching all this happen. I have to be that drop of rain, to challenge people’s misconceptions. Maybe this mess is my fault. He was right the first time. He should’ve shunned me. I should’ve walked away. “Mr Teale met with me a few times.”

She lets go of me and stares.

“He’s been helping me with some things going on in my head. Things I couldn’t understand on my own.” If I’m to make a change in this world, now is the time to start. I tuck my hands into my sleeves and stare at the floor. Coffee stains form a pattern around the chair legs, and I wipe at them with my sock. “Nan, how do you know when someone is the right one for you?”

“I’m not sure what you mean, sorry.” She shuffles the magazines on the table until they’re in a neat stack. She always cleans when she’s nervous. Maybe she’s been expecting this conversation for as long as I’ve been meaning to start it.

"Alex wrote when you were away. He's moving to France."

She takes hold of my hand and gives it a stroke, her new burnt orange nail varnish catching the strip lighting from above. "Oh, bless you. You don't want him to go, do you?"

I shake my head and tears prickle my eyes. "I'm being stupid."

"Not at all," says Nan. "Oh, come here."

I bury my head into her shoulder, my tears running onto the scratched leather of her jacket. "I don't want him to leave."

"Of course you don't. You two have been through so much together. Everything that has happened with your mum, and him with his parents' divorce. When you love someone, it isn't easy to let them go."

"I didn't say the L word."

"Sometimes, people don't need to say it." She moves my head so we're inches apart, and she dabs my eyes with a used tissue. "Does he know how you feel about him?"

"Neither of us have ever said anything. It's too late now. He goes next Friday. I doubt he feels the same, anyway."

Nan stands from the table. "You have to tell him."

"I don't think I can," I say. "He has enough going on without me complicating things."

"Theo, I think it's time I told you a story." She flicks the kettle on and rummages through her bag, bringing some Guinness flavoured fudge to the table. I take a bite, but it's not for me.

When she sits, she puts three spoons worth of sugar into her mug and lets out a few long breaths as she stirs. "When I was a child, I lived at the old farm on the edge of town. These days, it's all been swallowed by the housing estates. Used to be a dairy during the mid-war years you see, and my job was to bring the milk into town on this rickety old cart. The wheels were buckled and it was a nightmare. One day, I was carrying the urns across the yard to the storage sheds and a boy stood there, asking if I needed help. I'd seen him before. He used to sit on a low wall and watch me from a distance. Eventually he built enough courage to say hello.

"Every day after that, he would be there, same time, same place, every morning. It didn't take much for us to realise what we meant to one another. He would tell me about his family, and how he had been evacuated to Stokewood at ten. He wasn't very life aware. I taught him to sew, to make butter, and he used to help muck out the pigs and…" She tails off and wipes her nose with her sleeve.

"What happened?" I ask.

"One morning, he wasn't there. He was the first boy I loved." Her voiced is tinged with a longingness, as if wishing him to enter through our back gate. "A few days after he disappeared, he was there again. Stood in the middle of the path on the way out the farm. Told me his father had been killed in Egypt. He had come to say goodbye. His mother was taking him to Cornwall. I wanted to tell him I loved him, that he could stay on the farm with us."

"But you didn't?"

"I didn't." Nan sighs deeply. "I watched him walk away down the dusty gravel path back to the main road. He waved as he got to the hedgerow, and then I never saw him again."

I rub Nan's back. "I'm sorry."

"Henry. That was his name. Christ, I haven't thought about him for a long time. I have a picture of him somewhere. We're sat on hay bales in the blazing sunshine. I remember that day clearly because he fell off backwards and I thought he had broken his neck." She lets out a small laugh at the memory. "I never told Henry how I felt. If I had, then maybe he would have stayed in Stokewood and we would've grown old together."

"Do you think he remembers you?" I ask.

"I like to think so." She turns around and embraces me. "Theo, I need you to listen to me. In sixty years' time, I don't want you to be stood here thinking about Alex. Please don't make the same mistake as me." She taps me on my forehead with a finger. "If you do, then there will be something in here, nagging at you for the rest of your life."

"What if Alex doesn't feel the same way?"

"It's a risk you have to take. Nothing is guaranteed, but trust me, sometimes risks are there for a reason. It is always better to try."

"Mr Teale knew about Alex. He warned me how dangerous the world is for people like us."

"I can't deny that, but you've got a decent head on your shoulders. People like you will change this world. You can't make that change, though, without taking risks. It is impossible to know which small acts are the most important."

I picture Mum, sitting by me, holding my hand, willing me to do the right thing. *"You can't live life wondering about the 'what ifs?'"* It's as if she knew I'd need those words as we held our last conversation together in the hospice.

"I need to borrow another card, Nan. I have a letter to write."

Thirty-Seven

22nd May 1998

I sit back in the chair and stare at the clock, watching the final minute countdown. There are definitely better ways to spend a birthday. The tick of the second-hand echoes around the silent room. A few of my classmates still scribble furiously on their answer papers, but for me, I've done all I can.

"Pens down, please," says Mr Barrett. You can almost sense the relief seep out of everyone in the room. We all collectively let out the breath we've been holding for nine months.

As I exit the hall to make a swift exit, Sam grabs my arm. "We're heading to the tennis courts."

"I need to go get my stuff ready for tonight," I reply.

"Theo, look, we have plenty of time. We've finished our last ever exam so we should celebrate."

I look across as a rabble of students file out the main entrance. Some are tearing their geography textbooks and throwing them in the air like a paper snowstorm. "I think I'm good."

"Right, sit," Sam says firmly, pushing my shoulders until I'm on the bench. "It's your sixteenth birthday, you've finished your exams, and we never have to come to school again."

"I'm doing Sixth Form," I remind him. "And so are you."

"That was an example. These could be the best days of our lives, and with the party tonight, you need to cheer up. Sorry to be harsh."

I look at Sam and give him a dead leg with a clenched fist. "Thank you. I needed that."

"Does that mean you're coming with me?"

"I guess." He pulls me from the wall, but I hang back, playing with the zip on my rucksack.

"What is it now?"

"Alex is about to get in the car for France."

"Hey, Theo, he's gonna write. Just because he's out the country, doesn't mean he won't be your friend."

I stand in front of Sam and grab his cheeks between my palms. "You don't understand. I've been an idiot. I wrote to him at the weekend and told him I loved him."

"Shit, seriously?"

"I even put my phone number on the back."

"And?"

"He never called, Sam. He never called."

I walk into the front room and catch Nan eating another of my birthday cupcakes whilst engrossed in the television. "You'll ruin your dinner," I say. "And they're meant to be for tonight."

"They're too tempting. Your new shirt arrived, by the way. It's on the sofa."

I've been waiting for this to come from the catalogue for two weeks and pray it fits. It isn't every day you get your first Ben Sherman shirt. I've never had anything designer before, but the future is now, my school uniform days behind me. I yank my school shirt over my head and rip open the packaging.

Nan does a double take and leans a little closer.

"What the hell has happened to you? You're filthy."

I go to the mirror and stare at my shirtless torso. My skin is covered in the permanent marker signatures of my classmates, like I've been attacked by a dodgy backstreet tattooist. "We were signing each other's shirts after the exams. The pens must've soaked through."

"Well go and wash it off. You can't look like that at your party."

I spit on my hand and rub at the ink on my bicep. It smudges slightly, but barely fades. "Nan, I don't think it's coming off."

Any sympathy Nan had for my situation was hidden by the fit of laughter. Once she'd regained her breath, she grabs my hand and drags me into the bathroom. "I have a rough pad somewhere we can use. I'll go and get some make-up remover to see if it will help. How long do we have?"

"Sam and Barnaby are collecting me at six," I reply.

She looks at her watch. "That's twenty-five minutes. You are such a silly sausage. Right, wait here."

After ten minutes of extreme erasure, you can barely see the names on my arms anymore. My chest is mostly free of ink but glows red from Nan's furious scrubbing. "That will have to do," she says as she throws a tub of cream at me. "Take this moisturiser, quickly, and rub a load on."

I open the lid and recoil. "It smells like old people."

"It's either that or feeling like you're on fire all night."

"Fine," I grumble as I take a large blob and apply it all over my body. In one tray on the shelving unit, I spot Dad's aftershave in a small glass bottle. "*Coolwater*. Perfect!"

I remove the cap and spray a mist into the air, striding through it with confidence. The pain is unbearable when the liquid particles meet my friction burns.

I throw myself in front of my bedroom fan, lifting my arms high, waiting for the itchiness to subside. As I stand with my eyes closed, there is a roar of an engine from outside, followed moments later by the doorbell being rung furiously. At least when Nan leaves with Jon I can finish getting ready without any more jokey comments.

"Theo?" says Nan, tapping on my bedroom door but her head already looking around it.

"I'll be out in a minute!" I shout. "You can go now if you want and I'll meet you at Joshua's. Leave the cakes with me or there'll be none left."

Nan takes me in a hug and kisses the top of my head. "You better come to the front door."

I throw on a t-shirt and drag my feet behind her, hoping Sam and Barnaby don't spot my beacon like arms. As I get to the hall, Nan is stood smiling as if she's just won the pools.

"You could've at least let them in." I remove the safety chain and pull the door open wide.

In the middle of our driveway, he is there; dressed in his blue school blazer, his ginger hair neatly styled, and a bunch of red carnations in his hands.

"Hi, Theo."

"Alex?" This cannot be real. This seriously cannot be real. "What are you… I mean… why? How?" I poke his arm to make sure he isn't an illusion and feel the firmness of his muscles on my fingertip. "Things like this do not happen to people like me."

He throws the flowers to the floor and strides forwards, taking me into the tightest hug imaginable. "Well, here's your lucky day."

I don't care how sore my body is, this is worth it. As he loosens his grip, he presses his forehead against mine, tears falling down his cheeks. "You smell like, I don't know, Lily of the Valley?"

"Yeah, sorry about that. Long story." My smile is wider than ever. I hold his head in my hands and stare into his eyes. "Why aren't you in France?"

He shrugs. "On the way to the airport, you were all I could think about. Picturing you getting ready for your party whilst I was going hundreds of miles in the wrong direction doesn't make sense. I asked Felicity to turn the car around."

"But what about your family?" I whisper, my heartbeat punching against my ribcage.

"Who cares? I needed to put myself first."

"I don't know what to say."

Alex pushes his finger to my lips. "Say nothing. It's my turn to talk. I got your card last week. I'm glad I didn't reply as I get to tell you in person now. Theo Barker-Hall, I love you too."

Acknowledgements

Thank you as always to Stuart at SRL Publishing for believing in this book, being a champion of my writing, and for continuing to push for a sustainable future in publishing.

Thank you to my agent, Anna, at Intersaga, for trusting me as a client, and for sharing all the details of this book on socials, even though I was not a client when it was written.

This story started very differently, so thank you to David Brown and Jam Keane who have read most of it a number of times, and who were not afraid to be brutally honest in their feedback to make it the best it could be. It is definitely in a better shape with your support.

Finally, thank you to Wood Green School in Witney. Many of the silly bits on this story are based on incidents that occurred duing my school days there. We really did have a small fire in the science block, we had a very long journey to Aachen, and my maths tutor, Mr Askew, genuinely claimed 2I could've had someone's eye out" after I threw a Twix from his second-floor classroom window in Year Ten.

I was lucky to revisit the school whilst editing this book, and the positive steps they have taken have put the school in a strong position for diversity, inclusion, and ensuring all students are made to feel safe. It was extremely heart-warming.

SRL Publishing don't just publish books, we also do our best in keeping this world sustainable. In the UK alone, over 77 million books are destroyed each year, unsold and unread, due to overproduction and bigger profit margins.

Our business model is inherently sustainable by only printing what we sell. While this means our cost price is much higher, it means we have minimum waste and zero returns. We made a public promise in 2020 to never overprint our books for the sake of profit.

We give back to our planet by calculating the number of trees used for our products so we can then replace them. We also calculate our carbon emissions and support projects which reduce CO_2. These same projects also support the United Nations Sustainable Development Goals.

The way we operate means we knowingly waive our profit margins for the sake of the environment. Every book sold via the SRL website plants at least one tree.

To find out more, please visit
www.srlpublishing.co.uk/responsibility

www.ingramcontent.com/pod-product-compliance
Lightning Source LLC
Chambersburg PA
CBHW010432170726
48283CB00011B/3179